GILLIAN SCOTT

What Goes On Tour

A love triangle romantic comedy

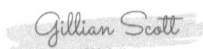

First edition

ISBN (print): 978-0-473-54409-6
ISBN (digital): 978-0-473-54412-6

This book was professionally typeset on Reedsy.
Find out more at reedsy.com

I'd like to dedicate 'What Goes On Tour' to all the wonderful people who work in travel and tourism. Working in Europe provided the best times of my life and also lifelong friendships. Let's hope the world gets back to travelling soon.

Foreword

Once upon a time, before Google Maps and Wi-Fi passwords, there were the map book and the trusty clipboard. And the person clutching them, usually juggling passports, counting heads, salving a hangover and coaxing everyone back onto the right bus.

That person was me.

In the 1990s, I worked as a tour rep, then a tour manager across Europe, guiding young travellers who were equal parts wide-eyed, weary, and wonderful. Those years were full of laughter, long days, dancing on tables, unexpected detours, and friendships that lingered long after the coach pulled away.

The *Terrific Tours* series grew out of wild, unforgettable experiences from various cities in Europe and creates stories from them. The *What Goes On Tour* series, where the chaos first began, follows Shaz, a tour manager navigating life, love, and a busload of drama.

While the stories are fictional, they're inspired by the heart and humour of real travel life of the time: the camaraderie, the chaos, the crushes, and the constant discovery of something new, often about yourself.

These books are love letters to travel, to the people you meet along the way, and to the beautiful, unpredictable journey that is life itself.

I hope you come along on the adventure.

Gillian

Acknowledgments

I'd like to thank my coffee group (Tresna, Fiona, Iva, Deb, Sarah & Sheryl) for being a brilliant sounding board to me over the numerous years it has taken to get this book completed.   A special thanks to Sheryl (S L Beaumont). Together we did a 'how to write a novel' course many, many years ago. She has gone on to write many fabulous books and provided inspiration for me to keep going to get my one, finished.

Thank you to BubbleCow for providing a valuable manuscript assessment. Huge thanks to Kirsty Morrison for pushing me to do better.

Some teachers have a lasting impact. Mr Iain McGregor, my English teacher in 1985, was one of those teachers. While I was one of probably thousands of students over his career, he instilled some self-belief at a challenging time in my life. For that, I'll be eternally grateful.

Thank you to my brother, Alastair. He didn't actually do

anything but he wanted a mention. Last but not least, a big thank you to my husband Murray and my offspring Kennedy and Christian, love you guys.

Chapter 1

London: Departure Day -2

Monday 13th May 1996

'What part of I'M NOT ON THE PILL did you struggle with, Skipper?' I ask, swatting him on the side of his strawberry blond head.

'Sorry... I... uh... Just got carried away.' He at least has the decency to sound sheepish. The small remaining glow from the fumbling bedroom encounter and the preceding nine (ish) large vodka and tonics evaporates like a drop of water on a hot rock. In that split second, I feel deflated and more than a little pissed off.

The trouble with the withdrawal method of contraception is that the sole chance of it working at all revolves around the person who is supposed to 'withdraw' actually doing so. But not only do they need to do it, they need to do it in a timely manner.

Shit, bugger, shit, bugger, shit.

Bugger.

Tomorrow I have to trek from one side of London to the other to go to the office and get, what I can only guess, will be a hauling over the coals for sins on my previous tour around Europe. I need to collect a ton of paperwork and instructions for my next tour, before a 5pm pre-departure meeting. And now, thanks to Skipper, I also have to fit in a visit to the local sleazy 'free for foreigners' doctor. Hopefully, I can get the morning-after pill without a lecture on the perils of casual sex.

Fan-fucking-tastic.

'Right, you better go then. Big day tomorrow.' I direct Skipper, pushing him off me and over the side of the narrow single bed with one impressive shove.

As he fumbles around the tiny hotel room's grubby carpeted floor for his clothes, I wonder three things:

1. How the hell DID I end up in bed with this guy? The answer to that question probably has something to do with the vodka, and;
2. Why do all coach drivers (you must call them coaches, not buses. Coaches don't stop to pick people up. Being a coach driver is supposedly much more salubrious than driving a bus), have ridiculous names like Skipper? Already I have worked on tours of Europe with a Dipstick, Blue (there is a little and a big one of those; I'd had the little one), Sandfly, Psycho, Boxo and Rasher.
3. What is it going to be like when we are all 80 and remi-

niscing about old times in Europe? 'Do you remember Russell Jones?' someone would ask. 'Hmmm… was that Sandfly or Rasher?' Bloody madness.

As a tidal wave of exhaustion pummels me, all I want to do is close my eyes and slip into a dream that does not involve accidental pregnancies.

'See you out there somewhere,' says Skipper, as the heavy off-white wooden door closes, clicking locked behind him.

Not if I can help it I think, as I fall into a deep and thankfully dreamless sleep.

Chapter 2

⚜

London: Departure Day -1

May 14th 1996

Tuesday dawns sunny. If I'm to be picky, it's a teeny bit too
sunny for my tired, bloodshot pale blue eyes. London is
experiencing a heatwave, which means today's temperature
could well be 24+ degrees Celsius. This would be great if I
were lying by a pool somewhere exotic. It's not so great with
a throbbing hangover and a long commute on the Tube and
British Rail with lots of hot, smelly folk wishing they were
somewhere exotic. Add to that the prospect of a bollocking
from the boss and an embarrassing doctor's appointment, and
my day hardly smells of roses. My Sahara mouth becomes
even more arid at the thought of it.

Damn you vodka.

Chapter 2

The gold and silver-plated Swiss Army precision timepiece on my wrist ticks over to 9.31am as I arrive at the ticket machine at Holborn Underground Station. Timing to buy an off-peak travel card... Perfect. Even if I do say so myself.

I scramble through my black leather wallet, which is handily fitted with dividers to cope with multiple currencies, and find some British money in amongst the French francs, Italian lira, Deutsch marks, Spanish pesetas and Dutch guilders. I feed the hungry ticket machine a slightly crumpled £5 note to buy a travel card for my trip to Orpington and back. I should have just enough time after the journey for a quick coffee when I arrive, to calm my nerves before I'm due to meet my scary supervisor at 11am.

The underground is in its usual chaotic state and I'm distracted from my woes as I focus on not being pick-pocketed and trying to preserve some semblance of personal space for the short ride. When I transfer to the rail, I get a seat on the train and enjoy some time to contemplate as I stare out of the grubby window of the 9.51 to Orpington.

Most of my fellow tour managers try to avoid having to see supervisors in the office as much as I do. Once you have a year or two's experience on the road under your belt, then, in theory, you shouldn't need to trek from central London to the office in the 'burbs' on your one and only day off between tours of Europe. Catching up on sleep and laundry are usually the preferred activities. The only good thing about coming into the office is that you also get to collect mail from home. Like me, most drivers and tour managers are from the Southern Hemisphere. We get a visa to work for a couple of years, and spend the Northern summer showing tourists around Europe. In between tours, we spend a couple of nights in a cheap hotel in London, but it is to the office that our friends and loved ones send our mail. Wafer-thin blue aerogrammes carry news of the life that I left behind in New Zealand.

Just about the only reason anyone with any experience is ever asked to go to the office is for a bollocking, which is what I fear today will be about.

Although my last tour hadn't been too bad, there were a couple of things that may have filtered back to the nerve centre of the company. After a fairly torturous few weeks with a tour group that was imploding and a driver who was in need of a personality transplant, there was that last night we were in Vienna.

I'd let my hair down…

Way down…

Like Rapunzel down…

And I had a little too much wine at a Viennese village 'heuriger' (wine tavern).

Feeling full of the joys of spring and zinfandel wine, I might have performed, in the middle of the quaint country restaurant, a stunning, if I do say so myself, rendition of that old Austrian favourite, *Do-Re-Mi*. This performance contained not only enthusiastic singing but was also accompanied with an interpretive dance that would have left Isadora Duncan speechless.

There had been a scattering of applause from the crowd for my performance that went as follows;

'*Do a deer, a female deer.*' I skipped between the heavy wooden tables with my hands on my head like deer horns. '*Re, a drop of golden sun.*' Waved my arm in a rainbow arch.

'*Mi, a name, I call myself.*' Pointed dramatically to myself while bouncing up and down with a ridiculous smile on my face.

'*Fa, a long, long way to run.*' I motioned into the distance and then jogged, pretending to run far, far away.

'*So, a needle pulling thread.*' Shamelessly overacted while imitating sewing, all the while smiling maniacally.

'La, a note to follow So.' I 'la'ed' at the top of my lungs.

'*Ti, a drink with jam and bread*'. Sipped an imaginary cup of tea with my pinky pointed stiffly skyward.

'*That will bring us back to...*' Me, energetically repeating my deer impersonation, skipping amongst the mostly amused diners.

When the evening had come to an end, I'd been leading my group of 50 merry clients back to our coach, when I'd become slightly geographically challenged in the tiny Austrian village with a single one-lane road. After exiting the *heuriger* under the gated archway smothered in ivy, I'd turned right onto the narrow road. I'd then taken the first right turn into what I'd thought was the parking lot where I'd thought our coach was waiting. This trip should have had my flock back in the safety of their multi-coloured coach seats in less than two minutes.

Unfortunately, I'd actually turned too early down a driveway that had no business looking like the entrance to a place where a bus would park. Although I could see the coach from this lookalike driveway, I couldn't work out how the hell to get to it without doing a 180-degree turn and giving away that I didn't know where I was going and had led my group the wrong way. Psycho (drivers with nicknames like this should be avoided at all costs), after seeing me Pied Piper-like leading the flock astray, had turned the coach hazard lights on to try and guide me, but to no avail.

Too embarrassed to double back and risk losing sight of the festively flashing coach, with alcohol-impaired judgement, I'd instead decided the most direct route was the way to go.

I'd led my merry little band across a vineyard, dodging grapevines and climbing fences along the way. There was only one teeny weenie minor sprained ankle, a ripped pair of tights and a couple of scratches that barely drew any blood at all. Surely none of the clients would have complained about that?

Once the train has come to a complete stop, I step off and walk briskly to the coffee shop opposite the office. The smell of bacon makes my stomach rumble but can it handle food? I weigh up the benefit of salving my liver with fatty foods to aid my hangover but deem the risk of regurgitating a bacon sandwich on the boss too high. I order a black coffee with two sugars.

Aside from Vienna, there was only one other small issue I can remember - Paris. I was impatient to get back to the hotel after a long night at the Moulin Rouge watching the cabaret show for the 500th time this year (okay, it was only the fourth time, but it felt like more), I thought I'd counted the requisite 50 passengers on board. However, I'd miscounted, and one slippery little customer hadn't reached the coach. Barry from Wollongong had stopped to relieve himself down an alley and had been left behind in the Pigalle, the raunchy red light district of Paris. He'd found his way back to the hotel after what he described as a 'magnifique' evening with a French lady of the night, so no harm done, surely?

I guess there's only one way to find out. I down the rest of my strong, sweet coffee and head into the drab, grey office building. I enter through the glass door decorated with a

'Terrific Tours' sign and the company logo of a frog wearing a beret and clogs. Seriously, marketing team?

Supervisors are indeed very scary people. All of them have, at one time, been tour managers themselves, so they know about the stress of touring Europe with 50-odd youngish folk who have often forgotten to pack their brains for their first big trip overseas. However, it seems that this knowledge, and any empathy for the hardworking tour manager, is sucked from their heads as soon as they enter this dull, concrete, office block on the outskirts of London.

I give my name to the gatekeeper at the front desk, a bored-looking bottle-blonde receptionist guarding the hallway to the offices, whose name is likely Sue or Karen. I make my way to the crew room to see if there is any mail from home and to scull a quick glass of water to try and unstick the inside of my mouth. The road crew room is hardly more than a large cupboard behind the receptionist's sentry post. It has an ancient metal cabinet on one wall with cubby holes alphabetised for mail. It contains mainly aerogrammes from New Zealand, South Africa and Australia, carrying news from home to the staff of 20-somethings who have converged on London from the colonies in search of adventure. It is also the place where the road crew leave messages for each other. The only other items in the room are a small, circular, dark faux wood table with two tatty desk chairs and, thankfully, in the corner of the room, a water cooler.

As I round the corner from the hall to the crew room, time slows, just like it does in the movies as a momentous moment is about to happen to the main character.

(Cue dramatic music…)

And then…

I...

See...

(Drum roll...

Clash of appropriate percussion instrument...)

HIM!

Perched on the edge of the faux wooden table, making paperwork look sexy, is Roger Martinez. Or as I like to call him, Ridiculously Handsome Roger, or RHR for short.

'Hi Shaz,' he says, his voice smooth as silk. He smiles and lights up the room, possibly the whole of Orpington, if not the whole of the United Kingdom. 'Rough night?'

Shit, shit, shit.

'You can tell huh?' I make my way past him to the water cooler, trying to stay composed as my pulse rate soars. I feel my neck and cheeks begin to change colour. The room suddenly feels much smaller than a large cupboard.

Be calm, Shaz, be calm, I repeat in my head to make sure it's registered. BE CALM.

In this moment, I wish I'd put a bit more effort into my appearance. I wish I'd chosen something other than a long-sleeved, heavy denim shirt and straight-legged black polyester pants (although, seriously, you can't beat polyester when you have limited access to an iron, right?). I could have put on something a bit sexier, something that would have clung in all the right places. I could have hoisted up my bra straps an extra centimetre. I could have spent some more time adding eyeshadow to make my pale blue eyes smoulder. I could have tamed my short hair with some styling product. I could have put on a sexy red lipstick. I could have shaved my bikini line.

Wait. Why would I do that? Let's not get ahead of ourselves here Shaz.

Still, I could have tried a little bit harder.

Done something.

Anything.

Mind you, that might have given the supervisor the wrong impression. It might have suggested, 'She's trying to keep her job with the offer of sexual favours.' That would be bad, very bad indeed.

Oh, for God's sake, Shaz (I mentally slap myself), concentrate on Roger.

I fill a tiny cup with tepid water from the water cooler (which is not a very accurate name given the temperature of the water), and take a perch on the edge of the low-quality table next to Roger in, what I hope is a seductive, alluring and intelligent way.

'Got any mail from home, Roger?' I ask, hoping to divert his attention from my less-than-pristine appearance. Instead, I probably just bathed him in my coffee breath.

Ridiculously Handsome Roger is originally from Sydney, where his family still live after emigrating from Spain well before he was born. He has a cool Aussie drawl and a devastatingly gorgeous Mediterranean visage. Skin the colour of milk chocolate, likely a gift from the Moors invading Spain hundreds of years ago. His dark, wavy hair frames his face in a way that would make Leonardo da Vinci want to repaint the Mona Lisa with curls. His rich brown eyes are like deep, muddy pools. He is, in my humble opinion, the most handsome man currently inhabiting Planet Earth.

'Nah, just sorting all this paperwork out. I'm off on tour tomorrow,' he replies in his deep, masculine timbre. The fog in my brain immediately starts to clear, and thoughts begin to whizz around my head, firing off little shots of electrical energy that I can actually feel through my hangover. If Roger is on tour tomorrow and so am I, then maybe we'll bump into each other?

My eyes glaze over as I drift into a lovely daydream about bumping into Roger at sunset in Paris. We would promenade the Champs-Élysées while holding hands and gazing deeply into each other's eyes, oblivious to the beauty of the city, interested only in each other. We fall deeply in love and leave Europe to move to my native New Zealand and...

'Shaz!'

A harsh, growly and overly shouty voice pulls me away from the Champs-Élysées and back to the sparse crew room. There stands Neil, 5'4" in his tan leather platformed boat shoes, looking none too happy.

'Come down to my office,' he snaps.

'Good luck,' Roger mouths with his oh-so-kissable dusky pink lips. I manage a weak smile as I fall into line behind Neil to, I am fairly sure, certain death, if not at least a flogging. Is it my imagination, or does every office cubicle I pass on the hallway to Neil's office contain a person giving me 'a look'? Some of the looks say, 'you'll be right', a couple say, 'good luck', and at least one says, 'good job, ha ha'. I resist the urge to slap that person around the head.

The nanosecond my polyester-wrapped behind hits the orange vinyl chair in front of Neil's desk, the verbal tirade begins.

'How did you do in math at school, Shaz?' Neil asks, illustrating to me that sarcasm is, indeed, the lowest form of wit.

I decide to be chirpy about it. 'Oh, not too bad, Neil. Passed school certificate anyway. 51% actually. Scaled up from 47%, must've been the year for the mathematically challenged. Still, a pass is a pass, eh?'

Stop talking Shaz, for the love of God, stop talking.

'Fancy being a dancer?' He continues, ignoring me. 'Because you'll need to find a new career if your next tour is anything like your last one. Your driver, Psycho, says you aren't a team player. Care to explain?'

This is the last straw. I see red. Bile rises, burning my throat. Damn you again vodka.

'Psycho, that son of a bus driver, is a fine one to talk.' My voice rises an octave or two and goes ever so slightly squeaky. 'That, from the man who got into a punch up with a passenger who took offence after Psycho shagged his barely 18 year-old sister that he was travelling with? Who backed the coach into a tree after he'd had more than a few beers? Who barely uttered two words to the rest of the group the whole 31 days, is saying I WAS NOT A TEAM PLAYER?'

'Yes,' Neil responds, serious face set like concrete. 'We have let *him* go. YOU are on your last warning. Make this next tour a good one or we'll be seriously looking at your future with the company. Oh, and I've docked your wages 50 quid for your unprofessional dance display. Here's your paperwork. Have a good tour.' Left unsaid is, 'Or else.'

Walking towards the office exit, I glance into the crew room. Empty. I do a quick 360-degree spin to see if I can see RHR. The only person I see is Sue/Karen smirking at me. I need to gather my thoughts. I slip into the crew room, close the door behind me and pour another plastic cupful of tepid water from the so-called water 'cooler'. I stare vaguely out the window for a moment, then cast my eyes around the room and over the crew mail pigeon holes. The 'G' spot (no pun intended) has an envelope in it. Maybe it's for me?

My spirits lift a little as I see a bright pink envelope with 'SHAZZA GREEN' in my best buddy Liza's neat handwriting. I rip it open and pull out the greeting card inside. On the front of the card in colourful writing is *Friends are like condoms*. I open the card and the message continues... *They cover you when things get hard.* Liza had written, '*Don't worry, everything will be okay,* and finished it with *xxxxxxxxxxxxxxxxxooooooo ooooooooooo.* For effect, she has also stapled a condom to the card. The staples go right through the middle of the packet and presumably will render the condom inside completely useless. Still, the thought was there. I tuck the card into my bag and head out of the office.

I am 50 quid worse off, and the return train ride to central London feels even longer than usual. Weighed down by the ton of paperwork and the burden of nearly being sacked, I drag myself in the stifling heat from Holborn to the sleazy (so I've been told) doctor's office near the Grand Hotel.

Although receiving free medical treatment is great as a non-British person, the lack of choice as a transient non-resident, as to who you receive this free treatment from, is a downside. This doctor's surgery is situated on a small square behind the Grand Hotel, which I use as my official address in the UK (even though I only stay there about 14 nights in total each summer). The square also houses a laundromat, a Boots chemist, an Italian restaurant, and an Asian noodle canteen called 'What the Duck'. It's a drop-in clinic so no appointment is required. I seem to have struck it lucky as the small waiting room is empty, apart from one bedraggled looking man who must be at least 50 years old. He's filling the room with the stench of stale urine. He's either asleep or dead. The receptionist doesn't look too worried though, as I give her my name and date of birth. I'm guessing he's just asleep. Excellent. Hopefully he's waiting for another doctor and I won't have to wait long.

The receptionist tells me Dr Jones will see me soon and waves her hand in the direction of the waiting room chairs. I find a seat as far away from the smelly sleeping old guy as possible and sit down, touching only the necessary bare minimum of my surrounds.

Don't think about the germs Shaz.

A pile of magazines on the low, veneer coffee table in the middle of the room tempts me. While I would love to catch up with all the Hollywood gossip, the thought of touching the dog-eared pages that have been fingered by so many sick people means I just can't bring myself to pick one up. Instead, I stare beyond the smelly guy, out of the small window at the vista of an unhealthy-looking tree.

'Sharrrrrrrron Grrrrrrrreen.' I break from my reverie to see a man, who I assume is Dr Jones, having emerged from his examination room, obviously ready to see me.

Dr Jones possibly has Welsh roots, given a) his name and b) how he pronounces my name. He is a man of perhaps 55 (although I'm not very good at guessing old people's ages), with long, wavy grey hair that needs a good wash. He has a pot belly, which stretches the buttons on his flannelette shirt, and an unnerving glint in his eye.

He ushers me into his examination room and clicks the door shut behind him. He indicates a chair for me and he sits himself down on the only other chair in the room, at his desk. He swivels to face me. He is now so close our knees are mere millimetres apart. I slide my bum back in my chair to try and create more of a gap. It's a largely unsuccessful exercise.

'So, Sharrrrrron Greeeeeeen, what gives me the pleasure of meeting you today?' He leans in, expectant on my reply, putting further pressure on his shirt buttons. Although I am 10 years over the legal age of consent, I suddenly feel very naughty and embarrassed, like a child caught with their hand in the cookie jar.

'I've... um... had... um... you know.' I shuffle in my seat, look at the ceiling momentarily and clear my throat. 'I... um... I...'

'Yeeeeees.' He leans in.

'I need a morning-after pill.' I finally manage to get it out. My cheeks heat up, and the room suddenly feels much warmer.

'Rrrrrright. Why is that?' He leans closer still, a smirk starting to crack through his serious, concerned professional façade.

'Um. Because I accidentally had... you know... um...' I'm hoping he'll fill in the blank... still hoping... no, right then... 'sex.'

'You accidentally had sex? You didn't *mean* to do it?'

'No. I didn't mean to.'

'Then why did you?'

'Vodka probably.' Just give me the bloody prescription, for fuck's sake.

'Rrrrrright. So you were drrrrrrunk and accidentally had sex?'

'NO!' I respond, offended at this statement. 'I... I was... well... maybe... okay... I suppose I was a little bit drunk... So... I guess... alright... okay... yes.'

'Are you in a relationship with this man?'

'Um…'

'Let me rephrase that,' he says helpfully. 'How long had you known him before you had sexual intercourse?'

'A while.'

'Can you define "a while" for me Sharrrrrrron?'

I look at the sliver of floor between our knees and mumble, 'About an hour and a half.'

'AN HOUR AND A HALF?' he says quite loudly. Unnecessarily loudly really, considering the size of the room. Obviously, when it's said in such a shouty way it doesn't sound great.

'Yes,' I say to the slither of floor, wishing it would just swallow me up.

'Do you often accidentally have sex after an hour and a half of meeting someone, Sharrrrron?'

'No! That was the first AND I hope, fingers crossed, the last time. It's not like he was a complete stranger after all, we do work for the same company. Sorry to rush you along, doctor, but I've really got a lot of work to do this afternoon. Can I get a prescription please?'

'But what about STDs Sharrrron? I really should give you a full examination.' The smirk widens a little bit too much and I get an icky feeling in my stomach.

'I'll make a deal with you, Dr Jones. You give me the prescription now and at the first sign of any itching or any other strange goings on in my nether regions, you'll be the first person I'll think of, okay?'

He must realise there's no way I'm going to consent to an examination, so he pushes himself back on his chair and swivels towards the desk, shooting me a final concerned, serious doctor look.

17

Less than a minute later, I'm out the door and on my way to Boots, prescription in hand, to pick up the little white pills that will save me from becoming the mother of Skipper Junior. Would I be so worried if the possible pregnancy was the result of a night of passion with Roger? Probably not. It could have happened once. I have been lucky enough to have had one night of passion with the divine Roger. The magic happened at a beautiful, romantic château in rural France. That's the big picture; the glossy version. The technicality of it was that it was in the luggage compartment of a coach parked outside a beautiful château in rural France, but tiny details like that should not be allowed to sully this precious memory.

I bask in the glow of that memory for a moment, remembering the musky smell of his skin, the feeling of his stubble rubbing against my cheek and how glossy his hair felt when I entwined my fingers in it, before I shake myself back to the present. I let myself into my small dingy hotel room, wondering how such a hovel could cost the same for one night as my weekly rent had cost back in New Zealand.

My room, A.K.A the scene of last night's crime, has a single bed, which sags limply in the middle. It's pushed hard against the wall, giving the door just enough space to open into the room. The sheets are white-ish and well-worn, threadbare in places. A burgundy woollen blanket is hardly enough to keep you warm on cooler nights, no matter how tightly you roll yourself into a ball. I often resort to using my sleeping bag. The chipped, white porcelain basin with tapware from the 1920s has a cracked mirror above it. As the nearest bathroom is down the hall, in an emergency or in situations of extreme laziness, it's not uncommon for the basins in these rooms to be used as urinals. Knowing this makes me a little anxious about brushing my teeth.

A set of dark wooden veneer drawers is the base for a small television. The carpet is multi-coloured with a swirly pattern and, if you walk on it with bare feet, you notice it's slightly sticky. I keep my shoes on. The small window that looks out onto Southampton Row is so grimy on the outside that it makes viewing anything through it impossible. It does, however, let in a little light and keep out a little noise.

The shared bathrooms are located some distance down the hall. Because The Grand is cheap, by London standards, at £22 a night, it attracts a diverse clientele of foreigners, wastrels and one crazy old lady with wild hair who endlessly wanders the corridors at all hours carrying an electric jug and asking anyone who passes her where she can plug it in. I try to avoid a trip to the bathroom after dark. Although, as yet, I've never resorted to using the basin, no matter how many vodkas I had splashing around in my bladder.

I check my Swiss Army watch, a gift to myself on my last visit to Lucerne. 4pm - I only have an hour and a half until the start of the tour pre-departure meeting. I grab the TV remote and flop down on the saggy bed. I toss my bag and the pile of paperwork I've carted back from the office down onto it in front of me. Slipping my shoes off, I place them beside the bed, ready to step back into in order to avoid stepping on the hotel room carpet, even for a stomach-turning second. Turning on the TV, I flick through the channels and find my favourite programme, *Countdown*. The cogs are ticking round the inside of the head on the screen; that means it's only just started. Yeah! The camera pans to the audience of geriatric clappers, before settling on the host of the show, Richard Whiteley, in his ridiculous round glasses that cover half his face, which is not such a bad thing. Today he's wearing a glorious baby poo yellow coloured suit jacket that does nothing for his sallow complexion.

Richard introduces the contestants: Steve, the defending champion, with a bad case of post-puberty pimples, is from Basildon, single, works in something called I.T. and is into collecting Star Wars figurines. The challenger's name is Janet. She has shoulder-length blonde hair that's in the end stages of a perm falling out. Her teeth protrude from under her top lip, covering the vast majority of her chin. She's from Dagenham, is an accountant, wants to travel to Antarctica, collects stamps and is, surprisingly, also single.

After some inane chatter, Richard introduces his co-host, Carol Vorderman. Carol is the Goddess of the Whiteboard. I have a huge girl crush on Carol Vorderman. She's graceful and gorgeous, with her blunt brunette fringe and widely spaced eyes. She's also very clever and articulate at the same time, a combination I aspire to achieve. Often, I struggle to string two words together coherently, while SHE can solve complex mathematical equations or word conundrums, all while smiling her brilliant smile and keeping up a witty repartee with Richard. Today, Carol's wearing a tartan suit jacket with shoulder pads so high they nearly reach her ears and a pencil skirt so sharp she could probably write with it.

It's a word puzzle to kick off the show. Steve asks for a vowel to start. Carol spins toward the pile of letters under her whiteboard, sliding one off the top and revealing it in dramatic fashion.

'That's an 'A', Steve,' Carol says, maybe for the benefit of the blind members of the TV audience, as she puts the letter tile onto the board.

With something familiar on as background noise, I fossick around the bottom of my cavernous bag until I find the small packet I had collected earlier from Boots, following my uncomfortable meeting with the lecherous Dr Jones. The instructions on the back of the packet state that these pills are to be used in an emergency only (check) and that one pill is to be taken, followed by a second pill 12 hours later. I read on: possible side effects can include headache, nausea, painful boobs and bleeding. I try to imagine how it would feel to have all these side effects while taking a group of people from London to Paris tomorrow, at the same time as remaining upbeat and with an ever-present smile. Oh well, needs must. I pop the little pill that offers salvation from motherhood into my mouth and wash it down with some tinny-tasting London tap water from the glass beside my bed.

Oh shit. Too late, I realise that now I have to set my trusty travel alarm for 4am to take the second pill the requisite 12 hours later, making an already long day tomorrow hideously longer.

Mentally slapping myself around the head, I turn my attention back to the TV and immerse myself in half an hour of joyous escapism. I am Carol, stringing entire sentences together without stumbling over my tongue and solving complicated mathematical equations without breaking a sweat. It's a fierce battle but in the end, Steve retains his title, dispatching Janet with an impressive display of 'geekery' and he does a double fist pump in celebration.

There's still plenty of time after *Countdown* finishes for a quick shower. Those are the only sort I ever have in the shared bathrooms with strangers' hairs of all lengths, textures and colours stuck to the cubicle walls. Then I will finish off my paperwork and make the short walk down the road to the bar/meeting room affectionately called 'The Pit'. This is where I'll see, for the first time, who I'm about to share the next 26 days of my life with.

Chapter 3

London: Still Departure Day - 1

Still May 14th 1996

5.25pm - My brown leather, open-toed sandals make a 'clop, clop' sound on the industrial metal stairs leading down to The Pit. I feel that familiar mix of excitement and apprehension that I have at every pre-departure meeting. Who, from anyone in the world aged 18-35, have the Travel Gods thrown my way this time? A fun, laid-back group of like-minded folk that will gel immediately and have the time of their lives? Or a bunch of people who having signed up for the same tour is the only thing they have in common and who will have me working my butt off to keep them all happy? Hopefully not a load of people whose doctors have recommended they go on a 'holiday' for their mental health. Sometimes you can tell at the very first meeting. It can be 'group love at first sight'. Sometimes it takes a day or two before the nature of the beast that is a tour group is revealed.

I pull open the safety glass door to The Pit. A wave of loud chatter and cigarette smoke washes over me. I weave my way through the crowd towards the people wearing the same lime green shirts as me, next to the bar, identifying them as staff. For some people, lime green is a colour that enhances their appearance, gives a certain *je ne sais quoi* and adds colour to their cheeks. Not so for poor Chloe. Chloe is clutching a glass of wine like her life depends on it. Her flame red hair and freckly complexion, in combination with the green shirt, gives her the look of an upside-down strawberry.

'Busy in here tonight, huh? There must be seven or eight tours leaving tomorrow,' Chloe says, before taking a larger than strictly necessary gulp of her wine. 'How long are you out for this time Shaz?'

'26 days. You?' I respond while waving to try to catch the attention of the surly, overly tattooed barman.

'Forty-fuckin'-five days.' Chloe spits this out like she's just swallowed something nasty. I hope she isn't drowning her sorrows on the eve of the 45 days or day one will feel like an eternity. Those long trips can be a killer: 45 days is a long time away from the English-speaking world, and tempers can fray within the group as travel exhaustion sets in. It's also a 'budget' trip: it's made 'budget' by skipping hotels and cabins in favour of the group putting up tents everywhere. I say a silent, 'Thank God that I've hopefully done my share of camping trips'. I'm safe in the knowledge that, when my head hits the pillow tomorrow, sometime around midnight, it'll be in a hotel room rather than on an airbed that, no matter how hot the weather, always feels slightly damp and chilly.

Finally having had a pint of slightly warm lager shoved towards me by the surly barman and handing over my £2.10, I move away from the bar and from Chloe, to scan the room for another friendly face. My scan takes me to the corner of the room, near the empty dance floor. My head jolts to a stop on the vision of loveliness that is… Roger.

Roger makes lime green look good.

Roger would look good in any colour, or no colour at all. Roger, as usual, is not alone. He's surrounded by a bevvy of beauties hanging on his every word. Just as I am about to drift off into another Roger daydream, a microphone clicks on with a screech of static.

A decidedly Australian twang says, 'Hi everyone, my name is Shelly and I'd like to welcome you to Terrific Tours. Tomorrow there are eight tours leaving, so it's important you take careful note of what your tour manager looks like, so you know who to look for in the morning. Could all the tour managers please come and join me on stage?'

I plaster on my 'I'm very friendly, approachable and fun while being organised and in control' smile and move to stand near Shelly on the low podium by the door. I'm joined by Roger and a few other tour managers, resplendent in green.

From my slightly elevated position, I see, through the crowd, a lime green blur zig-zagging through the human mass towards the stage. Chloe does NOT have her friendly, approachable smile in place; in fact, she looks decidedly unfriendly. As Chloe approaches the podium, she trips on some invisible bump in the carpet and begins to fall uncontrollably forward.

Time goes into movie slow-mo again; someone yells,

'Nooooooooooooooooooo.' Just at the moment when everyone in the room thinks that Chloe will land on her face, Roger takes a swift step forward and, in a masculine poetry-in-motion kind of way, catches and swoops her to an upright position in one magical movement. It's almost like they are dancing some very technical ballroom dance moves but without the sequins. I swear I can hear every woman in the room inhale and swoon simultaneously. Not only does Roger catch Chloe and save her from total embarrassment, he discreetly keeps her upright for the duration of Shelly's introduction. By the time Shelly has finished and directed everyone to where they need to go to meet their tour managers, Chloe's driver, Skitz, has arrived to keep her on an even keel.

I don't have time to dwell further on Chloe's fate as I move to my designated spot to meet my group of eager travellers. It strikes me that my assigned driver, Fitzy, hasn't turned up. Bastard. In this case, the nickname Fitzy is derived solely from him having the surname Fitzgerald. Not very imaginative. David Fitzgerald is 33 years old. At 5'6" tall, he's only marginally taller than me. He's balding and has slightly bowed legs. More than slightly, actually, but I'm not one to be unkind. Where the hell is he? The short, bald, bow-legged twat.

My group swarms eagerly around me.

'Hi everyone,' I chirrup above the general din in the room. 'My name is Shaz and I'll be your tour manager for the next 26 days on our tour, which is called the 'European Blitz'. Who comes up with these names, seriously? 'Our driver's name is Fitzy and he's awfully busy doing very important driver stuff right now, but you'll meet him at seven am, that's SEVEN A.M. tomorrow morning when we leave for Paris. Tonight, I need to see your passports, to check that you have the visas required for this tour and to have a laugh at your passport photo... Just kidding about that last bit. Please take time to say hello to your fellow travellers; you'll be getting to know each other well over the next few weeks.'

By the time I've finished checking passports and visas (South Africans are particularly tricky; they need visas for nearly every-bloody-where), it is nearly seven o'clock and even my hair is weary. My first impression of this particular group of tourists is that it's like the United Nations, with lots of different nationalities and a couple of odd bods. One odd bod in particular is Norman from Melbourne, who was very concerned about the size of his 'port'. Every time Norman said 'port', a spray of saliva would speed from his mouth, and it took all of my decorum not to gag and cover my face with my hands. Justin from Sydney, on seeing my confused look, translated that in the state of Victoria, a suitcase is commonly called a 'port'. I store that away as a useful piece of information for quiz nights. Sally and Margot (travelling together from Calgary) have requested a double bed. I make a mental note to check with them in private whether that was indeed what they wanted or if that was an error with their booking. One thing I've learnt during my time on the road is to expect the unexpected. Nothing much could take me by surprise.

In total, the group comprises 30 people: 18 females and 12 males, three couples (four, if Sally and Margot are indeed a double). There are four Canadians, ten Australians, seven New Zealanders, two Malaysians, two South Africans and five Americans. It should be an interesting 26 days.

7.07pm - The only people left in The Pit are about 20

excited travellers making the most of their first night on holiday. They have begun to gravitate to the jukebox and the dancefloor, with a few folk in lime green shirts. There's no sign though of heroic Roger.

'Who's keen to go to The Blue Pub?' asks Nathan. Strangely, tour managers didn't have nicknames anywhere near as often as drivers do.

'Not me. Big day today, early start tomorrow, you know how it is,' I try.

'Yeah, yeah, cry me a fucking river,' jibes Nathan. Before I know it, and despite my best attempt at a protest, I'm caught up in the crowd of green shirts walking the two blocks to the pub. I feel my willpower for an early night being swept away by the urge for some fun. The hunger pangs singing out from my stomach are telling me that food would also be a good idea.

'Okay, just for one.'

Famous last words.

11pm - Damn it. 11 o'clock already. Shit, shit and double shit. I down my sixth and final vodka and tonic in one gulp, bid my farewells to my fellow green shirt wearers and make the ten-minute walk back to my room at The Grand in a reasonably straight line. Probably wouldn't have passed a white line test, but would have managed not to vomit on the cop's shoes. My saggy single bed has never felt so comfy. As I drift off to sleep, I wonder what tomorrow will bring?

Chapter 4

⟨ornament⟩

Departure Day

Paris: Day 1

4am - My trusty alarm clock buzzes to life, almost shaking me off the saggy bed and onto the grimy, swirly carpet. What the..? The haze of the vodka from the previous night has rendered my brain temporarily useless... then it floods with questions. Why hadn't I gone straight home after the tour pre-departure meeting? Why had I drunk vodka again? Why was my alarm going off at 4 fucking am? Then it hits me - the pill. Having located and swallowed my tiny white saviour, I reset my reliable alarm and lay back down to catch another two hours of sleep.

Why is it, though, that when you really want sleep, and only have two hours to get it, you bloody well can't? Half an hour passes, and I'm still watching the back of my eyelids, waiting for oblivion to take over. Even my old faithful, thinking happy thoughts about being married to Roger, living in a mansion and having two smart and, of course, gorgeous children together, fails to help me into dreamland. It's a little after 5am when I give up trying and face the fact that my day has started.

I pull myself upright on the saggy bed and swing my bare feet onto the sticky carpet. Ewwww. This seemingly innocuous movement stimulates two simultaneous sensations:

1. A sudden, then continuing, throb in my head that feels a bit like having a boombox on your shoulder playing the Macarena with too much bass.
2. A wave of nausea.

I wonder if these are the side effects of the pills or side effects from the vodka? The answer makes no difference to how this day is going to play out, I decide, as I head for the shower, making an extra effort with the scrubbing for the first day of a new tour.

I spend a solid seven minutes in the cubicle jiggling about under the trickle of tepid water. I tip some creamy shampoo from my handy, compact and, most importantly, leakproof travel bottle onto my hand and wash my short reddish hair. 'Hellova Henna', the box was labelled. I don't know if it's 'Hellova', but it does give a bit of life to my normally mousy brown mop and hides those few pesky greys that are starting to appear. I blame bad genes. It's totally unfair to be sprouting grey hair at 26 years old. Before rinsing, I scoop some of the shampoo foam off my head and smear it on my tanned legs to give them a quick going over with the razor. Very cost-effective use of shampoo, even if I do say so myself. It's still a few weeks before we get to Paxos; the beach, wearing a bikini and the need to get out my armpits or flaunt my bikini line. So, they can wait.

Back in my soon-to-be ex room, I peer into the grubby mirror, dabbing foundation on my nose in an attempt to make it the same shade as the rest of my face, rather than the brilliant red it appears in its non-made-up state, and to hide the freckles scattered on my cheeks. I pull my lower eyelid down to apply some white liner on the bottom of my eyelids. I read somewhere that white makes your eyes 'pop' and makes you look fresh and alive. I may need all the help I can get today. I finish my make-up regime with some mascara, then knock back a couple of Advil with a glass of London tap water. It doesn't pay to think about how many times the water has passed through strangers and the Thames before making its way to my mouth. If I did think about it too much, I might not be able to hold it down.

I grab the lime green polo shirt off the back of the chair and give it the sniff test. There is a slight aroma of cigarette smoke and an undertone of burger. A spray of perfume and it will last another day or two. Trying to look smart and professional on day one, I team the shirt with a pair of navy blue polyester suit pants and slip on a pair of black Italian leather loafers I bought from Bata the last time I was in Venice. I throw all the remaining clothes from the floor into my multi-coloured Benetton suitcase and slam it shut, twirling the security lock. I put the shoulder strap of my ridiculously heavy briefcase, full of tour paperwork, over my right shoulder and the strap of my large black carry case packed full of music cassettes over my left shoulder. I set off, dragging my suitcase behind me along the two blocks to the coach park where I'll rendezvous with my new group, or 'the flock' as I like to call them, and my driver, Fitzy.

6.30am - The sun is weak in the sky, but the streets of London are already starting to hum with activity. Men in suits stride past, looking very busy and important, rushing to their work in some glass-enshrined office block. Blue-collar workers in boiler suits and high vis vests are buying takeaway breakfasts from the small café next to the hotel. Homeless Harry (that's not his real name... or maybe it is?) has set up a filthy mat outside the café. He's got a paper cup and has a bluntly written sign that reads, *Homeless, please help.* He waits, hoping to collect pennies from generous Londoners.

One of the suit-wearing, busy important men, not looking at anything other than where he is going, kicks Homeless Harry's cup, spilling the few coins he had. Homeless Harry is outraged enough to mumble, 'Wanker,' as the busy important man continues to where he's going without so much as a backwards glance. I try to rummage in my purse, without upsetting the delicate balance of bags on my shoulders, managing to pull out a pound coin to drop in Harry's cup. Hopefully, he'll spend it on food and not a can of that gut rot cider I've seen him with, although I don't hold out much hope.

I continue down the road, part woman, part donkey, with my heavy load. Or should that be part woman, part tortoise? I do have my life on my back, taking it with me everywhere, of no fixed abode. A rolling stone gathering no moss. Oh for fuck's sake, just concentrate on getting to where you need to go Shaz.

Rounding the corner into the coach park, I count eight lime green buses emblazoned with 'Terrific Tours', and I hear Fitzy's voice.

'SHAZZZZAAA. Over here maaate. Sorry, I didn't make it last night, you know how it is.'

I didn't actually, but for the sake of harmony on day one, I'll let it go.

'Hi Fitzy, how are you?' I ask.

'Any better and I'd be dangerous mate,' Fitzy enthuses, grabbing my suitcase and throwing it into the lockers under the coach. Just like there's no mystery as to how Fitzy got his nickname; there's not a lot of mystery to the rest of Fitzy either. He's 5'6", at full stretch, and he'd grown through the top of his hairline about three inches ago. His freckly complexion doesn't tan well in the European sun and his teeth are crooked and more yellow than white. A few years in the hands of an orthodontist when he was a teenager wouldn't have gone amiss.

'How many have we got on board, and are any of them hot?' He asks, looking hopeful.

'30, and none of them did it for me, Fitzy,' I reply, knowing that whether the girls were good-looking or not would have no bearing on how hard Fitzy tried to get, at the very least, one of them into his bed. Drivers, even the less-than-attractive ones like Fitzy, had a better-than-average chance of making it happen. The keys to the coach have some magical, mystical and mysterious power over even the most intelligent and beautiful of travelling girls that I can never quite work out. I wish I could harness this magical power of the keys for my own personal use on Roger.

6.58am - Having handed their luggage to Fitzy to stuff under the coach in his well-practised, jigsaw puzzle fashion, the whole bunch of travellers are aboard the coach, with no one hanging around outside. A couple of coaches have already departed as I heave myself up the steep coach steps and head down the aisle, counting in my head (look out Carol Vorderman), people in pairs: 2,4,6,8,10,12,14,16,18,20,22,24, 26,28,30,32…

What? Back down the coach, this time from back to front. 2,4,6,8,10,12,14,16,18,20,22,24,26,28,30,32.

Fitzy has now taken up his position in the driver's seat.

'Fitzy, how many are on your manifest?'

'Thirty, Shaz.'

Hmmmmm. I grab the microphone from the dashboard and stretch the tight umbilical cord that attaches it to the tape deck, so it reaches my mouth. I click it on, blow gently into it and hear a satisfying 'shhhhhh' through the speakers. All in working order.

'Good morning everyone. You're all looking gorgeous this morning. Can you please raise your hand if you didn't come to the meeting last night?'

A few heads turn, but no hands lift.

'Can you please raise your hand if you didn't come and see ME last night with your passport?'

A couple of hands midway back tentatively rise. I flick the microphone off, place it back on the dash and trot down the coach aisle towards them, passenger list in hand. I take up a spot in the coach aisle beside these stowaways, bending down to meet them at eye level.

'Hi.' Helpful, friendly smile in place. 'Do you remember who you saw at the meeting last night?' I ask the confused-looking Canadian couple. Their nationality is telegraphed by the cap with the maple leaf – him, and the 'Roots' t-shirt – her.

Heads shake.

'What are your names?'

'Larry and Lori Roy,' Maple Leaf cap responds in a Canadian drawl.

I run my finger down the alphabetical list of who should be sitting on my bus. No Roys.

'Why don't you follow me.' I lead them down the aisle, down the steps and off the coach. As I leap off the last step, I almost land on Chloe, who is running along the side of the coach. Chloe looks terrible; pale, even paler than normal, wild-eyed and with beads of sweat clinging to her forehead.

'Fucking fuckety-fuck, fuck, fuck. Forty-five fucking days and I've lost two fuckers already,' she gasps.

'I think I may be able to help.' I smile as I introduce confused Canadian One and confused Canadian Two to Chloe.

7.05am - Our flock of 30 is now complete. 'Flock,' as in sheep. As in, they travel en masse and don't think independently. It's mine and Fitzy's job to guide our flock through the next 26 days, showing them Europe, enlightening them as to the history and the arts, and instilling in them some culture along the way. That is Plan A, the gold standard. Plan B is to get them back to London alive.

We pull out of the coach park driveway, the fifth of the coaches to leave. I haven't seen Roger yet, I wonder if he's already gone? The race is now on to Dover. The two (ish) hour drive to the ferry is an intricate dance. The trick is to keep the temperature inside the coach cool enough so the jetlagged flock can stay awake, but not so cold that they turn blue and become hypothermic. This drive is when the longest talk I will give to these people on the tour will happen and will set the scene for how the next 26 days will go. It'll hopefully help them not to get ripped off, run over, robbed, lost, or worse, in the wilds of Europe. Luckily for me, I can read off notes and don't have to rely on my goldfish memory. Another delicate balance is to put the fear of God into the group, while still instilling the feeling they'll have the time of their lives. Tricky indeed. It goes something like this...

- This is not a democracy: Fitzy and I are in charge.
- In case of an emergency, follow our directions.
- Don't bring hot food or milky drinks onto the coach.
- Don't be late or you'll be left behind.
- No drugs or you'll be kicked off.
- No room parties (unless we're invited, of course).
- There will be lots of early mornings and late nights, so take vitamins.
- Look after yourself.
- Have a night off the booze every now and then.
- Don't bring random strangers back to your room.
- Things are done differently in Europe; get used to it.
- Don't wave your money around.
- Don't walk around looking like a tourist – tricky, as you are indeed a tourist.
- If you're going to throw up on the bus, put the handles of a plastic rubbish bag over your ears to catch the vomit.
- And finally, don't forget to have fun!

No need to mention that Fitzy and I will break most of these rules and just hope that we don't get caught. The full diatribe takes me until the coach has whipped around the white cliffs and dropped into the port of Dover to deliver, leaving our group of once eager travellers, by this stage, looking decidedly less keen.

I'm feeling continuously queasy, and am letting out the odd, very moist burp. I manage not to throw up during the drive, which I tick off as a win. While I battle the beast that is nausea, I try not to think about what will happen if the little white pills don't work their non-conception magic.

Hang on a minute... where is that damn plastic bag?

Chapter 5

~☙❦☙~

Paris

Day 1: Later the same day

9.10am English Time. We arrive at Dover a few minutes too late to board the 9.15am ferry. Bugger. I try to make the chat with Border Security as quick as possible anyway. I have my fingers crossed tightly behind my back, hoping they won't want to do a security screen of the coach, as that could mean missing the next ferry departure, and I am dying for some crispy bacon, fried eggs and a cup of strong coffee. Thankfully, they send us straight through and we're off to board for the 9.34am departure.

I explain to the flock what will happen on the boat and how they will know when they need to return to the coach. 'A booming voice on the loudspeaker will say very clearly... and in English, IT IS NOW TIME TO RETURN TO YOUR VEHICLE.' No matter how clear the message is, there is always someone who forgets, gets lost or gets on the wrong green coach. I have my money on it being Norman from Melbourne; he looks like he has a kangaroo or two loose in the top paddock.

As soon as all 30 of the flock have jumped off the coach and clattered up the steel staircase with the rising diesel fumes, Fitzy and I race one another to the commercial drivers' room. We both know this will be the last chance we have to be without the flock until around midnight tonight, and we're keen to make the most of it. No lining up for overpriced food at the cafeteria for us, oh no, complimentary is the way to go for commercial drivers and, in this case, tour managers too.

Usually, there are zero, or only a couple of other females in the commercial drivers' dining room. The majority of patrons are male, overweight, heavily tattooed drivers of heavy lorries. This morning, there is one other chick in the room. I make a beeline for her, balancing my plate loaded with eggs, crispy-to-almost-cremated bacon and a mug of steaming caffeinated heaven. Leering truck drivers' eyes follow me, which I note with just a tinge of satisfaction. I ignore them, put my nose in the air and sway my polyester-clad behind with just a little more sass.

'Hi Lizzy. How are your lot looking?' I ask as I put my tray on the table next to hers and slump down in the booth. Fitzy isn't far behind me.

'Average,' Lizzy replies, lifting a forkful of bacon to her mouth. 'One actually hurled on the way here, before I'd explained about the sick bags. Mad Dog's going to have a hell of a job to get that out of the upholstery.'

Mad Dog grunts and looks less than pleased. 'Bastards. It's going to be a long 15 fucking days.'

After an hour in which Lizzy and I discuss whether a single currency in Europe will be a positive thing or not, and Mad Dog and Fitzy weigh up the merits of shagging a Canadian vs. an Australian, a loud female voice with a posh English accent booms over the speakers.

'LADIES AND GENTLEMEN, IT IS NOW TIME TO RETURN TO YOUR VEHICLE. PLEASE DO NOT START YOUR ENGINE UNTIL ASKED TO DO SO.'

Then she switches seamlessly to French, also with a posh English accent.

'MESDAMES ET MESSIEURS, IL EST MAINTENANT TEMPS DE RETOURNER A VOTRE VEHICULE. S'IL VOUS PLAIT NE PAS LE MOTEUR EN MARCHE DEMANDE DE LE FAIRE.'

'I wonder where Roger is?' I ask no one in particular. 'I thought he might have been on this ferry.'

'Hoped, more like,' winks Lizzy, as she stands. She slings her expensive-looking suede Italian handbag over her shoulder as she starts to head back to her coach. 'He's probably trying to find his way out of his own arse,' she mumbles, just loud enough for me to hear. 'See you out there somewhere.'

And she's gone, before I can ask what she means by her disparaging comment about my future husband and father-to-be of our children.

11.15am English time / 12.15pm French time. All aboard, I think. I'll just walk down the aisle to check…

2,4,6,8,10,12,14,16,18,20,24 shit. Lost count. Back to the front of the coach I go: 2,4,6,8,10,12,14,16,18,20,22,24,28…

MERDE! May as well get into French mode. Back to the front of the coach again: 2,4,6,8,10,14. Oh, for fuck's sake. And again, I start at the front: 2,4,6,8,10,12,14,16,18,20,22,24,26,2 8,30.

'Put your hand up if you're not here.' Chortles from around the coach. 'Little bit of tour manager humour there.' All 30 of the flock are present and accounted for. Even Norman. The enormous metal mouth of the ferry creaks open and vehicles spew out onto French soil.

The drive from Calais to Paris takes three hours or so, depending on traffic, with a break at a motorway service stop on the way into the city. This will be the flock's first chance to try out their French and my chance to make some organisational phone calls before we hit Paris.

The coach hits the smooth asphalt of our first major European road, the E15/A26, which will take us to near Arras, before we join the A1 all the way to Paris. As we leave the industrial port area of Calais, we move through rolling hills and fields smothered in yellow rape seed flowers. For a while, we drive alongside the main train line. A TGV (Train Grande Vitesse), which translated means 'train high speed', whizzes past us, making our 100kms per hour seem *escargot* pace.

I spend some time on the microphone, telling the flock a bit about France; how big it is (big), how many people live here (lots) and what they like to do (eat cheese and drink wine, hoorah!). I also give them some downtime to chat amongst themselves or, as many do, take a power nap. An hour and a half flies by and we are soon near our first stop. Before we pull into the roadside services, I let the flock in on a few tricks.

Trick 1: Go to the bathroom first. This is crucial for a

successful motorway stop on a coach tour. Then, if five other coaches pull in behind us, they won't miss out on using the bathroom. After the bathroom, go for food.

Okay, so that's only one trick I share with them. I, on the other hand, formulate my own plan: it's a triathlon.

1: Sprint to the bathroom.

2: Trot to the reception area to utilise their free telephone to call the hotel and let them know what time we are expected to arrive, what time we'd like to have dinner and what the flock's dietary requirements are (one has no red meat, one vegetarian, two vegans, one allergy to shellfish). Also, I need to get room numbers so I can let the flock know where they'll be going when we get to the hotel.

3: Walk to the food counter for a croissant and a café au lait. The big question: will they sit well with my nausea? Maybe a bottle of non-fizzy water would be better than coffee?

All three triathlon events are to be completed in the 25 minutes allotted for this stop. Piece of cake for an experienced athlete like myself.

There is one other Terrific Tours coach in the parking lot of Assevillers Services when we pull in. It's empty. The nanosecond our coach comes to a halt, Fitzy flicks the switch that releases air pressure from the door. It makes a pftssssssss noise as it breaks its seal from the coach and gently pops open. The starting gates are ajar, and I'm off on the first leg of my triathlon. I bolt to be first in line for the toilet. Or, now that we're in France, *la toilette*. Come on high performance Italian loafers, don't fail me now. I'm in luck; no line yet.

I push the grubby graffiti-covered cubicle door open with my elbow and sidle into the stall, trying not to touch anything. I look around for somewhere to hang my bag. Nada. It only takes a quick glance at the floor to decide that I will not be putting my bag down there. I put the strap between my teeth, clenching tight. I unroll half a roll of scratchy toilet paper from the dispenser and line the toilet seat, lower my trousers and undies, and tentatively lower my behind onto the wrapped surface. As I glance down, I notice a spot of blood in my new, white cotton underpants. Damn. Surely it's not that time of the month already?

I desperately try to remember when I last had my period. I was in Venice, I think. But that was only a week or so ago. Can't be that time again already? Something sparks in my brain, and a connection is made. The possible side effects of the little white pills; bleeding is one of them. Hopefully, that's a good sign? I unclip the flap on my bag that's still clamped in my mouth and rummage around. Thankfully, I find a panty liner that's in reasonable condition. Quick check of my watch. Six minutes gone already. Shit, time is getting away from me. I finish my business, stand, unwrap the liner, peel the back off the adhesive strip and place it between my legs, pulling my underwear back into position in one swift move. How's that for speed?

I re-open the graffiti-covered door and, as I leave the cubicle and head to the basin to wash my hands, I have the feeling something isn't quite right 'down there'. Time is ticking by though, and I need to get to the phone before the next tour manager arrives. I wash my hands, smile at the female members of my flock who have entered the bathroom in my slipstream, and are now lined up waiting for a free *toilette*, and head out into the corridor.

I start to stride purposefully down the hall towards the telephone.

Ouch.

Oh.

Ouch.

Oh.

Something is definitely NOT right 'down there'. A bit of a twinge is happening in my underwear. A slight tugging. A bit of a pull. Then, a more intense tugging. Then a searing pain that stops me dead in my tracks. I bring my hands up to my stomach and double over a bit. Why do you do that? A pain in your 'bits' and you hold your stomach? I try to take another step, but doing so blazes another pain through me like someone is pulling at my pubic hair with tweezers. It shoots from my groin upwards, stopping in the back of my throat. Just as I do a bent-double, 180-degree rotational move back towards the bathroom, like a puppet whose master is too lazy to hold her up, who should appear out of the men's toilet, but Roger.

'You okay, Shaz?'

'Hi. Yip. Fine.' I groan and try to smile. Part of my mouth moves up in the corner, but pain prevents the other half from moving at all, and the smile comes out a little more like a demented grimace. I hope he doesn't notice. Straightening up as much as is possible, regaining what poise I can while trying to ignore the searing pain, I side-step Roger and hobble back into the bathroom. Thankfully, the line is now gone and when I bust into a cubicle, I get to the bottom (so to speak) of the source of my pain. No burst appendix or some terrifying pill-related side effect. Rather, in my haste to get to the phone, I have put the panty liner on upside down with the super sticky surface firmly attached to my lady garden of untrimmed and unruly pubic hair.

Chapter 5

Each step I take has been giving a good tug at my pubes, like some kind of medieval torture device. I peer down at my nether region and assess the situation. As I see it, there are two options here. Option one: gently disengage the super sticky adhesive strip, pube by delicate pube. Or, option two: rip it off in one go, with one almighty tug. I decide that I have to get this over with quickly: I have no time for delicate removal. I spread my legs a bit for better access and bend my knees a little for stability. I push my left hand onto the side of the cubicle, putting aside the thought of how many other grubby hands have been there and, with my right hand, take hold of a corner of the offending panty liner.

I take a deep breath in and release it slowly through my mouth. I take another deep breath in and out. For good measure, I take yet another breath in. I brace myself. I pull. Hard.

The panty liner dislodges alright, along with a good number of pubic hairs and a couple of small tags of flesh. The pain is quick, but oh-so-searingly intense. I feel hot/cold/sweaty and faint all at the same time. Stars pulse in front of my eyes, and my head spins. I clamp my lips together, but I can't hold it in. The raw pain comes from deep within, making my lips tremble before forcing my mouth open; in an ear-piercing scream. I lean back on the side of the cubicle until the feeling of faintness passes.

Fuck.

I wipe my sweat-beaded brow with some gravelly toilet paper pulled from the dispenser beside me and reset the panty liner with the sticky side to my undies, pubes still attached. I gather my composure and leave the cubicle. I find most of the female members of the flock are preening themselves in the mirror. They look at me in a very concerned way. I smile at them sheepishly and leave the bathroom with as much dignity as I can muster. Roger is waiting for me.

'Was that you screaming, Shaz? Are you okay?'

'I'm fine Roger, but I can't chat. I've got important calls to make.' I leave him in my dust as I race/hobble down the corridor, beating him to the lone telephone.

After making the requisite telephone calls, grabbing my café au lait, a bottle of water as a backup and a pain au raisin (I need more sugar than a croissant can offer to get over the shock), I only have time to race back to the coach without a chance to stalk, I mean find, Roger again. Damn. The other Terrific Tours coach is still empty in the parking lot as we pull out. They must have caught an earlier ferry to beat us here, yet are obviously not in a rush to get to Paris. I wonder who Roger's driver is?

Chapter 6

Paris

Day 1: Even later the same day

The rest of the drive into Paris is straightforward with no further pubic hair accidents, no vomiting and no other pill-related side effects to report. Fitzy parks up directly outside the hotel (pronounced in France as *'otel*). Terrific Tours are not renowned for flash hotels, and the Hotel Lyon, our home for the next two nights, is no exception. Dodging the numerous piles of French dog poo, I make a beeline to the compact reception desk to collect room keys for the flock. I hand them out as they make the transition from coach to hotel room.

Each of the rooms has a pretty wrought iron safety barrier over the bottom half of the window, which offers a 'street view'. This street view stretches across the Avenue Ledru-

Rollin and, depending on the room number, takes in either Café Lyon, purporting to offer the best steak in Paris, or a boarded-up sports shop covered in graffiti tags with an *A Vendre* (for sale) sign in the window. Not exactly the River Seine or the Eiffel Tower, but what do you expect when you book a budget tour?

I take some time on the coach to cue up my music cassettes for tonight's brochured 'Paris Illumination Tour'. I really think that 'theme' music can add a certain *je ne sais quois'* to the illuminations tour. I can get a flock eating out of the palm of my hand if I choreograph it well. If I can nail Paris, the rest of Europe should be a breeze. Paris only has a couple of thousand years of history and hundreds of monuments. How hard can it be?

To be a tour manager with Terrific Tours, you first have to survive the training. The six-week course is described as a cross between a university degree and an army training camp. Before I even attempted the training, my good buddy Liza and I spent a weekend in Paris, walking around backwards. We practiced the art of describing things for passengers on their right or left side, which, if you're standing up facing the group, is obviously opposite to your own right or left. ARGH! I'm sure Carol Vordeman could do it in her sleep! The weekend of backwards walking got us stared at a lot, but stood me in good stead for the tour manager training trip. To solve the 'whose right are we talking about?' confusion, which is often more than my brain can handle and leads to passengers completely missing a sight if I'm telling them to look to the right and I mean my right and they look to their right, I now tend to do the tour sitting down. That way, my right IS their right. Easy, right?

Chapter 6

With only 20 minutes to go until dinner, I lug my suitcase up the four flights of stairs to my own room. How can the bloody French make 400 different types of cheese and not put elevators in their hotels? And why do they insist on putting us road crew, as high up in the hotel as possible, when they know we have the most luggage and the least time? Bastards. I'm puffing and sweaty by the time I slide my key card into the slot and push open the heavy door with my hip. I throw my suitcase on the floor near the bed. Kneeling down, I open the suitcase combination lock and fossick around for a change of clothes for tonight. Enough of the green staff shirt. I find a fitting black top and a white skirt that'll be cooler than the polyester pants I'm in now.

Without time for a shower, I quickly check the bleeding situation (minimal), waft a spray of perfume all over and head to the dining room to make sure the flock are grazing happily. While the majority of the group have in front of them a quarter of a roasted chicken with some mashed potatoes and boiled to buggery carrots, Teresa, who is vegan, has a mountain of lettuce leaves on her plate. I note she's taken off the large wedge of cheese and placed it on her side plate. The lesbians… I mean, vegetarians… Sally and Margot have an omelette. The first of many I'm sure. Europeans really don't understand the concept of not eating meat, let alone not eating ANY animal products, especially cheese.

7.30pm - Paris really is a magical and romantic city. And never more so than at night, when the reflection of the illuminated buildings twinkle on the tranquil Seine. The only trouble with this romantic picture, which looks so amazing in the big colour brochure, is that in summer it doesn't get sodding dark until around 9.30pm. The Europeans are very strict on how many hours coach drivers can drive in a day, which is great for safety, but not so great for us as it means Fitzy has to be parked back at the hotel by 11.30pm. This gives a very tight one and a half hours for my keen travellers to get up and down the Eiffel Tower, allowing for a couple of speedy photo stops. The Parisian traffic means that the greater part of the 'Illuminations tour of Paris' will be undertaken in daylight. Still, Paris is a magical city; the city of love, and somewhere in this city of love, is Roger.

Once the entire flock is aboard the coach, I bounce down the aisle, counting and checking that indeed all 30 of them are present and accounted for. I do not want to give Neil any future ammunition by leaving someone else behind here. As I bounce, I plaster a smile on my face that emanates loveliness, friendliness, approachableness and, I hope, braininess; I wonder if there is a limit on how many 'nesses' you could display with one smile?

'Right-ho Fitzy, hit it. We're off like a robber's dog!'

The sun is still high enough in the Parisian sky to dazzle as our merry group sets off on its 'Illuminations' tour. Fitzy deftly navigates his way down Rue de Lyon, takes a right in front of Gare Lyon onto Boulevard Diderot and another right onto Quai de la Rapee. The buildings disappear from our left, being replaced by the Seine River. The coach is out of the maze of sandstone and onto Austerlitz Bridge, crossing the beautiful Seine from the right bank to the left. There is an audible sigh from the flock as these first-time visitors from the 'new world' get their first sight of the majesty of 'old world' Paris. I sit low in the front of the coach next to Fitzy, in what is commonly referred to as 'the jump seat'. I lift the microphone to rest it on my chin and slip into my patter about all the wonderful and amazing things they are seeing.

The drive along the Left Bank, the heart of Paris, is akin to watching a tennis match, for those sitting higher up in the coach. I point out monuments and places of interest to their left and right, left and right, right and left, slipping in interesting facts and important dates, as their heads whip this way and that to see everything they can.

'First, on our left, is the zoo and botanical gardens behind the high iron fence, where, mysteriously, animals disappeared during times when the people of Paris were starving. Next, on the right, the Musée de la Sculpture en Plein Air, a magnificent outdoor display case of sculpture. On the left, La Sorbonne University, of which Marie Curie is just one of the notable alumni.' As the road merges from Quai Saint-Bernard to Quai de la Tournelle, the traffic becomes one way. 'The numerous large coffin-like green-lidded boxes that now line the river,' I explain, 'will pop open during the day and street vendors will sell Parisian art, knick-knacks, postcards, old books and magazines.'

I try to bring the city to life. I tell of how the island in the middle of the Seine was where, in the 3rd Century BC, the Parisii tribe made their settlement, giving Paris its name. And how, now, it is home to the magnificent Notre Dame Cathedral, which is perhaps… and this is a quote straight from a guidebook… 'the best example of French Gothic architecture in the whole of Europe'.

Notre Dame is home to the relic purported to be the crown of thorns that sat upon the head of Jesus. I'm not really into religion. I mean, I find it interesting from a historical perspective, but I just can't believe the whole 'all knowing, all seeing, spirit in the sky' thing. However, chances are that some of my flock will be believers. Even though I'm not into religion, if Roger wanted to get married in a church, I wouldn't say no. I'd marry him anywhere. Church, beach, garden, naked… hmmm Roger naked…

'Its naked beauty… I mean, beauty …' Oh Shaz, I admonish myself. Is admonishing yourself the first or second sign of insanity? Shaz, focus… for fuck's sake. Fitzy sniggers beside me.

To get my brain to focus on Paris and not on a naked Roger, I get to my feet and bound up the three steps from the crew seats to where the flock sits, dragging the microphone on its springy cord with me. I put my feet on the raised ledges on either side of the aisle for stability, stretching my white cotton knee-length pencil skirt to its tightest. I bend my left leg slightly and push it into the seat occupied by Sheryl from Auckland. She shifts her legs ever so slightly towards her friend Deb to accommodate me. I gift her with my biggest, brightest smile. I lean back slightly, so my lower spine is firmly set against the safety barrier that stops people in the front row from falling onto my head in the seat below, if the bus were to stop suddenly. I am now safely braced and have my arms free to visually demonstrate how the elegant flying buttresses of Notre Dame help support this marvellous building, where construction started in 1163.

I move the microphone to my face to talk and then move it away to point something out. Something in front of the bus. Something to either side. I'm now slightly entangled in my microphone cord. Nothing too serious though. I can sort that out in a minute. Daylight is finally coming to an end, and the sun is setting on the horizon, beyond the front of the bus. The heat from this solar daily death throw warms my back through the large front windscreen. As I look down the aisle, I notice Colin from Newcastle leaning right out of his seat into the aisle to listen intently to everything I say. Very intently, in fact. He must be really into history. A client who cares about what I'm saying! Not completely unheard of, but quite unusual. This gives me motivation. I must feed his knowledge. Nourish his interest. Nurture this seed of... Oh shut up, Shaz.

Colin turns and whispers something to his mate Keith, who is sitting in the window seat next to him. Keith's head rises high above the seat in front to look at me intently also. A smile broadens over his tanned face. Wow! A *pair* of history enthusiasts.

Colin reaches across the aisle and thumps Muzza from Christchurch, who had, until that moment, been looking like he was about to nod off. Colin obviously doesn't want his new travel buddy to miss out on the fascinating stuff I'm sharing. Muzza leans into the aisle to also concentrate fully on me, no longer looking even a little sleepy. After a minute, when I've obviously enthralled them with my knowledge of Charlemagne and the Holy Roman Empire, Muzza gives his mate Pete next to him a prod. Pete stops digging for something inside his ear and pops his head up to pay attention. Pete also gives me a warm smile.

This is fantastic.

What an engaged and interested group of travellers I've got on board here. Buoyed by all this interest and enthusiasm, I continue.

'The Notre Dame Cathedral provided inspiration for Victor Hugo and his famous novel about Quasimodo, the hunchback of Notre Dame. Numerous kings and queens have been crowned in the cathedral, including my favourite short man, Napoleon, and his favourite, smelly wife, Josephine, who were to be crowned by the Pope. Napoleon though, anxious the Pontiff would change his mind at the last minute, grabbed the crown and plonked it on his own head.' Another example of a man with timing issues, maybe he and Skipper could have talked. Thankfully, I manage to keep *that* thought from whizzing out of my mouth unchecked.

Finishing my demonstration of Notre Dame on a high, I twirl twice in a clockwise direction to untangle myself from the microphone umbilical cord trap. I trot back down the three steps to my seat in the front of the coach, to give the flock an unimpeded view out of the front windscreen to soak up the sights.

'Shaz.' Fitzy, who has been keeping an eye on the inside of the bus from his rear-view mirror whispers when I sit, 'Your skirt is as see through as fuck. Nice knickers.'

'Fuck off, Fitzy,' I respond, feeling my cheeks begin to blush. Maybe Colin and his mates aren't so interested in history after all.

The coach crawls along the left bank in the heavy Parisian traffic as I continue to try and weave the colourful history of this magical city into the fabric of modern day Paris. Maybe I can still get Colin to be a history fan.

As I point out La Samaritaine department store to our right, over the river, I can actually hear the crack of ponytails whipping suddenly to view this Mecca of French shopping. I hear fervent whispers in American accents as a few of the girls decide this bastion of Frenchness will be their sightseeing trip tomorrow. We crawl past the massive museum of the Louvre and the Tuileries gardens on our right, with the glass awnings and vast arched glass windows of the Musee D'Orsay on our left.

With the golden statues guarding Pont Alexander III on our right, we make a left, away from the Seine, towards a magnificent building with a gold dome behind it. The building in front of the gold dome is the Musée de l'Armée, the military museum. The long taupe sandstone building is ringed by a brick-lined moat. Access to the building is over a cobble bridge, which is currently closed with solid iron gates. The far wall of the moat is lined with small, green copper cannons, at the ready to blow away any potential villain. In the vast front lawn are 50 or 60 shrubs, all trimmed to look like the pointy end of a missile. I attempt some more tour manager humour.

'Out to your right is the army museum. Looking at it, do you have any idea where the French hide their nuclear weapons?' I ask.

Silence, silence and more silence.

'Maybe under those shrubs?' I answer myself and give a hearty giggle to encourage those behind me to do the same. A few twitters and a bit of mumbling along the lines of, 'What is she talking about?', 'What's a missile?' and 'They have nuclear weapons here?' Fitzy and I exchange a glance and roll our eyes. Attempt at humour... Fail.

The sky is turning from a hazy burnt orange to a brilliant shade of red as the sun finally melts into the horizon. We take a right, then another right, heading behind the army museum. We pass Eglise du Dome, which holds Napoleon's sarcophagus, and get our first peep of our next stop, the Eiffel Tower. Paris's biggest erection. There isn't anything in particular to point out once we've passed the gleaming gold dome and drive behind the army museum on the Avenue de Tourville, aside, of course, from the café that serves the best *croque-madames* in Paris. What's not to love about a toasted ham and cheese sandwich with an egg on top?

Passing the École Militaire on our left, the flock looks to the right, down the Champs de Mars to get their first good look at the most famous of all Paris monuments, the 324-metre Eiffel Tower. I begin to recite everything I know about the giant Meccano set.

I also tell them, 'You will have an hour and 30 minutes. That's one hour and a half, yes, that's 90 minutes here, to go up and, more importantly, come back down the Eiffel Tower. Please make sure you are back on the coach at 10pm. That's 10 o'clock, 2200 hours. Fitzy HAS to be parked up back at the hotel before his driving hours run out, so it's really important you are back on time. Don't forget to watch out for pick-pockets. Take your camera and a warm jumper.'

'You're not their bloody mother,' Fitzy grumbles as he pulls the coach up beside the eastern foot of the tower on Avenue Gustave Eiffel, parking behind another Terrific Tours coach.

My heart skips a beat. Roger? Just in case, as the flock gathers cameras and jackets, I plunge my hand into the dark depths of my black leather handbag-come-rucksack (handy yet stylish) and rummage for a lipstick. Grabbing something that is long and cylindrical and feels like a lipstick, I turn my mouth into the shape of an O and lift it to my lips, ready to whip off the lid, twist up the colour and apply in seconds. As I form the 'o' shape, there is a bang on the glass of the coach door next to my seat.

I realise two things simultaneously: one, it is indeed the gorgeous Roger and two, it is not a lipstick I have held up to my lips. Instead of makeup in a shade like 'Berry Breeze' or 'Mauve Madness', I am instead wielding a tampon. A Carefree brand mini tampon to be precise, and one that has obviously been hiding in the depths of my handbag for way too long and is looking a little worse for wear.

On the downside, it is, without a doubt, not a good look to be holding a manky tampon to your mouth while said mouth is held in a taught O shape like you're about to suck on it. On the upside, it isn't a super plus-sized tampon. My hand drops like a lead balloon, and I feel a red-hot trail blaze up my neck and engulf my cheeks in a firestorm. Roger looks puzzled but manages to arrange his facial features into a smile rather than a gape. Why the hell does this stuff happen to me whenever he's around? Roger motions to Fitzy and I that he'll be at the café down the road, having a drink. I nod 'okay', tucking the offending non-lipstick safely back into my handy travel bag.

I wait by the front of the coach as the flock comes down the stairs.

'Shaz, will it be cold up there… should I take a jumper?'

'Should I take my camera, Shaz?'

'Oooooo, it's a bit chilly, maybe I should take a jumper?'

'Shit I forgot my camera… will I need it?'

'Why didn't you tell us it'd be cold out here? I'll just go back and get my jumper.'

ARGH. I give Fitzy an 'I told you so' look and simulate banging my head against a brick wall. He pretends not to see me as he pops the tachograph card, which records speed and distance, out from behind the coach speedometer and fills in details he needs to, in case we get pulled over by the police. Really, they don't need a mother? Maybe an ear clean would suffice. Once the flock has disembarked with warm tops and cameras at the ready, I lead eager sightseers through the mass of humanity towards the ticket office on the other side of the eastern leg of the tower. I have my handbag-come-rucksack on back to front, like I'm carrying a baby, to protect the hundreds of francs I have stashed in it from the deft hands of pick-pockets.

I instruct the flock to wait for me near the ticket booth. They can see the angry snake queue slithering back from the ticket booth for miles.

'Don't worry,' I tell them, 'I'll put my body on the line for you.'

Ducking under the guard rope, I stealthily slot myself into pole position at the head of the line, in front of a couple of swarthy middle-aged men. I turn to the previous first place holders.

'Je suis la guide,' I say with faux confidence, hoping that they do not speak French and will not challenge me on this. I often struggle with English, let alone crazy foreign languages that make every single thing in the world either male or female and expect people to remember which sex every single thing is. The previous first-place holder glares and mutters something to his companion in an unidentifiable language, possibly one from Eastern Europe, but thankfully, they do not issue me a challenge.

I often find that if you're confident enough, people assume you must have the right to do what you are doing, even if it seems outrageous. Reaching the sullen ticket seller, who obviously hasn't realised that hair perming really should've been left in the 80s, I ask for, *'Trente billets, s'il vous plaît.'*

The ticket printing machine appears to have come from the 1980s too; every painfully slowly printed ticket it labours over is accompanied by a loud, clunky processing noise, which leads me to imagine there is someone inside it cranking a handle. The crowd behind me in the line is getting restless. I can sense a riot brewing and pray (in a non-religious way) that some of the large lads in the flock will protect me if it turns ugly. I hand over the wad of francs for the tickets and quickly duck back under the rope. I don't understand Spanish, Italian, Romanian or Japanese, but I'm pretty sure I'd just been abused in all of them.

Even though the 900-plus people waiting in line for their tickets are clearly not happy with me, my flock now place me firmly in the 'Legend' category.

'Nice one, Shaz.'

'Good on ya, mate.'

'You rock, Shaz,' I hear from various members.

I see all 30 of them safely through the red elevator doors, while shouting, 'Don't forget you MUST be back at the coach no later than 10pm. Have fun!'

I scoot out from under the tower, turn left and rush down Avenue Silvestre de Sacy and diagonally cross the Avenue de la Bourdonnais, narrowly avoiding being taken out by a car so small it barely deserves to be called a car. I rush under the red awning emblazoned with 'Café Gustave' in gold writing and dodge around numerous marble tables at which stylish Parisian people sit on cane chairs, while managing to make smoking look elegant.

As I push through the brass-rimmed glass swinging doors and enter the café, I wish I'd given it a miss in favour of pulling out my fingernails or more pubic hair instead. Who, out of the hundred or so drivers employed by Terrific Tours in the whole of Europe and the United Kingdom, should be sitting next to ridiculously handsome Roger?

Skipper.

The one and only master of the 'non-withdrawing' method.

Shit. Shit. Shit.

Momentarily, I'm stuck, like a possum in headlights. Unable to process, move, or do anything, I settle on standing still and staring, with my mouth slightly ajar. Roger, Fitzy and Skipper are sitting at a square table on the right-hand side of the café. To the left is the bar counter and, directly in front of me, stairs lead down to *les toilettes*. I weigh up my options instantaneously and decide that buying time to compose myself is vital. I shoot a quick smile at the trio and signal with my hand that I'll just be a minute. I bolt for the stairwell and the haven of the toilets.

'Shit, shit, shit, bugger, bugger, bugger,' I mutter to no one in particular.

I brace myself on the bathroom vanity and stare at my reflection in the wide mirror. Deep breaths. That is what is needed here. Deep breaths and calm thoughts.

Breathe in...

Breathe out...

It's fine...

In...

Out...

No one knows about Skipper... Except me... And Skipper, of course... And even then, I'm a little hazy about it ...

Breathe in...

Out...

After a few minutes, I'm ready to face the boys.

Roger is sitting on a bench seat. Skipper and Fitzy sit on chairs on either side of the table. Conveniently, there is no chair on the fourth side of the table, so I slip around Skipper and slide onto the bench beside Roger. I rest my elbows on the table and say a silent prayer to the café gods that the waiter arrives immediately to ask *this madam* what she would like. He does.

'*Vin. Blanc. Grande. S'il vous plaît.*' I reply.

Skipper turns to me. 'Nice to see you, Shaz.'

'With her clothes on,' Fitzy mumbles under his breath. I swing my foot out to kick him hard in the shin. I connect, at force, instead with the ornate solid metal leg of the table, possibly breaking a couple of my toes. Fuck! Obviously it's hard to keep a secret around here.

'Nice to see you too, Skipper,' I lie through the pain, via orthodontically straightened teeth (I'd kept the teeniest gap between the front two to keep my smile interesting). I held Skipper with my interesting smile for a second before swiftly turning my attention to ridiculously handsome Roger. Skipper and Fitzy engage in some diesel talk, the way drivers do when they get together, giving me a chance to make a move.

'How is your group looking, Roger?' I ask, hitting him with my most beaming, interesting smile. My wine has arrived, and I take a dainty sip, making eyes at Roger over the rim of the glass.

'Pretty good,' Roger replies. He then spends the next five minutes or so telling me all about how many good-looking girls there are in his group and what he thought of his chances with a few of them.

Seriously, does he not get it at all? Did our night of passion mean nothing to him? Just as my mind touches on the devastating thought that this could be a lost cause, I feel a hand land gently on my knee. The hand moves ever so slowly and oh, so seductively, up my thigh to within an inch of my still tender, from the sanitary pad debacle earlier, pubic area. There it rests.

Tantalizingly. The touch light, yet the sensation it creates... electrifying. A shiver of excitement speeds up my spine, raising the hairs on the back of my neck.

Ah, I get it. The chat about other girls is a subterfuge by Roger. A cunning plan to divert Skipper and Fitzy's attention from his burning desire for me! I look at Roger and turn my beaming, interesting smile into a seductive, alluring one. At least that's what I'm hoping to achieve. Taken too far, it could be a smile that appears deluded or demented. It's a fine line and I hope I haven't crossed it.

I take a quick glance over at Fitzy and Skipper to make sure they're still deep in conversation. Check. I take my hand and place it gently on Roger's leg, giving his powerful upper thigh a playful squeeze. I then move my fingers further north to rest millimetres from his crotch. I add to my seductive and alluring smile, a sly wink. Rather than looking pleased, as I had hoped he would, Roger looks somewhat confused and just a little bit anxious. I break eye contact with him and let my hand slide off his thigh.

Roger excuses himself, stands up and moves away from the table towards the bathroom. The hand on my thigh, however, does not leave with him. Instead, it starts to slide provocatively up and down my leg. The realisation of what a twisted, thigh-grabbing *ménage a trois* this has been, dawns on me. I feel a little queasy.

'I'm heading back to the coach, Fitzy,' I say, standing up quickly so that Skipper's hand slams into the underside of the table, making him groan in a way that I find very satisfying. Ha! That's what you get for not withdrawing.

Roger is coming back up the stairs and we arrive near the café door at the same time. 'Shaz, I just want to have a quick word with you,' Roger says before I manage to get through the swinging glass door to safety. 'You remember that château thing?'

How could I forget, I feel like saying. The passion, the intensity, the moment when I fell head over heels in love with you… I just nod.

'Well, I don't think that should happen again, do you? We're going to be bumping into each other a lot on this tour and we should keep it professional, don't you think?'

NO! I scream, thankfully not out loud. The soul piercing, heart breaking noise is confined to my head and reverberates inside my skull while I manage to arrange my mouth into some semblance of a semi-smile.

I force my own head to nod and say, 'Sure, whatever,' in what I hope is a nonchalant way. I freeze the smile in place and turn to exit the café in a graceful, dignified manner. Instead, I walk straight into the glass door and nearly knock myself out, before I manage to negotiate my way through the opening. Tears sting the back of my eyes.

Chapter 7

Paris

Day 1: The longest day ever

10.15pm - We depart the Eiffel Tower only fifteen minutes late, after I had to run around to find a little lost member of the flock... You guessed it, Norman. He came down the west elevator instead of the east, was totally disoriented and about to head off over the river. As Fitzy eases the coach away from the tower, I begin to explain, again, more of the wonders of Paris, although after the café debacle, I have lost a bit of enthusiasm and a lot of focus.

One of the highlights of the tour this evening will be heading onto the roundabout that encircles the Arc de Triomphe. This monument is the ultimate in short man overcompensating. Napoleon's grand erection stands proudly in the middle of a roundabout with 12 roads shooting off it. The rules of the road are very different on this roundabout in Paris from most places in the world. Here, the cars coming onto the roundabout have the right of way, and anyone already circling has to give way, usually abruptly. With the flock not knowing this, the coach drivers love trying to scare the bejesus out of their passengers by speeding onto the roundabout. They thrive on hearing the gasps and screams as cars screech to a halt at the side of the coach. To add to the melodramatic theatrical experience, I will play some suitably exciting music. Sometimes I choose the *1812 Overture* by Tchaikovsky, with its dramatic beat. Tonight, though, I will play *Danger Zone*, the title track of my favourite movie soundtrack, *Top Gun*. What's not to love about Tom Cruise on a large motorbike? Or in a sexy jumpsuit, flying a fast plane? This is sure to get the adrenaline pumping. Not that I have the *actual* soundtrack, of course. What I have are cassettes I've spent hours and hours mixing, to provide theme music for just about every place in Europe I am ever likely to go with a tour group.

My mind flashes back to high school, 1986, when my first boyfriend made me a mixed tape after spending hours recording songs off the radio. It had all my favourites by the likes of Duran Duran, Split Enz and The Violent Femmes. That gift was a sign of dedication; a sign of true love. A sign of a relationship set to go the distance. And it did. A distance of about nine weeks. Which, in the sixth form, was akin to being married.

The coach turns right onto Avenue Victor Hugo. The flock lets out a gasp as, through the front window, they catch their first sight of the 50-metre illuminated Arc de Triomphe. Fitzy slows to snail's pace to allow the cars in front to get ahead, giving him a clear run up to the roundabout. I slide the mixed cassette three-quarters into the tape deck slot and hover my hand above it, ready to shove it in at the appropriate moment. Fitzy begins to speed up. The group begins to murmur, some excitedly, some with just a hint of apprehension. Tension is building.

What is Fitzy doing?

Is he mad? Is he trying to kill us all?

We're getting closer...

Closer...

The flock can see the traffic whizzing around in front of them and see that we are mere seconds away from joining the melee.

This is it.

Fitzy's moment of glory.

I shove the cassette in, so it'll start to play in time for our grand entry to the roundabout, at the climax of Fitzy's driving melodrama. The tension and excitement are palpable.

We speed onto the roundabout. Citroëns, Renaults and Peugeots screech to dramatic halts at our side, missing by millimetres, almost impaled in our luggage doors. As the drama reaches its crescendo, the music starts... And, rather than the powerful beat of *Danger Zone,* on comes the delicate strains of... '*Do a deer, a female deer, ri, a drop of golden sunnnnnnnn...*'

'Crap. Wrong side of the cassette,' I mutter. Desperately searching in the semi-dark for the little button with arrows on it that, if you hit the tape deck, switches to playing the other side of the cassette. Too late, the moment has passed. Skipper obviously isn't the only one with timing issues. Fitzy shoots me a withering look. Musical faux-pas or not, he'll still have half the girls fawning over him about being 'soooo brave,' and asking, 'How do you get that big bus through those tight spaces?' Makes me taste vomit in the back of my throat just thinking about it.

11.20pm - After the Arc de Triomphe, we meander down the Champs-Élysées and make our way back towards the river, to take our weary group back to the hotel. I take a mental recap of the day. It had some not very high highs and some rather low lows. One high has to be not actually vomiting on the coach after taking that damn morning after pill. Was that really only this morning? It feels like a week ago. The lows include ripping half my pubic hair out with a sanitary pad that had clearly been possessed by the devil. The lowest of the lows, without a doubt, was the thigh grabbing mix up at the café, which has now left me torn between being desperate to see Roger again, to see if he was serious about the whole 'professional' thing, and knowing that he comes as a package deal with Skipper, at least for the next couple of weeks.

'Quick drink at the bar before you hit the sack, Shaz?' Fitzy asks as we pull up outside the hotel.

'I really should get some sleep Fitzy... Maybe just one, eh?'

Chapter 8

Paris

Day 2

7am - When my trusty travel alarm clock bursts into life, it doesn't feel like my pillow has even had time to get warm. I split my eyelids a little to squint at the timepiece. 7am? The one drink last night turned into three, maybe four, and it was 2am before I knew it. Bugger. Time to get 'up and at 'em' if I'm going to have a chance to eat and be on the coach by 8.30am.

Before I rise, I take a few minutes to look around the room that I was in and out of so quickly in daylight yesterday. To the right of my comfy double bed is a window with a curtain that I didn't even bother closing last night. My suitcase sits, lonely, underneath it. The view through the window is of the back of another hotel. Scenic. On the opposite wall to the window is a door to the en suite, which is open, revealing a basin and mirror. The room's walls are painted off white, and hanging above the bed is the obligatory hotel artwork of a Parisian scene. In this case, the art stalls of Montmartre.

7.02 am - My brain is now mostly awake, but my body feels leaden. I try to wake it by stretching like a cat would in the sun. I extend my arms above my head, straighten my back, point my toes and let out a satisfied 'humph' sound as my body tenses. That's better. I feel taught, toned, and athletic. Fit and ready to face the world. Suddenly, the calf muscle on my right leg protests at being stretched so fully this early in the morning. It twitches gently at first, then more threateningly, then spasms violently. Argh.

Fuck. Cramp. I snap out of my stretch, and my back clunks as I reach swiftly for the toes on my right foot and pull them back to release my spasming calf muscle. Crap. My body protested a lot for one simple stretch. At 26 years old, I expect better from it. That's hardly athletic! Mind you, when was the last time I did any actual exercise other than running around looking for the odd lost member of a flock? I put that on my mental 'to-do' list – exercise more.

I get myself out of bed and hobble to the other side of the room. I open my suitcase and rummage around for clothes for the day. A pink Benetton collared shirt. Doesn't look too rumpled. A bit of a shake out and it won't need an iron. Perfect. And shorts, not see-through in the slightest. To go with the ensemble, I also grab a skin-toned bra. I throw my toilet bag in to the bathroom basin and balance my clothes on the edge of it, closing the door with my foot in one swift move.

I reach behind the slightly mouldy shower curtain to turn the shower on and take one step to the toilet. There's still some bleeding going on, bit of a pain, but at least that means it's fairly certain that I don't have a little Skipper growing inside me. I shiver involuntarily at the thought.

The water of the shower tickles more than massages, as it splutters out of the tiny shower head. Oh well, at least it's hot. After a quick lather up with the tiny bar of soap provided, I turn off the shower and grab the towel from the rail beside the cubicle. I give myself a good, brusque rub down to get my circulation going and remove any dead skin. I treat my arms, legs and décolletage to a generous layer of expensive cream and cover my face in high SPF moisturiser; I don't want to age before my time. I open my toilet bag again and find a panty liner. I tear the strip off the back to reveal the sticky underside, like a magician demonstrating a 'big reveal'. Ta da! I stick the end of the sticky bit on my top lip for safekeeping until I find my underwear. I'm not going to be sucked in again by any devilish sanitary product. My undercarriage is still tender from my last encounter with one. Okay underwear... Where are you? I lift up my shorts, no. Move the shirt, still no. Shit, bugger, bum. I've forgotten my undies.

I open the bathroom door and tentatively stick my head out. I'm still naked apart from the sanitary pad stuck to my upper lip, giving me the appearance of a St Bernard that is panting to cool down. Fortunately, no one has snuck into my deadlocked hotel room. Just to be sure, I cast my eyes left and right. My sanitary pad tongue sways as I do. The coast is clear. I make a dash for my suitcase, crouch down and rummage around frantically looking for a pair of knickers that's not a g-string. As I rummage, I have an uneasy feeling. I feel like

I'm being watched. Not possible - I'm alone in my hotel room. Just in case, I furtively turn my head to check behind me. No, still nobody has snuck into my deadlocked room.

As I turn back to my gaping suitcase, I glance up through the window. Staring back at me, through a window of the hotel opposite, is a businessman in suit and tie, his mouth wide open, gaping. He stares at me, obviously unable to make sense of what he's seeing. Surely he's seen a naked dog/woman with her head in a suitcase before? I try to smile, but the sanitary pad tickles my chin. I stand, unashamed of my nakedness, grab the curtains and pull them dramatically together. Magic act over. Curtain drawn. God, surely this day has to get better?

9.30am - Fitzy has battled Parisian rush-hour traffic to get us to Notre Dame. Terrific Tours hires a local guide in Paris to do an extensive tour of the cathedral. They do this for two reasons: One, it's illegal for foreigners to do guided tours of the city unless they have some complicated certification, which I don't. Two, they feel the local adds more 'depth and authenticity to the client's experience'. Bah. While I disagree, it does mean I have to do feck all this morning!

Today's Parisian guide is a woman who must be as old as Notre Dame itself. Okay, I'm exaggerating; maybe she's only nine hundred and ninety. The only authenticity she adds to the flock's day is her French accent; an accent so thick that most of the flock can't understand a word she's saying. I struggle to follow what she's talking about, and I've been here and heard the spiel a lot. At least the sun is warming the morning air as the flock stands watching her, whilst trying to nod in the right places. Mostly, they fail. It's like a Mexican wave of nodding that, after my late night and a couple of wines, is really quite hypnotic. My mind wanders. I wonder when Roger will be here? Oh shit, I remember, he doesn't want me. I...

'SHAZ.' Nine hundred and ninety year-old woman is shouting at me.

'*Oui?*'

'Ve vill meeeet ut ilevn a.m. - no?'

'No... I mean, *oui*. 11am. Tres bien,' I reply. I turn to the flock, 'We will meet out the back of the cathedral in the little park with the swing at 11am. Please be careful of pickpockets when you are in the church. Stick with your guide, she'll tell you everything you've ever wanted to know about the Notre Dame.'

And off they go. And off I go. Not into the church, but rather down the left side of the massive Gothic structure. I go beneath the gargoyles, which tower way above my head, their mouths gaping wide, ready to spit out rainwater to keep it from running down the side of the building. I dodge the piles of Parisian pooch poop on the cobbled footpath and cross the narrow road. I swerve around clusters of tourists from Asia, crowded around shop stalls that hold postcards, scarves and miniature Notre Dames.

I've arrived at my morning haven in Paris, Café Esmerelda. Here, not only can I satiate my need for caffeine, but I can also see when the flock is at the meeting point. That way, I can rush over with my clipboard looking very busy and important, like I've been working *tres, tres* hard while they've been learning about the church. Genius!

'*Oui*,' the grumpy-looking man behind the cafe counter with a dark monobrow enquires.

'*Je voudrais un café au lait, s'il vous plaît,*' I reply, hitting him with my most beaming smile.

'Sugar?' He grumps, switching seamlessly to English and clearly not fooled by my 'French' accent.

Not to be put off, I stick to the local tongue. *'Oui, merci beaucoup.'*

I find a stool at the polished wooden bar, with a view out to the back garden of the church and indulge in the creamy caffeine heaven that Mr Grumpy slides my way. I wonder if Roger will come here? Maybe he has another hangout. Not that I'm looking for him. But he wasn't one of the 300 or so people who walked past the café as I sat watching the world go by.

Chapter 9

Paris

Day 2: Later that day

6pm - I have time for a decent shower before I meet the flock at 6.30pm to drive them to a traditional Parisian restaurant (where I've rarely heard French spoken) for dinner, before we go to the Moulin Rouge. After making sure the curtain in my room is firmly shut, I undress, letting my clothes fall in a pile near my suitcase. The shower still isn't much more than a trickle, but it's enough to double wash and condition my hair and lather some soap with which to clean myself from head to toe. After I'm clean and dry, I dress for an evening out in 'the city of love'. Over my underwear, I slip on a fitted navy blue shift dress, which is long enough to be modest and short enough to show off my tanned knees. I choose black high-heeled shoes with a thin ankle strap to accentuate my shapely calves and slim ankles. To push the point home, I clasp a delicate gold anklet around my right ankle.

Anklets around the left ankle mean you're a prostitute. Don't want to give the wrong impression. Or maybe it's the right ankle? No, I'm sure it's left. Or maybe it's just an urban legend that prostitutes made up to stress high school students out?

I clip small gold hoops in my ears. Around my neck I hang a gold chain with a Pinocchio charm on it. Pinocchio's feet dangle on the crevice of my cleavage. If Pinocchio lets go of the chain, he's a goner. What would the gold retailers of Florence do without me? Hopefully, Pinocchio will send a subliminal 'liar' message to Roger, while also drawing his attention to my cleavage. Let it go Shaz, let it go.

Le Petit Oignon is located on a small street off the Boulevard Saint-Michel on the bohemian Left Bank. Fitzy drops us off a couple of blocks away from the restaurant. The flock follows me on foot, dodging yet more smouldering piles of Parisian dog poop and human Parisians charging determinedly in a straight line to wherever it is they are in such a rush to get to, until we arrive at the red wooden restaurant door. As we enter, Pierre (real name Peter, from Leeds) serenades us with his accordion while he ushers us upstairs, past the gathering of dodgy-looking men sitting at the bar smoking Gauloises cigarettes, to a large dining area filled with long tables covered in white tablecloths.

There is a tour group chatting and laughing at some of the tables at the far end of the room. I glance over to the corner of the room where a table is set up for the road crew. Skipper is sitting erect in his chair and is following me with his gaze.

He beams a generous smile my way when he sees me. I flick a quick, not-so-generous, not-so-beaming one back. Next to Skipper sits Roger, lounging back in his seat. He looks divine in a crisp white shirt that is held tightly at the neck by a thin black leatherette tie. Roger is smiling at a girl with big hair who has bobbed down beside his chair to chat.

I direct my flock to their tables. Rather than going to the crew table, I pull up a chair in between two male flock members. Not any random table, but one that is directly in Roger's line of vision. I cross my legs seductively, dangling a slim ankle towards him. Fitzy clunks up the stairs and, seeing me, stops dead in his tracks. He looks at me sitting with some of our flock, then looks to the crew table where Skipper and Roger sit. He looks back at me, confused.

'Aren't you coming to the crew table, Shaz?'

'No Fitzy. I'm getting to know these lovely folk better.' I hit my tablemates with a beaming smile.

Fitzy smiles nervously at them and bends to whisper in my ear. 'Why the fuck do you want to do that? Come sit with us. It'll be a laugh.'

A laugh is absolutely the LAST thing I think it will be.

'No, I'm good. You go though.' He's obviously not sure if I really mean it or if I'm setting some kind of tricky feminine trap. However, when the choice is between making small talk with his clients or talking shit with the boys, the decision is not even close for Fitzy and he saunters over to join Roger and Skipper.

Out of the corner of my eye, I can see the three of them questioning what I'm doing, with plenty of shrugging of shoulders. The entrée has arrived. While my tablemates have all opted for French onion soup, to broaden their horizons and show how European I am, I've ordered escargot. The clean white plate in front of me has the carcasses of six snails swimming in melted garlic butter in their shells. Not so much swimming, obviously, as they're dead, and I'm not actually even sure snails would be able to swim, given their lack of limbs. I think even if they waved their sticky-up eyes at light speed, it still wouldn't keep them afloat. It's actually more like they've drowned in garlic butter. The only utensil provided to eat the escargot is the world's smallest fork. My tablemates look at me expectantly. Why did I have to be such a bloody show off? Why didn't I just order the bollocking soup? My stomach is still not 100% after that morning-after pill. The memory of the pill prompts an involuntary turn of my head towards Skipper and a flash of a stern frown.

'Come on Shaz. Get stuck in,' Flock member number one chirps up. I must start to learn some of their names.

I grab the tiny fork, plunge it into a little snail carcass and lift it out of its shell coffin. It looks like an amputated labia. Just about the last thing I want to do is put it in my mouth, but I'll lose street cred if I don't now. I smile at my tablemates and place the morsel gently onto my tongue. All I can taste is garlic. Thank God.

Satisfied, my tablemates get on with their delicious-looking soup while I chew on the garlic labia-esque food in my mouth. The now overpowering taste of garlic mixed with the greasiness of the butter is turning my stomach. I start to feel a little ill. While conscious that I must now chew, I just can't make my jaw cooperate. I look around the table and weigh up my options. Spit? Chew? Swallow? I pick up the half-full glass of wine in front of me and finish it in one go, washing the drowned snail down. The snail doesn't slide down in the way you'd expect a slimy thing to, rather it ping-pongs off either side of my gullet as it travels south.

Just stay in my stomach… Please. A few deep breaths, and I feel confident the escargot won't be expelled in a hurry.

So I don't have to repeat the exercise with the remaining five snails, I excuse myself in order to go and work the room and chat to the rest of the flock sitting at other tables. Roger, on seeing that he is being out-tour-managed by me, moves reluctantly away from Skipper and Fitzy and begins mingling with his own tour group.

The rest of the meal is less gastronomically challenging; a main course of veal in marsala sauce and a heavenly crème caramel to finish. During dinner, the flock has been merrily swilling carafes of cheap, nasty French wine, and most members are well-oiled by the time we need to leave to meet Fitzy at the coach for the drive to the Moulin Rouge.

While the area surrounding the restaurant we just dined at is modern, edgy and chic, the Pigalle area that has been home to the Moulin Rouge since 1889 is anything but. Fast food joints, restaurants, souvenir shops and a *supermarché erotique* (don't need to speak French to work that one out) stand shoulder to shoulder along the Boulevard de Clichy, which is the main road through the area. Side streets on one side of the boulevard slope upwards to meet the feet of Montmartre, on top of which the gleaming white Sacre Coeur basilica sits virginal and disapproving of the sin taking place below. I remind the flock to be extra vigilant with their valuables as we leave the safety of the coach to join the heaving mass of humanity swarming around the Pigalle.

The glowing red windmill of the Moulin Rouge is a marker so prominent that even the most geographically challenged tour manager like me can't possibly miss it. Soon, I have the flock safely down the sumptuous red hallway, inside and sitting at small round tables towards the back of the vast, ornate theatre. Each table has a small, fringed lamp at its centre and a complimentary mini bottle of champagne opposite each chair. Those will be gone in no time, I'm sure. I get directed to a table for two in the darkest, dingiest corner of the room. I sit down wearily and wait for the show to start.

A dark figure lowers into the chair beside me. 'Hi Shaz.'

That voice. It makes me melt.

'Hi Roger.'

'Why didn't you sit with us at dinner?'

Because I'd rather have had my fingernails pulled out one by one than spend a single minute sitting with you and Skipper at the same table. I hope I only said that in my head. From what I can see of Roger's expression in the gloom, he's still waiting for a reply. Phew.

'I really like to spend time with my group early on in the tour, get to know them, let them know I care.' That sounds feasible.

'So where are they from?' Roger enquires.

'Who?'

'Your group, Shaz. The ones you just spent time getting to know.'

'Right. No idea.'

'No idea?'

'Sorry, did you say where are they from? I thought you said, where do they run?' That does NOT sound feasible.

'They're mainly from Oz and NZ, a couple of Saffas, a couple of Canadians and Malaysians.' I'm back on the right side of feasible.

'Shaz … About last night.'

'Look! The show's starting.' Thankfully, the whole theatre is plunged into darkness, and loud music heralds the start of the show. Further conversation is now impossible.

Sitting very close to Roger in the dark is fine for the opening song, the jugglers and the tightrope walker. When the full cabaret kicks in though, and the stage is covered in beautiful, toned and topless women jiggling up and down, the proximity becomes decidedly uncomfortable. As soon as the last dazzling sequin has dimmed and the last breast bounced, I bid Roger a cursory farewell and rush to gather my flock. Most are still trying to finish their alcohol as quickly as possible. Some are, without much subtlety, scouring neighbouring tables for anyone foolish enough to have left behind their complimentary champagne.

'Righto, everyone, time to call it a night. I'll meet you on the bus, which Fitzy will have parked close to the door.'

The responsible members of the group collect up their jackets, purses and cameras and begin to make their way out. A hardcore group of revellers don't appear interested in leaving at all.

'Come on guys, dodgy train ride back to the hotel at this time of night. Best get moving so Fitzy doesn't leave us behind.'

Gail from Kalgoorlie, Western Australia, plonks a solid arm over my shoulder and sways in close to the side of my face.

'Yor da besht too'ah manglar I've eva had Shazza,' she gushes.

'How many tours have you been on, Gail?' I can't help asking.

'Zish iz my firsht eva.' And away she sways towards her new best friend Belinda, who has a bottle of champagne to her mouth, her head tipped back to drain every last drip.

Laurent, the manager of the Moulin Rouge, is scowling in my general direction. There's a quick turnaround between the 9pm show we watched and the 11pm show, the last of the evening. The staff need to reset the tables and tidy the area for the hundreds of people lined up outside, and my lot of hooligans hanging about isn't helping. Roger, on the other hand, has his entire group out. They're probably halfway back to their hotel by now.

Time is ticking by, and Fitzy will be getting grumpy, as well as running out of his allowable driving hours. I stand between the stage and the flock stragglers, putting my arms out wide in the way a shepherd would. Talking in calming tones, I move forward with my arms wide, literally herding them towards the exit, out of the door and up the stairs to the coach where Fitzy sits with a face like thunder.

'I'll just do a count, Fitzy,' and off down the coach I go.

'Could you all sit down please? Just for a minute, so I can make sure you're all here… please…' The bodies in the aisle fall into the nearest seats.

2,4,6,8. Someone jumps up and switches seats. Shit. Back to the front.

2,4,6,8,10,12. No, the last 2 were empty seats with bags, so is that 10? Back to the front: 2,4,6.

'Here we are,' trill Sue and Paula as they squeeze past me and shimmy all the way to the back of the bus.

Back to the front I go.

'Can we just go?' Fitzy grumps. Memories of my last Paris tour debacle flood back, and Neil's stern words run through my head.

'Sorry Fitzy, I just need to be sure.'

2,4,6,8,10,12,14,16,18, someone pinches my butt, ouch, 20,22,24,26,28,29 ... Whose missing? A quick scan of the coach... Norman? Shit. Where's Norman?

'Don't let anyone off, Fitzy. I'll be back in a minute.' I rush off the coach and back down the plush red hallway into the theatre. I find Norman fast asleep in a back corner. One of the staff is trying to vacuum around him. I soon have Norman awake and on board.

Phew, that was a close call.

Chapter 10

En route to the Beaujolais region

Day 3

8am - It's been a couple of days now since I popped the pills that would stop any potential spawn of Skipper from sticking in my uterus, and I'm starting to feel normal, whatever that is. I've had no more spotting or queasy stomach problems, and my groin is almost recovered from the attack of the sanitary pad. My emotional state is in a less pristine condition, but as Roger and Skipper have headed elsewhere, today I'll have some time to work on that, before I bump into them again.

The Parisian traffic is kind to us this morning. Soon we have negotiated the chaos of the Peripherique, the road that encircles Paris, and are cruising south in the general direction of Lyon. Our final destination: a tiny speck of a village.

10am - I take to the stage, that is the aisle of the coach, facing the flock, and click on the microphone.

'Okay, folks, time to get to know each other better.' Equal amounts of happy and moaning noises accompany this announcement. 'Fitzy and I will start, then it's your turn. One person from your travel group can come up and tell us your name, where you're from and what you do. I'll start. My name is Sharon, but everyone calls me Shaz. I'm 26 years old. I come from a smallish coastal town in New Zealand called Whakatane.' There are some sniggers at this, as my home town is pronounced *Faka-TAH-ne*. 'You all know what I do; I take tours around Europe. Have done it for three summers now. Before taking tours, I worked in an office in Whakatane answering the phone, filing pieces of paper and wishing I was anywhere else. In the European winters, I either go home to see my mum or I travel somewhere different. My favourite drink is Chardonnay, hint hint, and my favourite band is Duran Duran. See, easy right? Fitzy, you're next.'

Fitzy multitasks; with one hand on the steering wheel, he takes a gamble that gear changes won't be required, and he takes the cordless microphone from me.

'Hi, I'm Fitzy. I'm 33. I'm a driver and I'm from Australia'. He hands the microphone back. Man of few words, our Fitzy.

'Who'd like to go first?' I ask cheerily as I wave the microphone in the general direction of the flock. Norman, bless him, shoots his hand straight up. He ambles down the aisle, sits in a vacant front row seat and I hand him the microphone.

'Hi, me name's Norman and I'm from 'Straylia. I'm 30 and I worked on an assembly line, but me doc said I needed a holiday. I live wiv me Mum. She wanted to come on the tour

84

too, but she was too old.' Norman passes the microphone one seat back.

'My name's Brad and this is Laura,' he says, nodding his head toward the seat next to him. 'We live in Vancouver, eh. We're both teachers. I teach high school PE and Laura teaches primary, eh. We got married two years ago and we're trying to make a baby.' This prompts enthusiastic cheering from everyone on the coach. He passes the baton backwards.

'Hi, I'm Hazdy and I'm travelling with my brother Mo. We are from Malaysia. Our parents wanted us to be doctors but we're rebels, so I'm studying architecture and Mo studies history.' This makes me panic; nothing worse than passengers knowing more about the history than you do. Mental note to ask him what area of history Mo's studying.

Next.

'Yeah, gidday. I'm Colin, and this is me mate Keith. We're both tradies from Newcastle.' Colin and Fitzy should get together and chat, it'd be fascinating. I notice Colin lingers whilst passing the mic on to Bianca. Looks to me like he's trying to make deliberate hand contact.

'Hi, I'm Bianca. I'm travelling with Candy and Paige,' two girls with equally 'Colgate' smiles and perfect skin wave enthusiastically. 'We're from California and we're cheerleaders.' No surprises there. From the way they look, they shine from the top of their shampoo advert hair to the clean white trainers that highlight their tanned legs. In stark contrast, next to speak is Teresa, who looks like she wouldn't even know what cheerleading was and certainly hasn't been touched by any sun recently.

'Hello. I'm Teresa. From Dunedin. New Zealand. I'm a vegan. I'm travelling with Jane. She's not a vegan. We do both love to read though.' Teresa passes the microphone over her head and it is accepted by the most enormous hand you'll ever see. The enormous hand is attached to Hennie.

'Ya, I'm Hennie,' he booms into the piece of equipment specifically designed to amplify voices. 'This is Zola. We are from *Suth Afreeka*. I'm 31 and Zola is 28. We are cattle farmers.' Hennie passes the mic across the aisle to a female who is as tough-looking as Hennie, but half his size.

'Yeah, gidday. I'm Gail, my mates call me G, or G-dog. I work in the mines in Kalgoorlie. This is me mate Belinda, she's from Perth.' Note to self: don't piss Gail off in any way shape or form. Gail passes forward.

'Hi, I'm Peter and I really need to take a piss.'

'Right, yes of course.' I had noticed a few people shuffling in their seats. I turned to Fitzy, hoping he'd back me up, 'Fitzy, how long is it to the stop we talked earlier about making?'

'Great timing as always, Shaz,' Fitzy responds. 'It's right here.' And, with that, he swerves the coach off to the right and down the slip road that leads to Beaune-Tailly Services. The flock unloads and files into the services to relieve themselves and refuel, as do Fitzy and I. Forty-five minutes later, we are back on the road, and Peter is ready to continue.

'Hi, I'm Peter and I feel much better now.' Murmurs of agreement and a few giggles. 'This is my friend Murray. We've been mates since we were ten years old. We both live in Christchurch. We're both 28 and we love rugby - go the mighty Crusaders!' I can sense some rugby banter in my future with Peter, as I most definitely do not support the Crusaders.

'Hi, I'm Sheryl. I'm travelling with Deb and Fiona. Deb and I both work for the New Zealand Government, and Fiona works in fashion.'

Fiona looks like she works in fashion. While Sheryl and Deb both have on the standard New Zealander travel wardrobe of Adidas three stripe tracksuit pants and t-shirts, Fiona has trendy dungarees over a white lacy singlet. Her hairstyle is 'the Rachel'. All Friends fans want to have this haircut, but not many can pull it off. Fiona can. Sheryl passes forward.

'Howdy, my name's Randy, and this here is my buddy Jake. We are from Nu Yawk. I'm 26, and Jake here is 27. We both work in banking.'

That'd explain the ironed shirts they've worn every day then. Randy hands on to a couple who are looking none too happy at either having to speak, or actually being alive. While both reach back to take the microphone, it's the female of the pair who snatches it from Randy. She gives her partner a death stare as she does.

'Hi, I'm Clara and I'm a teacher. This is my *boyfriend* Justin, he can speak for himself.' She thrusts the microphone into his chest, which takes the wind out of him momentarily. Justin looks sheepish behind his rimless specs.

'Hi, as Clara said, I'm Justin. I work in television as a reporter. Clara and I have been together three years now and, as you can see, it's going great.'

Does this man have an actual death wish? While there are a few nervous chortles from around the flock, Clara's death stare darkens momentarily before she turns to look, passive aggressively, out of the window. Lucky she does, as Justin gives Sue the biggest smile as he hands the microphone to her.

'Hi, I'm Sue, and this is my friend Paula. We live on the Gold Coast. We are both 24 and we love surfing.' They look like surfers. Both have long flowing hair in sun-kissed shades of blonde/beige. Their suitcases seem to be full of Billabong clothing, and they wear jandals (or flip flops as they call them), constantly. Sue passes forward to the final members of the flock to speak.

'Hi, I'm Sally and this is my partner Margot.' Suitably vague, could be business partners? 'We are from Calgary, Canada. I work in a coffee shop, Margot works in a movie theatre. We are both 22 and vegetarians.' Sally hands the microphone back to me, looking relieved that her turn has come and gone.

'That's fantastic everyone, thanks for sharing. I'll let you know when we get to Oingt, so sit back and relax.' I take my own advice and sit back in the jump seat ready to watch the French countryside slide by as my feet dangle in the stairwell.

Chapter 11

Beaujolais region

Still Day 3

4pm - I click on the microphone.

'Bonjour tout le monde! It's time to wake up, as we are nearly at our destination, the Chateau Vin Rouge. The Chateau is nestled in vine-covered hills and is near the village of Oingt. This is the Beaujolais region of France.' There is a buzz of excitement throughout the coach. 'Grapes were first brought to this area by the Romans, loads of years ago, and wine has been produced here ever since, meaning… they've had some time to get it right. The Beaujolais grapes are picked in September, whipped into Beaujolais wine and in bottles on the shelf by November. Hoorah!' I'm not the only one who's pumped; there is a murmur of excitement, with

whispers being shared among the flock. 'Terrific Tours have been staying at the Chateau Vin Rouge for more than twenty years, to educate and enlighten fine young people like you about the production of wine.' Sometimes people take the education and enlightenment seriously, most just quaff the wine at a great rate of knots and suffer the consequences of the 'Beaujolais monster'. Each to their own, I say.

'The Chateau itself is nearly five hundred years old. A magnificent sandstone building set on the side of a gently sloping hill with an amazing vista, which I'm sure you'll all love. From its grand cobbled balcony, you get views of the surrounding rolling hills, carpeted in vineyards. The Chateau has turrets on either side which, as you will see, gives it a fairy tale quality. Just wait 'til later when, in the setting sun, the building changes colour from light gold to burnt orange.' The excitement is building. Clara has even softened her face into something resembling a smile as she soaks up the view.

'The Chateau was originally owned by minor royals, distant cousins of the Bourbon monarchs. It was sacked and burned during the French Revolution in 1789 by local 'have-not' peasants, rising up against the 'haves' gentry. Legend has it that a young boy servant of the family died during the fire after becoming trapped in one of the turrets. It's said he continues to haunt the building to this day.'

I hear a few ghostly ohhhhhs from down the bus.

'The Chateau has been repaired and used over the years as a number of different things; from a nunnery to a hospital for war veterans. The building fell into disrepair in the 1970s, when it was snapped up by Terrific Tours to be used as somewhere for young people, like you, to experience the French countryside.' Twitters of excitement from the flock.

'There is a cuvage - wine cave - behind the Chateau, where we will have wine tasting before dinner. It also has wine for sale, which you can snap up if you're keen for a cheap bottle of plonk… I mean an authentic French wine experience. This dark, damp cave lined with enormous aged oak vats full of Beaujolais wine is our first stop this afternoon in Oingt.' Randy lets out a '*Yeehah*'. Peter and Murray '*Yeehah*' him back.

5pm - After throwing backpacks and suitcases into their assigned rooms in the Chateau, the flock follows me, crunching up the gravel driveway to the sealed path, which leads to the wine cave. The coolness of the cave is a welcome relief from the heat of the afternoon outside. No one is in a hurry to leave after the friendly barman, Nick, has given his talk about what makes good Beaujolais.

Nick is my favourite South African in the whole entire world. At twenty-three, he is three years younger than me. He has fallen into a job with Terrific Tours as he has a British passport, thanks to his homeland's colonial past. Nick is also the cutest South African I know. He is model tall and lean, with moppish sandy brown hair that falls over his forehead, to slightly cover his large brown cow eyes. His skin is a perfect organic free-range brown egg delicious colour, ever so slightly speckled with freckles, without the hard and shelly bit. His straight nose leads your eye to his perfectly formed, luscious lips. His dress sense is impeccable. He has made the lime green of the uniform shirt look amazing, teaming it with dark denim Levi 501s and a bandana casually hanging out of his back pocket, drawing my attention, every so often, to his rather beautiful behind.

Nick is also gay; as gay as a gay thing on gay day. And his boyfriend, Carl, is also an employee of Terrific Tours in another part of Europe. Because Nick is taken, I have adopted him as my little brother, best friend and boyfriend (without the sex) all rolled into one. We've made a pact that if I haven't had children by the time I am thirty-five, he'll father a couple for me. I'm not sure that Carl knows about our deal, but as 35 is YEARS away for me, I don't feel the need to worry about that small detail just now.

Nick also thinks Roger is 'to die for' and last year, after the end of season staff party, we left the funky Covent Garden venue together to try to find Roger, by roaming aimlessly around the streets of London. Despite our best efforts, Roger was nowhere to be found. Just as well, really, as I'm not quite sure what the two of us would have done with the one of him if we'd found him. I love Nick dearly, but I don't want to share my future husband with him in a sexual way.

Learning from Nick's spiel, the flock members hold their wine glasses up for an inspection of colour, give them a swirl to check if the wine has good legs and bury their noses deep in their glasses to assess the bouquet. The next step is sipping and, supposedly, spitting the wine after all the taste qualities have been enjoyed. This last step was unanimously skipped by the flock; they all swallow and follow up with another sip and swallow.

Nick gets into his sales pitch and soon most of the flock has shelled out fifteen Francs to take away their own bottle, or two or three, to enjoy later with dinner, or with a picnic on their free day tomorrow. My thirst is barely touched by the first glass of fruity red wine that makes it past my lips. I sip through a second and third as I chat to the flock and Nick, as he hands over bottle after bottle of wine. Soon, the last of the flock has wandered/swayed/staggered back down the driveway to get ready for dinner, to be followed by a quiet night in front of one of the enormous fireplaces. It can still be a little chilly in the evening in May inside this huge stone building, but the fires are mainly lit for ambience. Nick and I are now alone in the wine cave.

'How's Carl?' I ask, helping to tidy up by picking up a couple of glasses and putting them onto a metal dishwasher tray.

'He's good. He's just been visiting here for a few days, so I feel all satisfied and glowy,' Nick gushes.

'Okay, too much information.' I smile at him.

'How about you, darling Shaz? Do you have any action to report?' He enquires while doing a final wipe of the tasting table.

'I saw Roger in Paris,' I start.

'AND,' Nick screeches, stopping what he's doing immediately to grab my shoulders so he can study my face closely.

'And nothing.' I shrug my shoulders in a 'what's a girl to do' kind of way. 'He said he wants to keep things professional… after I grabbed his upper thigh under the table by mistake.'

'Seriously, Sharon Louise Green, what are you like? How do you grab a man's leg under a table, by mistake? Only you!' He laughs. 'You will have to tell me ALL about it later, but for now I have to get back to work.'

We walk, in comfortable silence, side by side down the driveway to the Chateau. Before parting, we arrange a rendezvous in his room after dinner, with a bottle of wine, so I can fill him in on the ups and downs of the last couple of days with Roger. And we can analyse what it all means.

At the Chateau, the flock has settled into the dining room, eating roast chicken with golden pomme noisettes and engaging in rowdy chatter. The volume is increasing as the wine flows. I wander into the large industrial kitchen and grab a plate of food, taking an extra pomme noisette to soak up some of the wine I've had on an empty stomach. I plonk myself at the wooden table beside the walk-in pantry to chat to Kerry from Perth, our chef for the evening. I skip the chocolate éclair for dessert, as all dessert calories will be used on wine, and head to the bar to wait for Nick.

'Hi Nick! Hi Gary,' I chirrup as I enter the large, dark mahogany-lined room, which is used as a casual bar and games room.

'Give me half an hour, Shaz,' Nick says. 'I just have to put all the board games out, stoke the fire, and then I'm all yours.'

Gary, a bear of a man, leans over the bar towards me, smiling. 'I could be all yours, Shaz. I could stoke your fire too, if you know what I mean.' He lowers his voice to a whisper. 'It may be small, Shaz,' he nods in the general direction of his groin, 'but... there's sixteen stone pushing it in.'

'You'd need more than sixteen stone to get IT anywhere near me, Gary,' I volley back. 'I'll wait for you upstairs, Nick.' I call over my shoulder, grabbing a bottle of Beaujolais and two glasses off the bar on my way. Walking up the first of three flights of concrete stairs, I ponder that even though I'd rejected him, as he'd expected I would, I know that Gary's unconventional pick up line has worked many, many times in the past. Obviously some women are curious to see whether IT really was as small as he says it is. Ewwww.

Nick's room is in one of the turrets on the side of the Chateau. It's accessed from the third-floor landing, through a low wooden door and up a narrow spiral staircase. I reach the top of the third flight of stone stairs, puffing ever so slightly, and turn right. I push open the cream wooden door, only just getting through without having to duck my head. The door slams shut behind me and I am plunged into total darkness. Shit. An involuntary squeak escapes my mouth, a shiver runs down my spine and my blood starts to pump audibly through to my brain.

There's no such thing as ghosts… There's no such thing as ghosts… There's no such thing as ghosts… I mutter to myself. I change the two wine glasses from my right hand to my left, beside the bottle of Beaujolais, and reach out with my right hand to find the wall. My hand bats the wall wildly searching for a light switch, panic slowly rising in my chest. I give up, and turn back towards the door to find the handle and escape, when something furry brushes against my ankle.

'Argh,' I scream at full volume. The door flies open, and I fall out onto the landing into Nick's arms. He stops me, and the wine and glasses from ending up on the floor. A flash of fluffy orange tells me that the ghostly ankle tickle is actually the Chateau cat, ironically named Blackie. I shudder in Nick's arms and struggle to get my breathing to return to normal.

'Shaz, are you okay?' Nick asks.

'Door… dark… ghost… cat,' I gasp. A smile spreads across Nick's face as he struggles to suppress the bubble of a giggle threatening to burst out of his mouth.

'Where's the bloody light switch? And what are you doing with that cat in your room?' I screech, whacking him with my free arm.

'It's the only pussy I'm ever going to want in my bed, Shaz,' he quips, as he flicks on the light to the stairs, grabs my right hand with his left and leads me up the winding staircase to his boudoir.

The view from Nick's bedroom is one of the best in the

Chateau. During the day, the valley of vineyards stretches out to the left and right; a huge shag pile rug of colour. White in the winter, as the snow covers the valleys. Green in spring, as the grapevines burst into life for the New Year. Into summer, the carpet darkens as the red of the grapes overtakes the green leaves. Autumn brings brilliant oranges and yellows and, finally, a solid brown, as the leaves fall to earth. Now, at night, the darkness is pin pricked with lights from winemakers' cottages and the only sound is the odd burst of laughter from the games room three floors below, as pissed Pictionary is in full swing.

Filling the two glasses with cherry red wine, we sit on Nick's queen-sized mattress, the only piece of furniture in the room, aside from a small wooden chest of drawers. We prop ourselves up with pillows so we can see the night sky out of the two large arched windows. I rest my head on Nick's shoulder, between sips of wine, as I go through the last week of my life. It starts with finding myself accidentally shagging Skipper and ends with the thigh-grabbing threesome and Roger trashing my hopes and dreams by declaring we should keep things professional. Nick puts his arm over my shoulder and gives me a squeeze.

'Do you think he meant it?' He asks. I shrug, taking another big gulp from my glass. 'You know, Shaz.' He pauses, rummaging in his mind for the right words. 'Roger's friendly with a lot of girls. He's always draped in them when he's here.'

'He's a good-looking guy.'

'I know that Shaz. I'd shag him in a minute.'

'But what about Carl?' I turn and look into his molten chocolate eyes.

'He could watch.' He laughs as I snort wine out of my nose

96

onto his aquamarine duvet cover. 'I just don't want you to get hurt, babe. Where is he now?'

'Not sure, gone south I think. They get back to London about the same day as we do, so I reckon we'll bump into them in some cities. I really *loooooooooove* him, Nick, I mean *reaaaaaalllly loooooooove* him.' I put my glass of wine down beside the mattress and snuggle closer into Nick. 'Why can't he be more like you?'

'Gay, you mean?' Nick puts his wine down too and envelopes me in a candyfloss sweet hug and plants a gentle kiss on the top of my head.

'What about Skipper?' he asks.

'What about him?'

'He's a good-looking guy, nice too.'

'Not my hose reel,' I murmur.

Chapter 12

~~~

Beaujolais region

Day 4

7.02am - The sun shining in through the arched windows wakes me and I realise I'm hot; very hot. I try to sit up, but I'm pinned across the chest by something heavy. Huh? I twist my head and see Nick's sweet face millimetres from my own, breathing hot air onto my cheek. As well as his arm pinning my chest, his leg is thrown carelessly over my hip, his foot twisted back and under my leg. I kiss Nick on the forehead gently and whisper his name to wake him up.

Nothing.

'Nick… Nick.' A little louder, 'Nick.' Finally, 'NICK!' He spontaneously levitates off the bed in fright and lands back beside me. He grabs me and then tickles me mercilessly. 'Stop

Nick, stop,' I plead.

'Never,' he says and laughs in an evil dictator kind of way, digging his fingers wickedly into my ribs below my armpits.

'I'm… going… to… pee… my… pants,' I finally get out. He stops immediately and envelopes me in another of his lovely hugs.

'Why can't you be straight?' I ask into his warm neck.

'B.e.c.a.u.s.e.' He starts like he's speaking to a two-year-old. 'I'm prettier than you.'

'Fair point, my pretty friend. Want to come on a picnic with me today?'

10am - I devour a bowl of cornflakes, moistened with creamy UHT milk, whilst sitting among some stragglers of the flock who are lingering in the dining room and planning where they should head for their picnic today. I check the weather forecast by jumping up and sticking my head out of the door. The morning air is crisp and cool, but the sky is blue. It looks like it's going to be a lovely day.

I grab a wicker picnic basket and a rolled-up, plastic-backed faux tartan (not very French) picnic blanket from the kitchen. I pop in a couple of serviettes, plastic knives and plastic cups, a baguette, two juicy-looking red apples and a bottle of sparkling water. From the large stainless steel industrial fridge, I grab a plump tomato, a round of gooey brie and four thick slices of ham. Next, I head to the bar, where I gather a bottle of rosé Beaujolais and a corkscrew made from an old grape vine.

Nick is on the front stairs waiting for me, looking divine in his white Levis and a dark blue denim shirt - very George Clooney. A strong sense of déjà vu washes over me, causing me to stop in my tracks. Seeing Nick's white jeans and being in the chateau whisks me back to this time last year, when another handsome man arrived at those steps. I was on my second night there, waiting for the next tour group to arrive so we could join our two flocks together and have a party. Who should step off the coach as it arrived that sunny July afternoon? Roger.

He lifted his tortoiseshell Rayban Wayfarers from his eyes, scooping up his fringe, and placed them on top of his head. He stepped onto the gravel driveway wearing a pink shirt, sleeves rolled up and unbuttoned just enough to see the sculpted muscles on his chest. His white jeans hugged him in all the right places, and my eyes were drawn, beyond my control, to his crotch. He saw me eyeing his nether regions and smiled.

'Nice to see you, Shaz,' he crooned. He could have taken me then and there, but it wasn't until the wee small hours of the following morning that I found myself behind the gracious building with Roger's tongue down my throat. His hands grasped my chest as I dug my fingernails into his back.

Breathless he asked, 'Your room?'

'I'm sharing,' I panted. 'Yours?'

'Same,' he said, pushing me back onto the sandstone building wall. He slid his hands up the back of my thighs and gave my bum a rough squeeze. His hand moved around to the front of my body and he slid a finger under the front of my underwear and between my legs. I groaned and bit his neck, moving my hips ever so slightly back and forward over his finger.

'Can we just do it here?' He almost begged. I shook my head, which made Roger gasp in pain as I'd forgotten to release my teeth from his neck.

'I know,' he said and moved abruptly away. My body, a

100

Chapter 12

second before so warm from contact with his, was suddenly cold.

'What are you doing?' I asked as he bent down by the bright green Terrific Tours coach parked behind the building. He tried the first locker compartment door, no luck. The second, however, clicked as he tugged it, and the door lifted open.

'Your chariot, m'lady,' Roger announced and waved his arm to usher me into the luggage compartment.

'Have you lost your mind, Roger Martinez? I am NOT going in there.'

'Where else then?' he asked. 'We can always forget about it and go back to the party.'

My desire, at fever pitch, was a horse running wild, and it was past the point of taming. 'No, no, this looks great. Let's go!' I sat at the entry to the underbelly of the coach, slipped off my shiny black court shoes and crawled into the bowels of the bus. Roger crawled in behind me and pulled the locker door down behind him, careful not to shut it all the way so it didn't lock. We fumbled to find each other in the dark and our foreheads collided painfully before our lips met and his tongue thrusted back into my willing mouth.

I wiggled, trying to get comfortable on the cold, hard floor. I tried not to think about how filthy it was and how many bags had been dragged along unhygienic footpaths before being hoisted onto the surface I was lying on. As I lay flat on my back, Roger straddled me, one knee on each side of my hips hunched over so as not to hit his head. He tugged at my t-shirt, dragging it over my head and tossing it aside. My turn. I tugged at his, until he took over lifting it off and whacked his hand on some unseen, under-coach support beam in the process.

101

'Fuck,' he moaned.

He wiggled back a bit so his bum was on my thighs and bent himself down towards me. The hair on his oh-so-chiselled chest felt divine on my nearly naked, not hairy chest. He's so warm. His mouth found mine again, and his tongue explored. Deeply. He may even have found a tonsil or two. I tried to meet his enthusiasm with my tongue, but his was quite bossy and shoved mine back. I stuck mine out more forcefully, but as I did, he shot his straight to the back of my undefended mouth and smashed into the back of my throat, making me gag a bit. I scooted my smaller tongue back into my mouth to defend my throat and concentrated instead on exploring his naked chest and back.

Roger's hand moved to his pants. I heard his zipper going down. A second later, I felt his manhood flop onto my thigh. He manoeuvred himself back a bit further so he could push up my skirt and pull my underwear down. He got them as far down as my calves. I squirmed and wriggled my legs to get them down to my ankles, then on to one ankle, and finally flicked them aside. Roger moved above me, taking his weight on his elbows and put his knees in between mine.

'Are you ready?' he asked.

Um, am I? Is that foreplay over? I wanted to demand. Would a bit more fondling be so wrong? How about a little cunnilingus? Would that be out of the question? Instead, I said, 'You bet,' in what I hoped was a very sexy voice.

Roger raised his hips and fumbled between my legs to find his intended target before he plunged into me. He withdrew a bit, then slammed his hips down again and again. I shifted beneath him, trying to find a spot that felt good both for my aching back and for where it was, you know, supposed to feel good. Couldn't quite get it ... I moved a little to the left ... Nope ... Not there either. I shifted to the right ... Nope.

Meanwhile, Roger was oblivious to me and was lost in his own pleasure, picking up his pace until he was a jackhammer at a tough piece of concrete. He pushed himself back for one last assault and, as he did, his foot hit the locker door we'd carefully left slightly ajar. A crack of light appeared under the locker door. He pushed back into me, and the crack of light disappeared. At the same time, a clicking sound told me that we were now entombed inside the undercarriage of a bus.

'Roger,' I screamed just as he withdrew and squirted his climax onto my torso, then collapsed on top of me. I felt the warm trail of his lust sliding down my stomach and pooling in my belly button.

'We're FUCKED Roger,' I stated, obviously referring to our entrapment.

'I know, amazing wasn't it,' he replied, rolling off me into a half-sitting position.

'No Roger, we're actually fucked. We're locked in.' I slid along the floor, not thinking about the dirt, and pushed on the door with my foot. Nada. Roger finally clicked to our predicament and crawled around frantically pushing a couple of the other doors. All locked tight.

'Help,' I whimpered. A bit louder, 'Help.' Then, much louder and with more conviction, 'HELP!' But the sound of the party drowned me out. I felt around for my discarded clothing. Putting my hand on something cotton, I grabbed it and turned it this way and that, trying to find where to put my head. Finally finding a hole that resembled a neck, I pulled it on. It immediately stuck to the goo on my tummy. Ewww. Pulling my skirt back down over my bare behind, I flailed my hand around on the floor of the luggage compartment again, not thinking about the dirt, but I couldn't find my underwear anywhere.

What seemed like an hour passed. We took turns shouting for help. Finally, we heard footsteps outside the coach, and some mumbled voices. 'HELP,' we yelled in tandem. The door clicked open and light flooded into the locker. I was momentarily blinded as I blinked my sight back. The shadows standing in front of us focused into Chris, the chateau manager and Gary, the head barman, returning to their rooms after closing the bar. I was sure our mumbled explanations about how I'd lost an earring and that was why we were half naked under a bus at 2am, together, and me with my T-shirt inside out and with a large semen stain on the front, were not convincing. Chris later told me my underwear was found by the driver, hanging off one of the supports under the coach, as he loaded the bags the next day.

I shake off the memory and, hand in hand, Nick and I wander off into the French countryside with a wicker basket full of tasty treats and the promise of a fun day with a good mate ahead.

Chapter 13

Bastardlona

Day 5

7.30am - The coach wheels crunch on the chateau driveway as we pull off, just as the sun is bringing light to the countryside. Nick, bless him, has got up early, almost unheard of for a barman, to wave me off. Even though he's up hours before he usually sees the light of day, he still looks like he's just walked off the pages of a men's magazine. His skin-tight, bright white t-shirt glows in the dawn light, his Levis are turned up at the ankle just an inch or two, and on his feet are smart brown leather boat shoes. As the coach crawls past him, he blows me kisses and waves to the bleary-eyed flock who can't believe being up at this hour is part of being on holiday.

But, up at this ungodly hour we are, because we are off

to Barcelona. Pronounced by the locals as 'Barthelona', pronounced by me as 'Bastardlona'. Why? Because it's a bastard to get to. Bastardlona is a good 700 kilometre drive from the stop before, and about the same distance again to the next stop. It can be a bastard to find, with confusing motorways, and it's a bastard to walk around, with the interminable heat and loads of confusing alleyways. Other than that, it's lovely.

In my earlier days on the road, when I was still pleb enough to be doing camping tours (the lowest form of touring life), my also pleb driver, Lamp Post (because he hit one in training) got extremely geographically challenged. Trying to find our way to the campsite south of the city involved some fairly complicated motorway manoeuvrings. We had to go from the C32 to the C61, onto the N11 and back onto the C32. Then on to the C60, C352 and C17, which would take us around Barcelona, where we'd follow signs for Tarragona and exit at number 617.

Herein lies the problem. When Lamp Post had been taking his notes on the training trip about how to get to the campsite, he'd left out one crucial teeny weenie piece of information; a small detail, but an important one. That detail? That we needed to exit at 617. We were almost in sodding Tarragona before he was able to turn around and find his way back to the campsite. After many, many stops to ask for directions. When we arrived at Camping Tre Estrellas at around 11.45pm, we had a load of very tired and unhappy campers putting tents up in the dark.

This time, we would have no such trouble, as we are staying in the middle of town in a hotel right on the Ramblas - Barcelona's famous, mainly pedestrian, street.

10.45am - The drive was slower than normal to our first stop. What should have taken three hours max stretched out to a bladder-straining three and a quarter hours until we pulled off the A9 at Remoulins. I handed over the requested amount of francs to Fitzy to give to the toll booth madame, then clicked on the microphone.

'Wakey, wakey,' I chirruped. 'We are about to make our first stop of the day.' Sighs of relief echoed around the bus from the flock, who had mostly slept during the drive but were now awake, and so was their desire to use the bathroom. 'Our stop is at the stunning Pont du Gard - a Roman aqueduct, which was constructed nearly 2000 years ago. Keep that in mind as you marvel at how they built the three tiers of archways on the bridge to carry water to the city of Nimes.'

'Shaz,' shouts G-dog (AKA Gail) from the middle of the coach, 'Can you please not say the 'W' word until we've used the loo?'

'Sorry, sorry, of course. There are only four toilets where we are about to stop, so those in most need go first. Two of the booths have your standard sit-down toilets, and two are squats. Good luck and see you back here in an hour.'

As soon as the coach grinds to a halt and the door opens, a tidal wave of human flesh pushes past me and bolts to the toilets. The cheerleaders, Bianca, Candy and Paige, are first off, and the scent of strawberry body wash follows them out. Candy and Bianca take up the sit-down toilets, and Paige opts to line up outside. G-dog can't wait; she is straight into the first squat booth, and Norman takes the second. A few others line up outside, shuffling their weight from foot to foot and crossing their legs.

G-Dog shouts, 'AW FUCK!' Norman squeals like a stuck

pig. They emerge simultaneously, both with wet footwear.

'What happened?' asks Peter, who is next in line for the squat.

'I pull down my shorts, stand on the foot things and squat down. I'm so busy concentrating on not getting it on my shorts, I piss all over my shoes,' moans G-Dog. I can't help but giggle as she squelches off in her travel sandals to rinse her feet in the river.

'I did me business,' starts Norman, 'then pulled the flush chain and the water came up out of the hole and went all over my sandshoes.'

The line for the sit-down toilets grows, and a number of the boys head off to find a bush instead of risking the squat. I wander off to the restaurant to get a café au lait and take a look at the gift shop, which is stuffed full of sachets of Herbes de Provence, brightly coloured fabrics sewn into aprons and table coverings, and I use their clean, indoor, sit-down toilet.

6pm - Finally, after a long day, we pull into our hotel on The Ramblas. The Ramblas runs from Placa Catalunya, over a kilometre, slightly downhill. It follows the path of a long-gone river and ends at the monument of Christopher Columbus, standing sentinel and pointing towards the 'new' land of America. The Ramblas is lined with leafy trees, giving a welcome respite from the overpowering Spanish heat during the day. The street is festooned with peddlers selling their wares and street performers keeping the tourists and locals entertained. It's also an easy walk to our first destination in the morning, a leather and fan shop just off Placa Catalunya.

That's tomorrow. Today, after a long and exhausting day on the bus... sorry, coach... we arrive at the hotel. And, after a quick dinner in the hotel dining room, I collapse in my room

Chapter 13

for the evening.

Chapter 14

Bastardlona

Day 6

9.30am - Jesús, pronounced Hey-th-oose (the 'th' comes with a spit of saliva), was born and bred in Bar-tha-(with a spit)-lona and is a third-generation seller of leather goods and handheld fans. He is a smartly dressed, attractive man of indeterminate age… could be twenty-five… could be forty… He has a great head of jet-black hair, and he's a natural showman. He has perfected his sales pitch over the years for the busloads of tourists visiting his retail premises.

'Hola Jesús,' I greet him as I arrive at his showroom, my flock and driver in tow. 'Hola Shaz. Cómo está?' He says, emphasising random syllables in words so it sounds like 'o-LA SHaz. CoMO eth-(with a spit)-STA.' He also says some words r-e-a-l-l-y s-l-o-w-l-y. I don't know whether the man has an actual speech impediment or whether he's just a messy talker, but every time he makes a 'th' or 's' sound, a barrage of saliva flies from his mouth. There are a lot of those sounds in Spanish. Some of the spit catches on his moustache, the rest flies over my head. I thank my lucky stars he's so much taller than me.

Jesús beckons the flock to him, with a graceful motion of his elegant index finger, and they gather around.

'I…' he starts, 'want to tell Y-O-U about the H.E.E.s.t.o.r.y of Bar-tha-lona.'

The first row of the flock cringes visibly as a machine gun round of spittle flies in their direction. They're about to experience the most amusing part of Jesús speaking English; his silent 'o' when trying to make the 'ou' sound. A French person speaking English usually has a silent 'h' so 'hotel' comes out as 'otel', not so Spanish Jesús, who inexplicably finds the 'ou' sound tricky.

'Bar-tha-lona,' Jesús continues, 'was FOnded by Charle-MAgne… you know C-h-a-r-l-e-M-A-g-n-e?' Cue nodding from the flock, most of it not very convincing. 'T-h-e-n FROm the ninth CENtury to the seventeenth CENtury Bar-tha-lona was ruled by a Cunt… you know C-U-N-T?' He asks, head cocked to one side.

I can't help but giggle as more than half the members of the flock have their mouths wide open in shock, trying desperately to work out what the hell this crazed Catalunyan man is talking about.

I enjoy their gaping for a moment, then pipe up, 'Count, it was ruled by a Count.'

There's visible relief from Sally, Margot, Teresa and Jane,

who are all very much on the conservative side. The laughter starts again every time Jesús mentions the word, with the silent 'o', throughout his history lesson, and now he's getting a reaction, he manages to get it in A LOT. When he's finished, he turns his attention to me.

'Who, Shaz, is this P-O-O-F you HAve with YOU?' he says, waving his hand dramatically towards Fitzy.

Another funky little quirk about Jesús, aside from calling every male he comes across 'poof,' is that he spends a lot of time either whacking men on the shoulder with the back of his hand, or smacking the back of their head with his palm. Fitzy, aware of this, is trying to hide in the middle of the flock.

'Come here P-O-O-f,' continues Jesús. 'I have a L-O-V-E-L-Y jaCKET for you to try on, that MIGHT make YOU look less of a P-O-O-F and more attractive to THESE b-e-a-u-t-i-f-u-l ladies you have with YOU.'

Cue giggles from the cheerleaders, Sue, Paula and Sheryl, and Deb and Fiona.

Fitzy approaches Jesús cautiously. He puts on the jacket he's holding out to him and steps up onto a small platform that elevates him slightly for better viewing for the crowd. The jacket is in the 'bomber' style, stone-washed brown leather. It's covered in lots of badges and pockets for useful things like packs of cigarettes or lighters. It's very cutting edge and fashionable, and all the hippest people are wearing them.

'Now, girls,' continues Jesús, whacking Fitzy on the shoulder with the back of his hand. 'How does this GUY l-o-o-k. Hot, NO? He NO look like a P-O-O-F now, does he? But girls …' he says, lowering his voice and completely ignoring the fact that the group is about a third male. 'To fully apPRECiate how H-O-T this former p-o-o-f now IS, you must F-E-E-E-E-L the leather. It is S-O-O-O s-o-f-t. Come you,' he pulls Fiona from Auckland out of the crowd, 'f-e-e-l the leather.'

He places Fiona directly in front of Fitzy, so they face each other. Jesús stands behind Fiona and takes hold of her wrists then places her hands on Fitzy's shoulders.

'Does it FEEL g-o-o-o-o-o-o-d so far?' He asks, not waiting for her to answer. He drags her hands slowly down the jacket to where it ends at Fitzy's waist. 'Is IT s-o-f-t?' He asks.

The flock is spellbound. What's going to happen here with this madman? Then he, ever so slowly, pulls her hands down further until they slide off the bottom of the jacket and onto Fitzy's denim-clad thighs.

'Stop it, you N-A-U-g-h-t-y girl!' Jesús lets Fiona's hands go and jokingly admonishes her. He gives Fitzy a whack on the back of the head for good measure. 'THAT is N-O-T the leather!' A now red-faced and giggly Fiona tries to blend back into the crowd.

'Do YOU see b-o-y-s?' Finally, Jesús addresses the menfolk in the crowd. 'How e-x-c-i-t-e-d THIS lady got to see a man, who BEFORE looked like a P-O-O-F, but when wearing THIS jacket is NOW so H-O-T? I think THIS girl NOW n-e-e-e-e-e-d-s one of these, no?' And he makes a seamless transition to showing the flock the handmade fans he also sells. The man is a genius. Within minutes of him finishing his speech, half the boys in the flock have put their credit cards through the zip-zap machine to buy jackets, to make them H-O-T too. And the girls are trying on leather suits, skirts, shoes and slinging various handbags over their shoulders. All are picking up fans to take home to their mothers, or grandmothers, or to use themselves to fend off the heat, which threatens to become oppressive later in the day.

After some frenetic spending on leather and fans, Fitzy and I have given an open invitation for the flock to join us for a tapas lunch at a small place we know just off the plaça. Fitzy is keen to make the most of the fact that the coach is parked up until tomorrow and the hotel is only a stroll away.

11am - We have set up base at the tapas place, sipping sweet sangria and waiting to see if anyone will join us. By midday, twenty-six out of thirty of the flock have plonked themselves around us and are enjoying either fruity sangria or ice-cold cerveza (beer). The mass of tables that we have haphazardly joined together on the footpath as people arrive are covered with red checked plastic tablecloths and small plates of *aceitunas* (olives), *calamares* (squid), various versions of chorizo sausage and *papas* (potatoes) smothered in creamy mayonnaise. Some of the braver members are trying garlicky snails, which they dig out of their shells with toothpicks. I learnt my lesson in Paris: I'm leaving them well alone! There are many convivial conversations going on around the tables, and a lot of them include Jesús impersonations.

I love this time of a tour. At the start, a new tour group of people are beads of mercury rolling around in the palm of a hand. Some beads are bigger than others, as some people are travelling together. There are also a lot of individual beads of people who come alone. At the beginning of the tour, the giant hand starts moving, and the beads roll around and bump into each other. Some of the beads join together as people get to know each other. Some break apart and join another bead. Some even join multiple beads during the trip. After a week, where we are now, there is pretty much one big mass of mercury on the palm of the hand as the group has bonded together. There is always the odd little bead that will never quite become part of the mass, either by choice or because they just don't quite fit in.

Here, now, is one pretty big mass of mercury, eating tapas. And, having helped this mass to form, I feel proud. I love its energy. The trick is to keep the mass as one until the end of the tour, before the little beads of mercury have started to tire of each other and become a rabble of numerous beads rolling uncontrollably.

Most of the flock stop by for an hour or so, before continuing their sightseeing mission around Barcelona. Some go to the Picasso Museum, some go shopping at the massive El Corte Inglés department store in Plaça de Catalunya, and a few visit Gaudí's Sagrada Familia to decide for themselves if it is art or madness. Some members of the flock drift away, only to return hours later to find that there are still a hardcore group sitting at the same maze of tables enjoying yet more *sangria, cerveza* and tapas, still watching the world go by telling taller and taller tales, as the sun peaks and then lowers in the Spanish sky. Some never leave and the entire time, Fitzy and I hold court, keeping the conversation flowing. The more *cerveza* and *sangria* we drink, the more it flows.

7pm - It's time for two things: dinner back at the hotel and for Fitzy to stop drinking, as he has to drive in twelve hours time. We hand piles of crumpled peseta notes to our friendly waiter with what is probably a ridiculously large tip. We're all happy and, it seems, in generous moods. Luckily, it is a short stroll downhill to the hotel where dinner (if we can fit it in) awaits us.

8.30pm - After brushing the remnants of sangria staining off my teeth, my head hits the pillow, and I fall quickly to sleep.

Approx. 10pm I am jolted awake by noises coming from Fitzy's room. It's obviously a thin wall that separates his room from my own, and it's doing little to block out noise. It sounds like he's moving furniture. What the hell is he rearranging his furniture for at 10pm? The hotel rooms' floors are covered in terracotta tiles to help keep them cool in the heat of the Spanish summer and it sounds to me like wooden legs are being dragged across them. The noisier it gets, the more awake and annoyed I become. I listen more closely, waiting for a break in the noise to yell at Fitzy to shut the fuck up. Wait a minute... maybe he isn't moving furniture? But there is definitely moving going on, on some furniture.

Back and forward, back and forward, squeak, scrape, squeak, scrape and then a voice; Fiona's voice. Shy, quiet Fiona from Auckland shouts out, 'It doesn't feel s-o-f-t NOW, Fitzy.'

Ew, ew, ew, ew! That is something you can NOT unhear. Ever. Not only did Jesús's sales pitch work a treat on the leather, but Fitzy has managed to bag Fiona with it too. I do NOT need to hear any more of this. I roll over in my bed, pull the heavy feather stuffed pillow over my head and push it down hard, to try and block out the sound, and the picture forming in my head of what's going on in the next room. Ewwwww. Ewwwww. Ewwwww.

Chapter 15

On the way to Nice

Day 7

Driving days can be a drag on tour, especially with over 700 long kilometres to tick off. Often, the flock takes the opportunity to catch up on missed sleep, but Fitzy and I don't have that luxury, particularly Fitzy. There is only so much paperwork and changes of music I can do to fill the time. I take care of an hour or two by staring blankly out of the window at fields smothered in the yellow flowers of rapeseed, or lilac-coloured blankets of lavender that have inspired the likes of Cezanne and Van Gogh.

Maybe Fitzy can help me uncover the inner workings of the male mind, so I can work Roger out. I look behind me to make sure the coast is clear and everyone is asleep.

'So, Fitzy… you and Fiona, eh?' I say, winking slyly at him.

'Got something in your eye, Shaz?'

'Nooooo. Last night, you moron. You and… Fiona…'

'What are you talking about Shaz?' He replies impatiently.

'Oh, come off it, Fitzy. I heard you last night. I was right next door, you know, and those walls are paper thin. From the room on the other side, I could hear the person combing their hair, for fuck's sake.'

'Okay. Yeah, she was in my room.'

'A-N-D…' I say, hoping to encourage him to spill. This is like pulling bloody teeth. Men. Honestly. If Fitzy were a girl, she would have given me all the info, as well as her predictions on where the relationship might end up by now.

'And… nothing. We had some fun, end of.' He's hoping to fob me off by looking out the window seriously, like at any moment, he might have to save us all from certain death by performing some kind of dramatic driving manoeuvre.

Actually, I'm quite happy to see a driver with his eyes on the road. Last summer, I'd had the misfortune of working with a driver who had never been to Europe before. You'd think that would be kind of a must for the job. The advert should have read: 'Coach Driver wanted for European coach tours. Must have a coach licence and have been to Europe'. Sadly, some genius forgot the last bit.

Pork Chop (that was just my nickname for him - he had another name, but I've erased it from my memory) was from South London, and his work ethic was: he didn't like to do it for too long, or too often. After a week on tour, with early starts and late nights, not to mention having to load and unload bags, he was exhausted with the work, and I was exhausted with him. Usually the driver and tour manager work as a team: the driver drives the coach, does the luggage and knows how to get to places, the tour manager books the hotels and excursions, does the walking tours, hotel check-ins, gets the parties started and educates the group on the places they're visiting. Pork Chop was able to drive, could (when forced) load bags, i.e. when there were fifty bags in front of the coach, so he couldn't drive anywhere until he put them all under the coach), but had absolutely no bloody idea how to get anywhere. And, like a typical man, would not ask for directions or advice from other drivers, or from anyone for that matter. The responsibility fell to me to guide him through every turn, to bypass every low bridge and to get him to every gas station and coach park, for thirty-three days.

On a driving day, ten days into that thirty-three-day tour from hell, we were on a long straight autostrada (Italian motorway) where he couldn't possibly get lost. I had my nose buried in paperwork when I felt the coach moving unusually on the road. I looked out of the windscreen to see if it was windy. It didn't appear to be. The trees on the hills surrounding the road were still and stiff as the Swiss guards at the Vatican. It was a calm, clear, sunny Italian day. I looked behind me to see if any of the people in the front four seats were noticing anything out of the ordinary. They were all in the land of nod, sleeping off hangovers from a late night at a nightclub and missing this dramatic scenery. I looked over to Pork Chop to ask him if he felt it was windy, as the coach again swerved dramatically on the road. Lo and behold, Pork Chop was asleep too, his head lolling about like one of those nodding dogs you see in the back windows of old ladies' cars.

A bolt of sheer panic gripped my chest and, for a second, I

couldn't speak. Looking through the glass panel of the coach door, I could see that the long motorway bridge we were on was hundreds of metres above the ground. The only things stopping us from plunging to certain death were warning signs and a teeny, very frail-looking barrier.

My life flashed before my eyes in movie-like fashion. It wasn't a full-length feature movie. My life hadn't even started properly. What about Roger? What about our imaginary kids? What would they do without me? How would they all cope?

'PORK CHOP,' I yelled, and swung my arm out to whack his shoulder at the same time. His head snapped up, and as it did, we took a terrifying lurch away from the edge of the road, towards oncoming traffic and back into our lane, narrowly missing a red Ferrari speeding towards us. I made Pork Chop stop at the next service stop to mainline some espresso. I never took my eyes off him for the remainder of the tour.

I have nightmares about it to this day. In my dream, I'm in the front seat of the coach, as it crashes through the barrier and plummets off the road. The sensation of falling tightens my gut, as we hurtle towards the pine trees below, my mouth open in a silent scream. Thankfully, I wake up just before the coach crashes to the ground.

Anyway, back to Fitzy… 'What do you mean 'end of'? Fiona seems a nice girl.' Bit dull, but no need to mention that to Fitzy. She should certainly be deemed a catch by the man whose face resembles a run-over pizza. 'You don't think there could be something there?'

'I've got a girlfriend at home, Shaz.' He says that like it should now be obvious to me, that he would not be pursuing anything further with his conquest, and that should be the end of the conversation right there.

'What then…' I start, trying to keep my voice calm, 'are you doing FUCKING someone else.' Okay, so the calm fell away a bit there.

'We have an agreement. As long as I don't go silly and screw everything that moves, she doesn't want to know about it and she'll wait for me,' he says. He may as well have told me that Simon Le Bon's hair isn't real, for that is how unbelievable and shocking I find this arrangement, Fitzy and his girlfriend have.

I wonder for a moment what a woman who agrees to a deal like that might be like. Desperate? Two heads? A nasty skin disease, which means she can only come out at night? Fitzy fishes his wallet out of the compartment beside his seat and passes it to me. It contains a photo of his beloved, and I am, let me be honest, surprised. Shocked even. Definitely only one head, skin looks fine, quite nice even, and there isn't a hint of desperation on her face; just a pleasant smile and nice, straight teeth.

'How do you do it, Fitzy? Don't you feel guilty? She looks lovely.' Too lovely for him, but again, I don't need to tell him that.

'She is lovely,' he says, 'and she's 2000 kilometres away. And… I have needs.'

A little bit of vomit rises into the back of my throat at the thought of Fitzy's 'needs'.

'She doesn't want to travel, never has. She understands that I want to and she knows that, one day soon, I'll go home, settle down and we'll have a house full of little Fitzys.'

I stare out the window as fields of lavender and bright red poppies swaying in the breeze blur as we whizz by. I ponder whether this situation would ever happen if the genders were reversed. I can't imagine me saying, 'Hey Roger, have I got a deal for you! You go home and set up house. Doesn't have to be anything fancy, but I do like good linen on the king-size bed and flowers in the garden would be nice too. Not roses, though, too pretentious. I'm not quite done travelling, so I'll be home in a year or two to join you. Until I do, I'll be shagging the odd bloke here and there, you don't mind, do you? I have, you know… needs.'

Would I put myself on the other side of the situation? Would I sit home waiting for the man I love to come home, knowing that he might, at any given moment, be sharing himself with some wanton slapper (no offence, Fiona) on the other side of the world? I think the urge to know would eat me up. I'm far too nosey not to shine a bright light in his eyes, get the thumb screws on and get all the details of what he'd been up to. And I'm far too insecure and controlling to be able to deal with it. More power to Mrs. Fitzy, I guess, hopefully she's getting her rocks off with the lawnmower man, pool guy or some other local bloke, while she waits for Fitzy's return.

My pondering continues until we pull off the motorway and pass Nice airport. Then we're onto the Promenade des Anglais and, as we hit traffic, we start crawling into Nice. Nice: the jewel of the French Riviera. Expensive real estate, on and off the sand. Where you have to pay for a prime spot on a beach lounger. Personally, I prefer the beaches at home in New Zealand. Pristine stretches of glistening sand washed clean by rolling surf. Acres of space per beach towel, whole oceans to yourself (well, it feels like that anyway) and all for free. One time in Nice, after laying down my giant blue and white striped beach towel and making a comfortable nest on my side in the stony foreshore, I fell soundly asleep. I don't know what was worse when I woke up; the sunburn down one side of my body or the rock-shaped indentations that were moulded into my other flank.

The highlight of our visit to Nice is a night-time trip to Monaco. It's a chance to see the money, feel what it'd be like to have the money, and gamble away your money. If you prefer to hold onto some money, you could gamble on bagging Prince Albert, surely the world's most eligible bachelor. Maybe in a few years, he'll lose that title to Prince William. At thirteen, I guess he's a bit young for that yet. Prince Albert, though, is in his mid-thirties and is prime pickings. Prince Ranier must be desperate for his boy to produce an heir. If I can't have Roger, Albert would be my second choice. I've never even managed to catch sight of the man, however, no matter how much lurking around the palace I did.

7.30pm - The flock members are dressed to the nines as they board the coach, which is an interesting visual experience. Some enter the coach looking like they've just walked off the pages of *Vogue,* a lot though, look like they've fallen off the pages of *Bogan Weekly*. Dresses are shorter and cleavage lower than would usually be considered decent, highlighting some particularly tacky shoulder tattoo work. For the occasion, I have gone for a navy-blue shift dress and a pair of black wedge clogs. Sensible for walking on the cobbled streets.

There is a twitter of anticipation as Fitzy puts his pedal to the metal. We roll out of Nice and start climbing the Moyen Corniche. This is one of the prettiest drives in Europe. As we wind around the side of the hills, Nice shrinks below us. The large striped beach umbrellas become tiny lollipops stuck in the sand. Looking down the steep drop off the side of the road, we get glimpses over the roofs of mansions into their aquamarine jellybean-shaped swimming pools and, further down, to the Mediterranean glistening in the setting sun. *Money, Money, Money* and *If I Had a Million Dollars* blast over the coach stereo, and the excited flock snaps pictures, this way and that.

Monaco is not a city/country that is easily navigated by a big, long bus. You can't just rock up to the doors of the palace and park. All the windy roads and postcard stands make that impossible, so we park in a coach park and walk. The coach park is cunningly cut into the hill that the palace is on. There's a complicated system of elevators and escalators to get to the top of the hill to navigate, before a walk through winding streets to find the pinkish palace. After we've seen the palace, we repeat the whole process backwards to return to the coach. We will then drive to be dropped off in a tunnel to do another complicated set of elevators and steps, and take another walk to find the casino.

Driving into the under-palace coach park, I have a familiar feeling of dread deep in the pit of my stomach. In times of stress, I find it hard enough to remember the difference between an elevator and an escalator, let alone that I have to ride an escalator, exit left, find the elevator, go up, exit right, take the escalator then wind my way to the palace. Working with a large group of people is the same, in principle, as working with wild animals. If they sense fear, they'll attack. Even a seemingly friendly house-trained group can attack if provoked or if they smell weakness. My plan: baffle them with bullshit and do it with an air of confidence.

'Righto, folks, you can leave your bags on the coach. Fitzy will be here. But bring your cameras.' I click the microphone off and drop it on the dashboard of the coach.

From the dark recesses at the back of the coach, 'Can we leave our bags on the coach?'

I pick up and click on the microphone, and put on a cheery voice. 'No problem, you can leave your bags on the coach.' Click.

Then, from someone sitting directly under a speaker. 'Should we bring our cameras?'

Click. Through a slightly forced smile, 'Only bring your cameras if you want to take photos of the beautiful palace and the stunning scenery.' Click. And I jump out of the door in one fairly smooth, gazelle-like move.

The flock follows along behind me through the glass sliding doors. I see a moving staircase in front of me: escalator, right, check. As we ascend, I run through the next move in my head: escalator, then exit right... No, left... or is it right? Oh shit.

As we arrive at the apex of the staircase, I step off to the left and see it's about a 10-metre walk to a wall, and there are no visible means of escape. In a move that an All Black winger would be proud of, I do a mean sidestep off my left clog, doubling back on myself and into the melee of the flock, who'd followed my lead but not been so fast on their feet. I swerve a couple to get to the front of the pack and stride off confidently as though nothing untoward has just happened. I'm now facing a long corridor that, for the life of me, does not look familiar, but, with no other obvious option, I continue walking. With each clomp of my clogs (surely a fashion nightmare in anywhere but Holland), my heart picks up five beats. I reach the end of the corridor and, as it bends left, I see an elevator door. Thank you, God.

Thankfully, the next escalator is blatantly obvious when the elevator doors open, and I manage to get everyone up and outside into the fresh evening air. I try to commit what we've just done to memory in reverse order for when we come back. This is where having the brain of a goldfish has some serious disadvantages, and I get myself even more confused, so give up trying.

The first part of the walk up to the palace is straightforward and very beautiful. We pass the Nautical Museum, with the funky yellow submarine out the front, and head towards the church where Prince Rainier married his movie star wife, Grace Kelly. On our left, the cliff drops away over stunning botanical gardens, down to the ocean where luxury yachts bob merrily. I turn to the flock to point out the church and tell them about Rainier and Grace's love story.

When I finish, I hear from the back of the group, 'I wish she'd told us to bring our cameras.'

11pm - No one manages to bag a prince, or a fortune at the casino tonight, but I do manage to find our way to all of the places we needed to go and back to the hotel, and that was a win enough for me!

Chapter 16

Nice

Day 8

It's a totally free day for the flock today, so that means a great day for me. A bit of a sleep in, a lazy breakfast, then Fitzy and I are meeting for lunch in the old town of Nice, nice.

9.57am - I amble into reception on my way to the breakfast room before they finish serving breakfast at 10. As I enter, Fiona looks up, her face bathed in hope. The hope slides from her face when she sees me.

'Hi Fiona. Everything okay?'

'Yes, fine, thanks,' she replies, but her body language speaks of being less than fine.

'Are you waiting for Deb and Sheryl?'

'Um... No. I thought I might catch Fitzy.'

'Have you left something on the coach?' I ask, and then it dawns on me. She's after more than one night of passion with my two-timing driver. The poor deluded soul thinks there could be a chance of something more going on. I sit down beside her.

'You know Fitzy does a lot of tours, right?' I try to give her the idea that Fitzy is a man whore, without crushing her directly or giving away the fact that I overheard their fornicating.

'What are you saying, Shaz?' She asks, probably knowing the answer but not wanting to believe it.

'That you should get out and have fun in Nice. Don't wait around here.'

7.13pm Arm in arm, Fitzy and I sway together through the hotel door, tripping on something invisible and laughing hysterically at our clumsiness. Our liquid lunch turned into a liquid afternoon tea and finished with a liquid dinner, and we're both slightly wobbly. Sitting in front of us, in the same place she was sitting this morning, is Fiona.

'Hi Fitzy,' she almost whispers. Fiona flicks a smile at him, then glares at me. If looks could kill, I would most certainly have dropped dead to the floor right here. Fitzy and I untangle our arms, and they drop guiltily to our sides. I hope she doesn't think I'm trying to cut her lunch. Eww.

'Hi...' Fitzy starts, then stops. There's an uncomfortable pause.

I turn my head casually from Fiona towards Fitzy.

'Fiona,' I whisper out of the side of my mouth.

'Fiona,' Fitzy repeats loudly in acknowledgement. 'Well, it was nice bumping into you. I'll see you tomorrow.' We make our escape to the lifts.

When the doors close behind us, Fitzy slumps against the elevator wall and mutters, 'Fuck.'

I can't help but laugh. 'You've got a bunny boiler on your hands there, Fitzy.'

Chapter 17

On the way to Florence

Day 9

9am - A mostly refreshed-looking flock boards the coach after handing their luggage to Fitzy, who is struggling to lift each suitcase into the underbelly of the vehicle, under the weight of a mild hangover. He's sweating way too much for this time of the morning.

'Morning Shaz.' Randy greets me as he and Jake hop on board in their crisply ironed collared shirts.

'Hi Abang,' says Hazdy as he moves past me. He's told me 'Abang' is an affectionate term in Malaysian. I'll have to take his word for it.

'Shazza, how are ya?' Colin asks, greeting me with a beaming smile. The next person to board does not give me a smile; she doesn't even make eye contact. While Sheryl and Deb both say hello, Fiona mopes past me and moves as far towards the back of the coach as she can. It's not my fault Fitzy's a dick!

Soon enough, we are all present and accounted for, and we're on our way out of Nice. We get on the A8 motorway that climbs up behind Monaco. It's the road that will take us all the way into Italy.

The great thing about this motorway is the number of tunnels we pass through.

'I've got an idea,' Colin pipes up to those around him, 'why don't we hold our breath every time we're in a tunnel?'

'Sounds fun to me,' agrees Keith.

I can hear a lot of huffing and puffing behind me as breath is held and then expelled. It's not long though, before the constant changing from darkness in the tunnels to the light outside makes eyelids droopy. Before long, most members of the flock are sound asleep.

1.15pm - We turn off the motorway and onto the SS1 towards Pisa. I click on the microphone.

'Okay, everyone, we are only about 10 minutes away from Pisa, where we will stop for lunch and to see the thing that leans.'

We travel along the SS1 through a taste of the Italian countryside, and past a few AGIP service stations with their distinctive six-legged dog signs. Oddly, we also pass a few 'ladies of the night' plying their trade in the middle of the day, before we head under a bridge and pop out somewhere Fitzy can drop us off.

'We'll meet Fitzy back here at the coach at 2.15pm. Fitzy can't stay here, so please make sure you have everything you need when you get off.' I place the microphone on the dashboard and jump onto the dusty cobblestones.

'See you in an hour Fitzy,' I say as I move away from the coach a little to give the flock room to disembark. Once Colin is off, I whisper to him, 'Colin, can you do me a favour?'

'Sure,' he says willingly.

'Do you mind keeping an eye on Norman? I don't want to lose him here.'

'Your wish is my command,' Colin replies and bows at the waist slightly like I'm The Queen.

I lead the flock down Largo Cocco Griffi - a small pedestrian street lined with stalls selling *genuine*, I use the word loosely, Italian gifts and souvenirs. We make a left turn. Shops continue along our right-hand side, but on our left is green space with grass so perfect you could bowl on it. The green space is protected by a low chain fence and Polizia armed with whistles, ready to admonish anyone who sets foot on it. Past the grass are the spectacular Pisa Baptistery and Cathedral. And, further along, the flock get its first view of the Leaning Tower of Pisa. I see a tear in the corner of architecture student Hazdy's eye.

'It's so beautiful Shaz,' he says wistfully.

I gather the flock around me.

'The amazing leaning tower is nearly 56 metres tall. It started to lean during its construction in the 12th century. At the moment, there is construction work underway to try and stabilise it, so we can't go up. You have an hour here to take photos and have some lunch. See you back at the coach at 2.15pm.' I wait until the flock disperses, then I backtrack to a local café, which I know has a payphone I can use to make some calls ahead to Florence.

2.15pm

'Thanks, Colin,' I whisper as he arrives back at the coach with Norman in tow.

'He's a slippery sucker,' he says to me grinning. 'He tried to ditch me a few times, but I stuck to him like glue.'

3.45pm - Arriving in Florence is always wonderful, and dealing with the Florentines, a pleasure.

'Here we are folks, the wonderful city of Florence. Here, the food is delicious, there's great shopping and knowing that you're walking the same streets as the likes of da Vinci and Michelangelo once did, makes it all the more special. Actually, if I could bring one person back to life for an hour, it would be Michelangelo. I'd love to ask him probing questions about his life and art.' The flock looks around in wonder as we drive into the city. 'I'd ask him, how did he cope being upside down for so long, painting the ceiling of the Sistine Chapel? If he had such a low opinion of painting as an art form, why did he agree to do it? What was life like in the renaissance? Did they even know it was a renaissance? What was his inspiration for the beautiful Pieta?' Most members of the flock are nodding, looking like they too are pondering these big questions. Norman, though, is still sound asleep, his head leaving a greasy mark on the window above the line of drool that's snaking from the side of his mouth. Most importantly, though, why did he give his most famous statue, David, such a small willy? I keep this question to myself.

Michelangelo had enough marble to make decent-sized feet for David and possibly even slightly oversized hands, but where it matters most, David comes up a bit short in my opinion. Roger could have been Michelangelo's model for David; he too is perfectly proportioned. Unlike David, Roger is not short in the willy department, again, my opinion, and he definitely does not have David's slightly freakishly large hands.

Terrific Tours' Italian operations are run from Florence by Giuseppe Russo. Giuseppe runs the business with a firm hand, a booming voice and little tolerance for fuck-ups. He also likes to keep his finger on the pulse of what's going on, by calling meetings in a local café and plying road crews with alcohol until loosened tongues wag and he gets all the information he needs. My hyperactive imagination has him pegged as a Mafia boss, and we are his hitmen or soldiers, or something. This is fuelled by the fact that he looks like a mafia Don, with slick black hair and a finely trimmed moustache. He's a bit like Marlon Brando in *The Godfather*, carrying a few extra pounds.

Giuseppe's second-in-command is a meek man by the name of Matteo. If Giuseppe is the mafia Don, then Matteo is his underboss or *caporegime* (right-hand man). They're an odd pairing. If Giuseppe is an Italian stallion - fine and proud, Matteo is more of a Shetland pony - unthreatening and innocuous. Matteo's wife, though, is a Clydesdale - enormous, with quite hairy ankles.

Each time I'm travelling from Florence to Rome, Matteo gives me a shoebox-sized package securely wrapped in miles of sticky tape to make it impenetrable. As he hands it to me, he stares intently into my eyes and says, 'You see this gets safe to Habriella, no?'

Gabriella (Italian's pronounce it 'Hab-ree-ella') is a guide in Rome. She's a short, officious woman with a nose like a beak. I have created two likely scenarios for the packages. Either they contain loads of cash that Giuseppe and Matteo have made smuggling people out of North Africa into Florence (probably in trucks with false walls), to sell fake belts and handbags. Habriella is his Roman contact who has family in Sicily with boats to bring men over from Tunisia. Or, the packages are full of drugs. I haven't quite worked out how that would happen, or why he'd be smuggling drugs south, but that doesn't matter; I'll solve it eventually.

In the meantime, I'll continue being Matteo's mule, mindlessly carrying his packages to Rome and handing them over to Habriella, with no consideration for the danger my own life could be in. The trip from Florence to Rome is already hazardous enough, dodging Italian truck drivers who've had one too many vino rosso with their lunch. Carrying the contraband probably adds the risk of being intercepted by a rival Mafia family and becoming involved in a shoot-out, which would be rather one-sided, as we have no guns. So I guess that means we'd just be shot and they'd speed off in their black bulletproof Alfa Romeos with the spoils of their kill.

Chapter 18

ॐ

Florence

Day 10

Today, Giuseppe wants to meet with Fitzy and me for lunch. I know two things for sure: one, Fitzy will be kept safe from the alcohol, as he has to drive the flock back to the hotel this afternoon. Two, that means double trouble for me as Giuseppe will not take no for an answer.

12.30pm - After handing over the flock to a local guide for the afternoon, I amble through Piazza Santa Croce in no hurry to be at the mercy of Giuseppe and his limitless bar tab. I take some time to admire the façade of the Basilica; the midday sun shining off its white marble facade serves to highlight its simple, classic beauty. I browse the stalls set up outside small shops, covered with tarpaulins to fend off the vicious sun.

They're filled with leather goods and paintings of Florentine scenes. I stop to feel a black leather belt and contemplate buying one... or two... Wait, no time for shopping. The tables outside the cafés that encircle the piazza are already starting to fill with the lunch crowd, stopping to rest from the heat and vigorous sightseeing.

I leave the hustle and bustle of the square and head down Borgo de Greci. This wide, dark alley is lined with shops of my favourite variety - leather and gold. It's also home to the café I have been summoned to; Francesco's, named after its owner. I warn the couple of tourists distracted while taking photos outside, that they are being lined up by a family of five gypsies looking to bolster their vegetable picking income by pickpocketing tourists who stand like corn in a field. I cop some abuse from the gypsies for my trouble and duck into the café. Good deed for the day, check. Sitting in the far corner, I see Giuseppe holding court with Fitzy, another driver, Fluro (because he used a fluorescent coloured pen a lot on his training trip. Seriously, the inane ways drivers got their nicknames), and my best friend in the wilds of Europe and partner-in-crime, Liza.

I arrived in Europe six months after Liza. We met in a hotel in Greece, where we worked together cleaning rooms for most of the summer. With our work over by lunchtime, we spent the rest of our time catching rays and the occasional Greek God. We decided, at the end of that summer, to try out at being tour managers together. We survived the rigours of the six weeks of training hell, which can only be described as being a cross between a university degree and an SAS training camp. It consisted of trying to learn the history of the whole of Europe, from day dot to the present, including learning all about each individual country's geography, political system, currency and language. All the while, being kept up until 3 or 4am to drive around cities, learn landmarks and, alternately, be deprived of alcohol, then locked in a bar with limitless supplies of free booze, to see how we coped. It was amazing that we lived to tell the tale, let alone make it out the other side to be let loose on unsuspecting tourists.

Last winter, when we were not working, Liza and I travelled through Africa together, the highlight of the trip being Liza setting what was possibly a Guinness World Record in the shagging category. We were sitting in a café in Windhoek, killing time waiting for a bus to Cape Town that was delayed by half an hour and during this small window of opportunity, Liza managed to chat up and shag the waiter of the café in the time it took me to finish my coffee. Admittedly, it was a large coffee, but still! Alas, it turned out there was no section in the Guinness Book of World Records for this amazing feat. Originally from Brisbane, Liza had left a bad marriage in her mid-20s and run away to Europe. She had more bounce than anyone I knew and could make the Energizer Bunny look like a sloth on a slow day. She literally bounded to greet me with a rib-breaking hug and a kiss on each cheek.

'Hi Hun, it's so nice to see you. Where have you been since March?' She asks, linking her arm with mine and walking with me to the table, where I say hello to Fitzy and Fluro. I give Giuseppe a kiss on each of his stubbly cheeks, the sides of his moustache tickling my stubble-free face.

Giuseppe continues with his story, explaining to the boys why he does not believe in seat belts. 'Bloody ridiculous things. I drive to Rome for a meeting and my shirt is all messed up in the front,' he booms.

It crosses my mind that if he went through the windscreen of his car, it would also have a negative impact on his shirt, but I'm more interested in catching up with Liza than issuing road safety tips to Giuseppe. We race with our words, trying to catch up as quickly as possible on where we have each been so far this summer.

Me: a 20-day tour with two days off, followed by a seven day tour with two days off, then a 31-day tour with one day off (to get a bollocking at the office and end up in bed with dodgy driver) and on to this 25-day-er. Liza has had a 14-day tour, then three days off, a 21-day tour with no days off, onto a 12-day tour, one day off, then on to the 15-day tour she is now on, which went the opposite way to most other tours, hence our not seeing each other en route. We moan about the usual things: not getting enough sleep, not having enough money to spend at Benetton, and drivers in general. I recount my bollocking from Neil, and Liza tells me how she's avoided going into the office all summer. Bitch.

'Get it out,' Liza directs me, pointing at my stylish black leather handbag purchased right here in Firenze. Not only is it a stylish handbag, but it can also be worn as a backpack, gorgeous, stylish, yet functional. Seeing the puzzled look on my face, she continues, 'Your diary, get it out!'

'I don't know what my next tour is yet.'

'I know,' she says, 'but I know what mine is. This one finishes in four days, then I'm doing another backwards one starting in Amsterdam.'

We flick through the pages of dates for the next couple of weeks until, 'There,' she says, '3rd and 4th of June. We'll both be in Hopfgarten!'

Yeah! Liza and I can have a schnapps or ten, washed down

with a wine or two, and have a real catch-up. Speaking of wine, Giuseppe has ordered a couple of carafes of vino rosso and interrupts our girly gossip with a call of, 'Salute!' This, of course, encourages us all to start drinking. Fitzy and Fluro take a sip to be polite, then move back to their Cokes.

As the boys are all engrossed in their conversation, I lean in close to Liza to quietly ask, 'So... any eagles landed lately?'

This is our code for 'Have you got laid?' It started back in the summer, we worked together when, one night, after quite a few muddy waters to drink, Liza had lined up a local man who frequented the bar we often drank at. She told me that night, she thought this man might be a 'hose-reel' (a hose-reel, she explained was a man that you could get serious with; one that you could set up home with and settle down with, so much so, that you'd be willing to go out and buy that most mundane of products - a hose-reel. This one, she had thought, would not be a 'fly by nighter', not an eagle landing. This one may be serious. From that day on, men were divided into hose-reels and eagles landing. The Greek man, as it turned out, was not a hose-reel. He was very much an eagle landing, and one who, Liza enthused, landed frequently, and with great skill.

Liza leaned in closer to me. 'I bumped into Roger Martinez on my last tour.'

My heart plummets into my red Italian suede loafers. Although Liza is my best friend, I wouldn't leave her alone with my boyfriend for long. Not that Roger is my boyfriend. Obviously I've told Liza that I've shagged him, but I haven't admitted to her that I *like him, like him* (and, well, that's an understatement). Liza doesn't know that he's my hose-reel; the man I want to reproduce with, live in matrimonial bliss with and grow old together with.

'Well…' she continues.

I do NOT want to hear that Liza has had her wicked way with my future husband, but at the same time, I need to know. I take a sip of my vino rosso and steel myself for what is to come.

'He was working with Skipper. Do you know him?' She asks. The red wine I have just sipped into my mouth is propelled out of my nose at terminal velocity. I cough and splutter, while reaching into my pocket, desperate to find a tissue and end up grabbing the one off the neck of the near-empty carafe on the table.

'Are you ok Shaz?' Liza asks.

'Just… went… down… the… wrong… way. Skipper? Blond, blue eyes, a bit lame?' I manage.

'LAME?' She screeches, stopping the conversation on the other side of the table. The male threesome opposite us turns to see what wound Liza up, decides it's nothing of interest to them and moves on to Florentine football. 'Lame?' She says, much more quietly this time. 'I think…he might… be a… a… hose-reel.'

What the fuck is going on with the world? Seriously? Liza - cool, funky, gorgeous Liza - thinks that shy, lame, non-withdrawing Skipper is a hose-reel? Jesus!

'Did you… You know..?' I ask, nodding my head to the side, not quite sure why this side nodding motion indicates naughty business, but it seems a fairly international signal.

'No,' she replies, 'I wanted to. I actually tried really hard, but he was playing hard to get. Has he got a girlfriend, do you think?'

'Don't know,' I say, not in the least bit interested whether

Skipper is attached or not. Given what happened between the two of us in London, I'd guess there's no girlfriend. But, considering Fitzy's revelations the other day, you obviously never can tell. I don't tell Liza about Skipper, as I'm still a little embarrassed about the whole accidentally shagging him situation. I silently vow to tell her another time. 'What was Roger up to?'

'You mean *who* was he up to?' She says. 'Nearly everyone.' Giuseppe calls for another toast and Liza and I are sucked into a chat about dull work things, killing my chance to dig further into what she knows about my future spouse.

Giuseppe quizzes me on what he has heard from the London office about my bollocking after my last tour.

'How's this one going, Shaz?' He asks in a fatherly way, placing his hand over mine and patting it gently.

'Great,' I enthuse, 'really coming together nicely. Haven't lost anyone and haven't done any interpretive dance. Yet, still early days though, eh?'

'Molto bene,' Giuseppe replies. 'You're too nice to get fired. Because I know you are a nice and trustworthy tour manager, Matteo has asked me if you could deliver this box of important papers to our colleague Habriella, in Roma.' He hands me a box, but there's something different this time; there's no sticky tape. As if reading my mind, he says, 'Matteo did not have time to wrap it, but he knows he can trust you.' He winks at me, and his eyebrow of wild, unruly hairs jiggles as he does.

'Sure Giuseppe, no problemo,' I say with a smile. I wonder what it is this time - drugs or cash?

4.30pm - After lunch, Liza had to go, so I spent some time wandering aimlessly around the city, until it was time for me to meet Fitzy and the flock at the Ponte alle Grazie bridge, which straddles the slow-flowing, muddy green Arno river. The bridge has a strictly 'no stopping' policy, so Fitzy will pull up in the coach, we will all jump on and he'll be off before the polizia can issue a ticket. Checking my Swiss army watch (I love my precision timepiece), I can see that I have five minutes to get there; that'll be a little tight. I approach the river near Ponte Vecchio, turn left and pick up my pace. I flip my handbag from my shoulder onto my back. It's actually damn heavy with Giuseppe's secret package.

With two minutes to go, I break into a sweat and start to panic that I won't make it. I launch into a jog, dodging from the narrow footpath onto the equally narrow road, lined with thousands of parked motor scooters. Thank God for rubber-soled loafers! Brilliant invention, thanks Italy. I trot alongside the sluggish, green river and glance up to gauge how far left I have to go. As I do, a rogue paving stone jumps up out of the footpath and catches the toe of my loafer. As I tip forward, the thought that this landing is going to hurt flickers through my brain.

Movie slow-motion mode kicks in, as I fall towards the unforgiving cobbled road. And hurt it does. It really fucking hurts. My knees are somewhat protected by my three-quarter-length cream Benetton pants, which now have large dirty marks on both knees. My hands stop my head from hitting the ground, and are painfully skinned; with gravel embedded in them, they are beginning to bleed. The contents of my handbag spew out onto the footpath in front of me: lipstick, tampons, my wallet and Matteo's box hit the ground. It bursts open. The contents of the box scatter in front of me. Rather than being wads of lira notes or tightly wrapped packets of cocaine or other illicit drugs, however, what spills onto the footpath is a box of chocolates and a red card with a love heart on the front. As the card lies open on the road, I see a handwritten message inside. This footpath debris scene debunks my previously well-thought-out theories, and I struggle to make sense of it as I scrape myself off the cobblestones and gather everything back into my handbag. I dust myself off and start to sprint-hobble towards the green coach, which has stopped on the bridge, to a cacophony of car horns urging it to move on.

'You took your sweet time,' Fitzy says, as I clamber up the coach steps. I hoist my handbag into Fitzy's lap for safekeeping from purse snatchers and hobble painfully down the coach, counting the flock.

'Good to go, Fitzy,' I instruct, as I grab my handbag from his lap and lower my behind gingerly into the jump seat. Into the coach cassette player I slot my new Andrea Bocelli tape. It probably won't take long before someone moans about my choice of music, but it suits the surroundings and, for the moment, I enjoy it. I sit back in my seat and start to pick small stones out of the palms of my hands.

'Are you okay? What happened?' Fitzy asks.

'I'm fine, I just fell over, that's all. Pretty standard Shaz stuff, you know,' I wink.

Hey, Fitzy…'

'Y-e-s,' he says.

'You know Matteo?' I continue.

'Y-e-s Shaz,' he replies.

'He's married, right?' I ask.

'Y-e-s, to the hairy scary woman. Why?'

'You know that package Giuseppe gave me from Matteo to

give to Habriella?' I continue.

'What is this Shaz?' Fitzy says impatiently. 'Ask the fucking obvious day? Yes, I know the package.'

'Very funny,' I carry on. 'When I tripped over it fell out of my bag and opened up on the footpath. Guess what was in it?'

'Drugs?' He asks. I shake my head.

'Money?' Obviously, Fitzy has the same overactive imagination as me. 'Sex toys?' He tries again.

'Now you're just being silly. It was…' I pause for dramatic effect. 'Chocolates!' I declare like I've just discovered who really killed JFK, or that I have proof that aliens really exist.

'Well, that's pretty boring. Can we turn this shit off?' He refers to the Italian tenor's dulcet tones wafting through the speakers.

'Fitzy,' I continue, ignoring his criticism of my taste in music, 'Matteo might be having an a-f-f-a-i-r.' I spell it out, to add to the sense of mystery that this revelation should, in my mind, cause.

'Well, he is I-t-a-l-i-a-n.' He replies, joining in my spelling theme. However, I'm not that great at spelling, so it takes me a minute for the realisation to sink in: Fitzy is condoning this set-up. Mind you, given his own twisted domestic arrangements, I shouldn't be surprised. He's saying that if you're an Italian married man, then it's a fait accompli that you will have a mistress. That it's totally fine, okay, expected even. I decide, then and there, that I will never marry an Italian man, even if he were the biggest hose-reel I'd ever met. I will not play second fiddle to anyone, especially not a short, loud woman with a dramatically Roman nose.

What are they like, Italian men? They come straight from

mamma's breast, aged about thirty, never having cooked or cleaned a day in their lives. Move to their wife's breast, to continue being looked after and, as soon as the Mrs gets a pasta arse and a moustache (sometimes even before), they take up with a newer model. I want more out of my relationship! If I ever get one, that is. I mean, WHEN I get one. There's no way Roger would get away with running around behind my back once we were joined in matrimony. Mind you, I'm hoping that my genetics, a bit of exercise and waxing, will help me avoid a pasta arse or a moustache. So, by taking this package to Habriella, I will be complicit in aiding Matteo's matrimonial perfidy.

I think I would rather the package contained drugs.

Chapter 19

Roma

Day 11

Rome - the eternal city. Eternally hot, eternally crowded. Roads are eternally being dug up and taking ten years to be rebuilt, because each time a hole is put in the ground, some amazing buried relic thing is found, and archaeologists flock to sift around with tiny brushes, halting any progress for months.

4pm - We arrive at our hotel on the outskirts of Rome at exactly the time I told the hotel we would, when I phoned their reception at lunch time from the bustling Autogrill service stop that spanned the *autostrada*.

'Si, Miss Shaz,' the receptionist had understood our estimated time of arrival, before adding, 'We no have you room numbers yet, but we give to you later, okay?'

I was slightly suspicious, but what could I do? Italian hotels, like most in the world, work like airlines: they overbook by about 20%. If everyone doesn't turn up, there's no harm done. If everyone does turn up, they panic. Because the hotels in Rome don't like to upset you with information that your group has been moved to a different hotel, they delay having to pass on this difficult information until the last possible minute. Usually, that minute is when you arrive at their hotel to check in. It's been a long day driving into the sun and all I want to do is hit the shower.

The receptionist tries to placate me as steam begins to pour out of my ears, 'But Miss Shaz, the new hotel is much nicer than this hotel, and it has a pool.'

'Yes, I know that Paola,' I reply, barely keeping my wafer-thin veneer of calm intact. I saw it on the sign as we drove past it - half an hour ago! Now we have to drive half an hour back to it. If you'd told me on the phone earlier, we could have had an hour lying by the lovely pool. Now we'll barely have time for dinner!' I turn on my heel and stride out of the reception, back to the coach, to break the bad news to Fitzy and the flock. Of course, I don't tell the flock it's bad news or that we drove past the hotel half an hour ago. I hope they won't have noticed that. I tell them how fantastic it is that we'll be staying in a nicer hotel, with a pool, all the while smiling through gritted teeth.

On the way to the new 'with a pool' hotel, Fitzy puts a further dampener on my day.

'Shaz, I'll be over my driving hours for today now, so you'll have to have a shuttle driver take you into the city tonight for the walking tour.'

European driving laws are very strict, and I can't argue the point. Can this day get any fucking worse? We check into our new hotel, which is actually very nice. My super big room has enough floor space for me to be able to put my suitcase down and still have space to walk around it to the bathroom, which has a bath. Luxury. From my room, I can see the kidney-shaped pool; the water sparkling crystal blue in the sun. I tilt my head, and I'm sure I can hear it calling my name. 'Shaz,' it whispers to me. I give my head a shake. Seriously? Now, swimming pools are talking to me? No time to listen to the talking swimming pool, however, we need to shove dinner down and drive into the heart of the city of Rome for an evening walking tour.

6pm - Our meal for tonight would test the strongest of elastic waistbands. A gut-busting affair that starts with 'il primo' (the starter) of macaroni, smothered in a fragrant tomato sauce. Secondo is a thick steak, with a side of crunchy green beans and to finish ('dolce'), a lemon gelato. I'll never understand the Italian way of eating pasta as an entrée. I'm always so full after that, I can hardly do the steak justice. Somehow, miraculously, I can always squeeze in the gelato though. A fiasco (a traditional style of bottle, half-covered in a tight-fitting straw basket) of Chianti sits in the middle of the table to share. And I do make sure I get my share. I fear I'm going to need all the fortification I can get for tonight.

7pm - After dinner is devoured, the flock waddles back to grab cameras, while I go to meet the driver replacing Fitzy for the night. Massimo is leaning against his coach, a cigarette hanging dangerously out of the corner of his mouth. His shoulder-length, greasy black curls fall carelessly over his face, and he has a cell phone in his hand. His tanned fingers, with immaculately manicured nails, dance over the keypad as he whips up a message. My guess is, it's sent to either his wife or mistress, or maybe, as he's Italian, it could be to his mamma. I really wish I could afford a cell phone. Alas, my twenty pounds a day wage will not stretch to cover phone bills, and who would I text or call anyway? I don't know anyone else who has one, apart from the odd Italian shuttle driver, and I don't fit into the wife, mistress or mamma category.

'*Ciao Massimo.* I'm Shaz,' I say to him by way of introduction, offering out my unmanicured hand to shake his. He takes my hand and puts it to his mouth, narrowly missing the burning end of his cigarette. His overly moist lips linger on the back of it for slightly longer than I feel comfortable, leaving a damp patch when he lets it go.

'*Ciao bella,*' he replies, looking me up and down in a none-too-subtle manner. '*Comé stai?*'

'*Bene, grazie.*' I have now almost completely exhausted my Italian repertoire, so I move on to English. 'Do you know where we need to go tonight, Massimo?'

'*Massimo, si,*' he says, smiling and nodding, ash drops off the end of his cigarette as he does. He removes what is left of his cigarette from his mouth and stubs it out under the toe of his white leather loafers, which appear to be high-quality and hand-stitched.

'Massimo,' I try again, this time much more slowly and a bit louder because, let's face it, volume always helps someone understand a language that's not their own. 'You drive us tonight, where?' It also doesn't help people's understanding to make simple sentences nonsensical by changing their word order, yet I do it anyway.

'Si,' Massimo replies and gives me a big smile while moving

his hands like they are on a steering wheel. 'Me drive,' and then slower and louder, while smiling and nodding, 'MASSIMO D.R.I.V.E.'

Shit. Shit. Shit. I rummage in my handbag/backpack for a map of Rome.

'Massimo, we are h-e-r-e,' I say slowly. I point to the hotel and draw a mark on the map. 'You take me h-e-r-e.' I point to him, do my own driving action and put another dot on the map in the centre of Rome near the large monument known as the wedding cake. 'You pick me up at 10 o'clock from h-e-r-e.' More pointing at him, more driving imitation and yet another dot, this time beside the Tiber river opposite Piazza Tribunali. 'Bring me back h-e-r-e.' I point to myself and then the hotel.

'*Si*,' he says with more steering wheel actions, just as the flock arrives at the bus. Massimo stands sentinel at the door of the coach, nodding to each of the males and offering his hand to help each of the females onto the first step. He also takes the opportunity to check out each of the girls from the rear, as he helps them up the stairs.

When everyone is on board, Massimo says, '*Andare!*' And *andare* we do, we are off at speed. The first part of the drive goes well. I recognise that we are indeed heading towards the centre of Rome, although I have never been this way before. I enjoy the sights out the window, taking the time to talk to the flock about how Rome was founded. I love a good tale. The story of twin brothers, called Romulus and Remus, who were suckled by a wolf and fed by a woodpecker before going on to found a city, is as good as any tale gets. I only just get to the bit where the twins fight and Romulus kills Remus, leaving him to name the city after himself in a stunning display of narcissism, when I realise we have travelled through Trastevere and have arrived at the River Tiber.

Driving alongside the river, the vast brick fortress of Castel Sant'Angelo looms ahead of us. It won't be long before we take a left turn, over the river and head towards the Victor Emmanuel monument, also known as the Wedding Cake. But, we don't make a turn; Massimo keeps driving along the river. I start to feel a little nervy. I look over to Massimo to see if his hand is about the flick down the indicator switch to indicate we are about to make a turn across the river. Obviously this is a pointless exercise. Italians do not indicate. We pass Piazza della Rovere, which would lead us to Corso Vittorio Emanuele II and to our destination. Maybe he's planning on crossing over Ponte Mazzini. This is a slightly trickier route for a bus, with a few more twists and turns, but he's a local, so maybe it's a shortcut he knows?

The movement of the river below us is imperceptible; it's a mill pond reflecting the ancient brick walls, buildings and trees that line it. If I wasn't so fucking stressed about when we're going to cross the damn thing, I'd be quite enjoying the vista. We whizz past Ponte Mazzini, and Massimo doesn't drop a kilometre an hour below the terminal velocity he has his bus travelling at. Ponte Garibaldi is our last chance. That must be his plan. Show the flock the jewel in the river, Tiber Island, with its picturesque ancient bridges linking it on either side to the mainland. It's still a fairly straight run from there to our drop-off.

However, we also pass Ponte Garibaldi, and we are now alongside the island with the hospital in the middle.

'Massimo.' I turn to him, every nerve ending in my body pulsating with nervous tension. *'Reste maintenant?'* Massimo looks confused. No, shit, that's French for 'left now' I think, or it could mean something else, no wonder he looks confused. '*Queda ahora?*' Nope, still no reaction from Massimo, maybe that's Spanish? '*SINISTRA, Massimo!*' I almost shout with the relief of remembering the damn word.

'*Quoi, pensaveo che volesse andare al colosseo,*' he replies.

I catch one word, '*Colosseo*'.

'NO Massimo, NOT The Colosseum!' I gesticulate wildly, pointing over the river, '*Vittorio Emmanule*.'

'*Vaffanculo*.' Massimo curses, then performs a fine bit of Roman driving, crossing two lanes at once without indicating, prompting a chorus of screeching brakes and horns around us and a herd of motorini riders part like the Red Sea. I'm pretty sure half the coach wheels are off the ground at this point, *Dukes of Hazzard* style, as we take a left turn onto a bridge that I'm pretty sure has a weight restriction, which should exclude our coach. It could possibly also be one-way, but I have, at this point, closed my eyes and braced myself against the dashboard. The flock is tossed like a coachload of rag dolls as we make the turn. From somewhere down the back, I hear a 'YEE-HA!' At least someone's having fun.

The coach clatters over the cobblestones that probably predate Jesus. I cross my fingers that the bridge won't collapse under the strain of this heavy modern chariot. I can see the headlines in the Roman paper tomorrow, '1000 year-old bridge collapses due to Terrific Tours' illegal spree!'. Or perhaps the headline could be, 'Terrific Tours topples bridge' or 'A Terrific tumble!' or, in Italian, '*Terrifico tumblo*'. Thankfully, we make it across before any collapse and, with a few speedy left and right turns, we finally arrive at the massive white monument. I breathe a huge sigh of relief. Massimo screeches to a halt in Piazza Venezia, opposite the balcony from which Mussolini once addressed the crowds.

While Mussolini was obviously a bonkers fascist, he did say one thing worth quoting: 'It is better to live one day as a lion than 100 years as a sheep.' As my own flock gets off the coach, I get the map I marked for Massimo earlier and, beside the dot I made for the pick-up point, I write as big as I can - 10 PM. For good measure I circle it. To be extra sure, I add an exclamation mark.

'*Dieci. Si, Massimo?*' I ask him, pointing to my watch and then to the map.

'*Si Shaz dieci, no problemo.*' He smiles and nods. I shelve my concern about what will happen at 10pm to the back of my mind and concentrate on getting myself and my flock to where we need to go. Italian drivers tend to see the lines on the road, which would normally indicate pedestrians can cross safely, as a way to line them up for a direct hit. With some intense eye contact and a few frantic hand signals, I manage, through sheer willpower, to get an Alfa Romeo, a Fiat and about twenty-five motorinis to stop, so that we can file across the pedestrian crossing. We take a right and meander down Via IV Novembre until its end, before swerving left into Via della Pilotta, which is barely more than an alley and is crossed overhead by several white brick pedestrian bridges. Even though cars use the 'road', it feels much less likely that one of my charges will be taken out this way than if we were walking on a more main vehicular thoroughfare. It also gives the impression to the flock that I must really know Rome like the back of my hand if I can lead them down the back streets.

A city that, up until this point, seemed devoid of other human life, now comes alive as we pass 'Il Caffe'. The giant plastic ice cream cone stuck to the side of its building leaves the tourists in no doubt as to what it serves. We emerge from the shade of the alley into the brilliant sunlight of a square and arrive at one of Italy's most important icons - Benetton. No wait, the Trevi Fountain. It's 8.10pm and the setting sun is giving the monument a glorious orange glow. The flock rushes to chuck three coins in the fountain and to make wishes of wealth, happiness and a return to Rome. The female members of the flock mostly find themselves having to fend off dodgy-looking men selling single-stem roses as they do. While they take on this tourist tradition and take some time to have a gelato, I rush into the nearby Benetton store and admire the fine lines, cuts of cloth and classic colours with a modern twist. It isn't unheard of for me to actually buy a thing or two in the fifteen minutes we have here. That's why I bring my handbag/backpack with me, so I can shove my purchases into it and hide the fact I've been shopping while working, genius. Tonight is no exception. I can't resist a rather lovely sea green mohair wrap-around cardigan and a sparkly singlet that shows both gold and blue depending on how the light catches it. I hand over my 100 000 lira note and get a 1000 lira coin in change, which I use to pay for a quick toilet stop at Il Caffe. If chucking the coin in the fountain would guarantee me everlasting love with Roger, I wouldn't have hesitated. As there is no such guarantee, spending it on emptying my bladder is a much wiser investment.

After the coins have been chucked and wishes made, we meander through more back streets of Rome, popping out of the shade only to cross the Via del Corso. We then take a right and head back into the maze of buildings, with ancient structures around every corner. I pray that no one asks me what most of them are, or I will be forced to make up a Roman Emperor story or two. Who could possibly know what all these relics are? Roger, probably. He would know every emperor that ever lived. Maybe on our honeymoon, we'll come to Rome and wander around, him holding my small, delicate hand in his large, strong one, while he regales me with witty anecdotes about the history of Rome. We'll stop often to kiss and eat gelato, or maybe kiss while eating gelato, or maybe smother ourselves in gelato and take turns licking it off, or...

'Shaz.' Mo, the history student from Malaysia, interrupts me from my daydream. 'What's that?' He asks, pointing to a tall, carved marble column.

'That, Mo, is a very good question,' I begin, giving myself time to think. 'It's a victory column, in honour of...' I try to summon up a suitable Roman emperor... um ... hmmmm... Actually, at this point, any Roman emperor will do... 'Marcus Aurelius,' I finish with confidence.

'Victory over whom,' the curious flock member persists.

'Well... Mo... over thousands of years, alas, that information has been lost. Those Romans had lots of fights, all over the show.' I hope that will end this line of questioning and also hope that there isn't a plaque on the damn thing that he'll find tomorrow, debunking my information.

We do a little more back alley wandering before we arrive at a piazza with a fountain in the middle, a couple of quaint restaurants on its edges and, perversely, a McDonald's. The reason we're here, though, is to marvel at the building directly opposite the Golden Arches. I turn my flock away from the shrine of the hamburger towards the great ancient structure.

'This, my friends, is one of the most amazing buildings

in Rome. It's nearly 2000 years old.' As they marvel at the Pantheon, with its rounded hulk, grand entrance and towering Corinthian columns, I continue. 'It is, I believe, hard to grasp how old 2000 years is. The best way...' I lean in towards them and lower my voice, like I'm about to impart some very important information, a deeply held secret. I look around furtively to make sure no one other than my flock is listening. They buy into my melodrama and huddle closer, tilting their heads towards me, straining their ears to catch this gem. 'The very best way... is to... FEEL it! Rub it... Hug it... Be at one with the building. Then you'll really get a sense of how long this amazing building has been standing on this very spot.'

I tell them this for two reasons:

1. It's true, by touching the enormous cool columns, you really do get a sense of how long they have been holding up the entry to this amazing building.
2. It's really fun to watch the faces of the other people milling around the monument as my thirty keen tourists rush up and enthusiastically hug, and in the case of Peter, hump, the pillars.

We have sufficient time here to allow the flock to explore the inside of the building and gaze at the twilight sky through the enormous hole in the roof of the dome; a dome that has been a window to the sky since the days when the earth was 'flat'. Time to soak up the ambience of the piazza and time to buy another gelato.

It is a short distance to the last stop on our stroll - the

fantastic Piazza Navona. The most beautiful baroque square in Rome. Home to the Fontana dei Quattro Fiumi (Fountain of the Four Rivers), Borromini's church of Sant'Agnese in Agone and... yes... fuck it, why not... why don't you get another gelato?

9.55pm - From Piazza Navona, it's an easy stroll down Via Giuseppe Zanardelli towards Ponte Umberto I, where Massimo will be waiting for us. Except he's not.

Nor is he here at 10.05pm.

Or at 10.10pm.

Or at 10.11pm.

By 10.12pm, I'm pacing.

I'm still smiling and maintaining a façade of calm. On the inside, though, I'm a frenetic mixture of stomach-twisting anxiety and boiling rage. The flock is getting twitchy. While at first they were huddled in small groups chatting in an animated fashion, they now shuffle silently from foot to foot. Occasionally, one of them will scowl in my direction. The natives are getting restless.

'How much longer will he be Shaz?' Asks Fiona, with distaste in her voice as light rain starts to fall.

'Oh, not long now. He's probably just stuck in traffic,' I trill. Where the fuck is he?

At 10.17pm the coach, driven by Massimo screeches to a sudden stop beside us. The door opens, and a cloud of cigarette smoke rushes out into the Roman night air.

'Shaz! Bella!' Massimo beams at me, showing off his teeth, which are lightly covered in red wine stains.

Fucking Italians.

Chapter 20

Roma

Day 12

6.30am - My trusty alarm jolts me awake. 6 fucking 30 in the morning! Not much of a lie in for the flock who have paid good money for their 'holiday'. However, we need to get into Rome to see the Pope's pad. I also have to deliver the ever-so-slightly battered package to Habriella.

By 8am, there is already a long, agitated snake of a line winding from the left of the Vatican Museum entry. We duck to the other side of the entry door and join the much shorter line reserved for groups. Habriella soon tracks us down. It's her job, for the morning, to guide my flock through the vast Vatican Museum into the Sistine Chapel and on to St Peter's Basilica. There, the flock will view the magnificent and graceful Pieta, carved by Michelangelo's hand, some five hundred years ago. It is my favourite statue in the whole of Europe. The Pieta is a delicate depiction of Mary holding a dead Jesus (the real one, not the bloke from 'Barthelona'). Then Habriella will set the flock loose on the city of Rome, before the intended meet-up with Fitzy and me at 4pm.

'*Ciao* Shaz,' Habriella chirps, as she leans in to greet me with the traditional kiss on each cheek. She doesn't put her face close enough to actually touch mine, and six inches of polluted Roman air separate us as she puckers her bright red lips and makes a smooching sound, which I reciprocate with a bit of extra pucker for good measure.

'*Ciao Habriella, come stai?*' I enquire, not actually caring too much about her answer. I'm fairly keen to hand over both the package and the flock and enjoy a day alone. Well, not completely alone. I'll be with Fitzy, but I can ignore him easily enough.

'You have the papers for me from Matteo?' she asks.

I turn the choking sound that involuntarily escapes from my mouth into a cough and nod combo. I reach into my bottomless backpack and pull out the slightly battered package I have been charged to deliver to this pocket rocket Roman woman who is spinning Matteo's wheels.

'Here you go Habriella,' I say, handing her the box. Her face lights up.

'*Grazie*, I'll get on to these this afternoon.' I'm sure she will. Yuk.

'*Arrivederci Habriella, grazie,*' I say to her, and to the flock, '*Arrivederci.* Have fun and I'll see you at the big monument at 4pm.' I flash them a friendly smile that broadens to a gleeful one, as I turn and nearly skip down the road to where Fitzy is double-parked, cursing me for taking so long.

Rome has many attractions at which to spend a free afternoon. There are the catacombs, where brilliant white human bones line the walls of a church. The Colosseum, a Flavian amphitheatre, where Christians once fought lions. One could indulge in the amazing shopping along Via del Corso. Hours could be spent people-watching while sipping café latte on the Spanish Steps. You could soak up the sun and have a gelato from the best gelato shop in Rome, next to the Trevi Fountain. Thousands of years of history could be consolidated while strolling through the numerous sites of ruins. You could test your fidelity by placing your hand in the gaping Mouth of Truth. I, however, will be doing none of these things. I will stay with Fitzy and the coach and travel to a vast coach park on the outskirts of Roma. There is a dodgy little café on the edge of the coach park, frequented by Italian bus drivers. And there's a restaurant for lunch just up the road. But for most of the seven hours of free time, I will just sit on the coach. Maybe I'll read a novel, maybe I'll help Fitzy wash the windows, and maybe I'll drink café latte all day with my feet up. My options are endless.

By 3pm, I have covered all of my options. I've read a bit of my new novel, *Bridget Jones's Diary*. Boy, can I relate to how Bridget feels! Her dilemma around whether or not to wear nana undies for a big night out is a problem I wrestle with most nights I'm heading out on the town. I've helped Fitzy wash the windows, had lunch and a couple of café lattes. I've possibly even improved my tan by having my legs dangling out of my shorts and hanging them over the barrier between the front row of seats and the jump seat, soaking up some Roman rays. Though tomorrow will tell. I'm just finishing some paperwork, Fitzy is sitting in the driver's seat of his now gleaming green machine, when a motorini chugs up beside the open coach door.

'Mr, Mr, Mr,' the driver says, as he dismounts his red bike and steps tentatively onto the first step of the coach. He has one of those army-type canvas bags slung over one shoulder. He lifts the flap of the bag to show Fitzy what's inside, all the time looking nervously from side to side as he does, to see if anyone is watching him.

'Do you want a video camera?' He asks. 'Brand new, but shhhh,' he says, indicating that it was likely hot and that Fitzy will need to be quick to get this great deal.

'How much?' Fitzy asks.

'450 000 lira,' the mobile electronics salesman says.

'How do I know it's real?' Fitzy asks, interested but wary. Motorini guy pulls the camera out of its case from inside his bag and turns it this way and that, showing it to Fitzy from all sides. He turns it on to show Fitzy that it indeed works, as he pans it around the inside of the coach. Fitzy looks at the viewer, impressed.

'350 000,' Fitzy counters.

'400 000,' the motorini guy shoots back.

'Hey ATM,' Fitzy says, turning to me, 'can I get some money?'

Terrific Tours' tour managers are given funds at the start of each tour to pay things like road tolls and parking. It's also okay for drivers to get money from the tour manager and this is deducted from their wages at the end of the tour, thus tour managers were known as ATMs (or automated teller machines) by drivers.

'Are you sure Fitzy?' I ask. Buying hot goods off a random

motorini driver doesn't seem like such a good idea to me. The Roman police and the Carabinieri were not to be fucked with; they have guns and everything.

'Yes, Shaz, I'm sure,' he insists.

I reach down to the floor for my backpack and find my wallet with sections for multiple currencies, super handy for Europe. I pull out four creamy brown centomila notes and hand them to Fitzy. He holds them in his hand and waves them towards the camera salesman. He keeps a tight grasp on the notes until the camera bag is pulled out of the army bag and is in Fitzy's other hand before he lets go of the cash. Fitzy looks down to open the bag. By the time he's opened the lid, the driver of the motorini has gone, in a puff of petrol fumes.

'F-U-C-K,' Fitzy yells. 'Mother fucking Italian fucker!' I look over my slightly more tanned than this morning legs, to see Fitzy glaring at a camera bag that contains a 1.5kg bag of farina (flour). 'I'm gonna kill him.' He viciously turns the key of the coach and gives the switch a hard flick to close the coach door. He revs the engine, like a racing car driver on the grid waiting for the start lights of a championship grand prix and moves, at breakneck speed, to the driveway of the coach park and onto the road, leaving a cloud of possibly ancient Roman dust behind us.

'Fitzy... Fitzy...' Slightly louder, 'FITZY, what are you doing?' I ask the back of his balding head, as I pull my legs down off the barrier and plant them firmly on the coach floor, bracing myself as best I can.

'Gonna fuckin kill him,' he replies, and begins what can only be described as a James Bond-type chase through the streets of Rome. The only trouble is, he doesn't actually know who he's chasing. There are hundreds, thousands of motorinis in

Rome and the one he wants to squish under his sixteen-tonne bus is long gone.

'Fucking mother fucker,' he mutters, swerving in and out of traffic and glaring at every driver of a red motorini to see if they have an army bag over their shoulder.

'Get me out of Rome before I kill someone,' Fitzy growls. Luckily for the Italian motoring public, we are leaving the next morning, and Fitzy has kissed goodbye to a good week's worth of wages.

Chapter 21

❦

On the way to Paxos

Day 13

10am - After leaving behind the hustle and bustle of Rome, our first stop today is at the small town of Monte Cassino. I click on the microphone.

'Is everybody awake back there? Have you all had your post full night's sleep nap? Are you ready for some culture? Well, we're about to arrive at Monte Cassino.'

There is stretching and yawning, heads peel off the coach windows where they have come to rest, leaving behind greasy marks. Fitzy will have the joy of cleaning those off later.

'Can you see, out to the left of the coach, that hill with a building on top?' General nodding, mainly from those actually sitting on the left. Those over the aisle on the right have had to lean over so far to look up and out of the window that they've almost got their heads in the laps of the people across from them. Muzza finds his head very close to the lap of the very gorgeous Candy. He takes his chance to lower his head further still, until it rests on her bare, tanned thigh. She gives his ear a quick flick with the long, bright red nail of her middle finger, and Muzza bolts upright, giving his ear a rub in pretend agony.

'That building on top of the hill is a Benedictine monastery that was heavily bombed by the Allies during WWII. They bombed it because they thought there were Germans hiding there. There weren't. After it was obliterated, the Germans did move in and use it as a bit of a lookout point.'

'Why do we care?' Pete moans from the back.

'Well, Pete, you may care because it was many of your fellow countrymen from New Zealand who mounted attacks to run the Germans out in 1944. Many died for their efforts and are buried here.' That showed him.

By now, we have made our way off the Autostrada and have skirted around the town past various hotels, restaurants and an Agip service station with its weird six-legged dragon dog sign hanging outside. Fitzy brings the coach to a halt at the gates of the Monte Cassino Cemetery. The flock members are chatty and jovial as they get off the coach. After they enter the gates of the cemetery and are confronted with over 4000 crisp white gravestones in neat rows, each one marking the death of a Commonwealth soldier, an eerie silence descends. They splinter into small groups, pairs, or wander off alone to spend some time reading inscriptions on the headstones. Many of the soldiers beneath the headstones are a similar age to the flock and had come to this country, on the other side of the world, to fight a war they didn't start and died trying to regain this hill in the middle of nowhere that meant nothing to them.

I approach Peter, who's kneeling down in front of a grave inscribed with the name 'A. Brown. NZ Infantry. Age 22.' Under the name is an indented cross and, through the middle, is written 'New Zealand', with a fern above. In front of the grave, a previous visitor has left a small New Zealand flag, a poppy and a postcard with a picture of the All Blacks, laminated to protect it from the weather.

'He was only twenty-two,' Pete says, his voice ragged with emotion. 'Same age as me. He should have been drinking piss and trying to get laid but instead he got shot up in this shit hole.'

'I know,' I reply simply and give Peter's shoulder a squeeze. I leave him to his thoughts.

1.30pm - Our bellies are full of panini when we leave our service stop, just south of Naples. I've just finished talking about the dodginess of the southern part of Italy, where the Mafia supposedly has its roots and still operates today, and I've sat back in my seat to stare blankly out the window for a while. In the distance, on the side of the autostrada, I see a car in the distinctive lilac blue of the polizia. Parked in front of the car is a motorbike of the same colour. As we draw closer, one of the officers moves away from his position of leaning against the car, talking to his friend, towards us. He is decked out in his very swanky uniform of nicely tight blue/grey pants with a red stripe, tucked sternly into a pair of 'don't mess with me' knee-length black leather boots and, on top, an ink blue motorbike jacket with a couple of white horizontal stripes. He swaggers into the middle of the lane in which we are currently driving.

'It's The Village People, Fitzy, but probably not as friendly,' I jest.

The polizia officer, who, although this is no time to get distracted, could have seriously just stepped off the pages of *Italian Vogue*, shifts his weight to one leg, putting his left hand on his hip and striking a pose. He lifts his right arm and, with his index finger erect, points directly at us, then swipes his digit towards the side of the road, indicating that we should pull over.

'Fuck, here we go,' Fitzy mutters, giving me a look as he clicks on his indicator, puts his foot on the brake and slows the coach down towards the side of the road, giving me some time to act. Below window level, I slide my hand into my handbag and retrieve my wallet, being careful to keep it below the dashboard level and out of sight of anyone outside the coach. I slide out five blue 10,000 lira notes and a couple of burgundy 1000 lira notes and slide them back into my bag. I leave behind the rest of the currency, which probably adds up to around 1000 pounds. While continuing to smile out of the window at the polizia, I talk out the side of my mouth to Jane who is sitting directly behind me.

'Jane, pass this back a few rows and ask someone to sit on it.' I move my wallet discreetly behind me to Jane's feet. She reaches down slightly to take it and nods silently. Once we have come to a complete stop, I take my handbag with me and step out of the coach onto the slightly loose road chippings by the side of the autostrada.

'Buon giorno officer, problema?' I try with my best flirty smile

Vogue model guy's sidekick makes his move and saunters up the stairs of the coach. He stands on the top step, right next to Jane, who now has the look of a possum caught in headlights. He casts his gaze slowly down and around the coach, eyeballing each and every one of the flock. When he has finished his intimidation, he turns to Fitzy.

'Tacho.'

Fitzy undoes the speedometer key on the dashboard behind the steering wheel and removes the paper disk behind it that records the coach's movement and speed. The coach has a safety feature called a speed limiter, which means it can't go faster than 100 kilometres per hour; the speed limit on the road we are travelling on. This should mean we will have no problem. It would definitely mean we would have no problem if we weren't in southern Italy.

'Inglese?' Vogue guy says, staring at me intently. Well, at least I think he's staring. It's a bit hard to tell, looking into his mirrored Chip's type sunglasses, where all I can see is my reflection.

'No, not *Inglese*. New Zealand. Well, I speak *Inglese,* but I'm not from *Inglese*.' Oh, shut up Shaz, I admonish myself. This scary model guy with the large baton attached to his pants does not want your life story. Stop staring at his baton, Shaz. *Sidekick* takes the tacho and issues another command to Fitzy, who is remaining very cool, calm and collected.

'Out.' *Sidekick* exits the coach, and Fitzy follows him.

The four of us are now standing in the sunshine. We could have been having a perfectly lovely chat if it wasn't for the fact that, on the other side of their pants from their big batons, are equally big guns. *Sidekick* stares at the tachometer, turning it this way and that, until he points to some small blip in the speed graph line.

'Speed,' he says. Obviously not one for too much conversation.

'No,' Fitzy says, shaking his head. 'Limit is 100, line says 95.'

'SPEED,' *Sidekick* shouts, and *Vogue* guy moves his hand ever so slightly toward the handle of his gun.

'Righto Fitzy, well obviously that was an accident and we certainly didn't mean to speed, being law-abiding citizens that we are. We're very, very sorry, officers. Will you give us a ticket so that we can pay at an official office somewhere and get a proper receipt?' I babble, staring at the general area of *Vogue* guy's crotch, willing his hand to stay away from the gun, while simultaneously marvelling at the size of what else he must be packing in his pants.

'No ticket... You pay fine now,' *Sidekick* demands.

Ah, the old southern Italian poliza red wine fund... Of course.

'Do you have any money, Fitzy?' I ask. Fitzy shakes his head dramatically and pulls out the lining of his shorts pockets to demonstrate that indeed he has no money. None at all. Not even a single lira. I take over the lead role in this melodrama. I delve purposefully into my handbag. I pull out a comb, which I hand to Fitzy to hold. Next is a lipstick, also given to Fitzy to hold. He shrugs his shoulders to the officers in a 'what's a guy to do' kind of way. I find a random piece of folded paper and hand it to Fitzy. A half-eaten packet of chewing gum and a tampon (unused, of course) also get handed over. Finally, I pull out three of the worn blue 10000 lira notes I had stashed there and hold them out to *Sidekick*.

'Basta?' (Enough?) *Sidekick* slowly and sternly shakes his head.

'No *basta*,' he spits out.

I dive back into my bag, rummage around a bit more for effect and pull out another two 10000 lira notes and two 1000 lira notes and hand them over.

'*Finito.*' And I hold my bag open so they can see that there is nothing left other than one piece of chewing gum that has escaped its wrapper.

Vogue guy and *Sidekick* chat animatedly for a few minutes, waving their hands and pointing at both the coach and at the two of us. Finally, *Sidekick* shoves the tacho back towards Fitzy and *Vogue* guy snatches the 52000 lira from my outstretched hand.

'No more speed,' *Sidekick* commands and wanders back to lean on his car and wait for the next victim.

Fitzy heads back into the coach to replace the tacho and start the engine, so we can get out of here as quickly as possible before they have time to reconsider. I scuttle along behind him. My hands shake ever so slightly as I buckle my seatbelt.

'Get me the fuck out of Italy,' Gail pleads from behind me.

5.15pm - Fitzy glides the coach to a halt alongside a row of parked cars outside the small travel agency on the main street of Brindisi, where I'll collect tickets for our overnight ferry to Paxos. A small table partially blocks the door into the agency. At the table sit two elderly Italian gentlemen. Both wear golf-type flat caps; one is tartan and the other a dark green. They're engaged in what appears to be a very intense game of cards. As I approach the door, tartan cap throws his hand of cards down in disgust, and green cap raises his arms in the air in celebration. They banter animatedly but pause as I walk past, to look me up and down, and greet me with a '*Ciao bella,*' in unison.

'Gentlemen,' I acknowledge, as I slip past them and into the narrow store.

Behind the bench at the back of the small office space sits a middle-aged man. He's balding and more than slightly overweight. Towers of paperwork lean precariously on the bench on either side of him; a small television showing some kind of soap opera is at full volume on a small table. A cigarette waiting in an ashtray on his other side trails smoke up to a yellow-stained ceiling. Obviously not the only cigarette that's ever been smoked in here. I stand in front of the bench for a minute and wait for him to notice me. From outside, I can hear car horns blaring as the locals begin to get impatient with our large green coach partially blocking the road.

I clear my throat. Nothing. No reaction whatsoever. The gentlemen in the doorway have erupted into a full-blown argument over their card game. Still, there's no reaction from behind the bench.

'Ciao,' I venture. The travel agent doesn't lift his head or deviate at all from the very important task of cleaning his fingernails.

'What company?' He gruffly quizzes.

'Terrific Tours,' I reply sweetly. He retrieves an envelope from somewhere under his bench. Without looking up, he slides it onto the bench top in front of him and goes back to picking at his fingernails. That's what I call good customer service. No wasting time on idle chit-chat.

'*Grazie*,' I call over my shoulder as I head out the door, past the old men in hats arguing and back to the bus.

'Is the ferry on time?' Fitzy enquires upon my return.

'Yes, it is Fitzy. It's on time... Greek time. It will leave around 6.30-ISH!'

8.30pm-ISH. We are indeed now on Greek time. As I predicted, the 6.30ish departure time became more like 7.26pm before we actually left Brindisi. After waiting for the dining room to open, I shovelled down a quick Greek salad, a crusty bread roll and washed them both away with a large glass of retsina, before heading straight to my womb room. I love womb rooms. Warm, cosy and you get rocked to sleep all night. In this case, by the rise and fall of the Mediterranean Sea. And I don't even have to share with Fitzy. Bliss.

Chapter 22

Paxos

Day 14

5.30am ISH - Dawn has barely cracked and the morning sun is only just peeking over the hills blanketed in olive trees, turning the buildings lining the entrance to the port pink, as our ferry pulls into the harbour of the island of Paxos. The somewhat shell-shocked-looking flock stumbles down the gangplank carrying their overnight bags to wait on the dock for the coach to come out of the bowels of the boat. Colin, a plumber from Newcastle, sidles up to me.

'Shaz. Couple of questions for ya.'

'Hit me with them, Colin, but remember it's early in the morning and I haven't had my coffee yet,' I reply, smiling my best, helpful tour manager smile.

'Righto,' he begins. 'Does the sun rise in the east here? And… is this island completely surrounded by water?' He looks at me expectantly.

'Colin,' I start, then pause a moment to compose myself and suppress the snigger of laughter that threatens to escape my mouth. 'You do know that the sun doesn't actually move, right? That the sun coming up is just the Earth turning and that the Earth keeps turning the same way all the time, rotating on its polar axis.' I've lost him. His eyes have glazed over, and he has a completely blank look on his fresh and freckly face. 'Yes, Colin, it does,' I go on. 'Now to your other question, Paxos is an island.'

'So does that mean it's completely surrounded by water, it's not attached to the mainland at all?' he asks again.

'Yip. To be able to get the "island" into a place's name, the residents have to prove that it is indeed completely surrounded by water, by having someone swim right around it. Only then can "island" go in the name.' I freeze my smile in place.

'Oh, cool. Thanks.' Off he goes, to share his new found information with his travelling companion Keith, the beer-swilling building apprentice, also from Newcastle.

The flock members are obviously not used to being up at this ungodly hour; many are wiping sleep out of their bleary eyes and still have unruly bed hair. They huddle in small groups on the dock, waiting for their chariot to appear. Meanwhile, Fitzy is on board the coach, reversing from the depths of the ferry to the orders of a squat, Greek port worker who, even at this early hour, has huge wet sweat marks in the armpits of his navy blue boiler suit. Sweaty Boiler Suit Guy fires directions at great speed and with great volume.

'Go malákas, píso malákas, aristerá malákas, aristerá malákas, aristerá malákas. Stási malákas! GO malákas, dikaíoma malákas.' (Go, back, left, left, left. Stop, GO, right). Each direction from sweaty boiler suit guy ends with 'wanker'. Fitzy will be completely ignoring him, I'm sure, and using his state-of-the-art reversing camera and fly-eye rear-view mirrors to navigate the big green machine safely down the ramp onto dry land.

Once we are all on board the coach and on our way south to the Paxos Beach Hotel, I flick on the microphone.

5.55am ISH - 'Kalimera, everyone. Kalimera means good morning in Greek. Welcome to Greece! As we have changed time zones, we need to perform a complicated time adjustment for this country. Please take the old, skanky watch off your wrist... don't worry, we'll be in Switzerland soon and you can buy a new flash one like mine. Now what you need to do with your watch is put it forward one hour and...' I pause for dramatic comedic effect, 'put it BACK twenty years!' Some of the flock's brains are obviously waking up a little, as there are a couple of giggles from around the coach. I wonder if they'll still be giggling when they find out I'm only half joking. They'll have a rubbish bin in their bathroom for USED toilet paper for the next three days, as the ancient Greek plumbing can't cope with this modern convenience.

The lack of plumbing isn't evident as Fitzy pulls up outside the Paxos Beach Hotel. The flock 'oh' and 'ah' at the picture postcard whitewashed building. Tall, arched windows have Oxford blue-coloured shutters closed to keep the heat of the day out of the building, when the day heats up, that is. Large cobblestones form a low wall, dividing the hotel grounds from the road and providing paving up the steps to the main door. Vivid splotches of deep pinks are provided by the bougainvillaea clinging to the stairs. All in all, a very good first impression, even in this low morning light, and the flock happily drag suitcases up the three flights of stairs, as the elevator has a 'temporarily out of order' sign on it.

The elevator, I am told by Christos, the hotel manager, will be fixed '*methávrio!*' *Methávrio* means the day after tomorrow. I don't bother to point out to Christos that the yellow aged piece of paper looks remarkably similar to the one that was there when I was last at the hotel a month or so ago.

10am-ISH. Rest is scheduled for the remainder of today, followed by a toga party in the hotel bar tonight. Most of the group takes the 'rest' part to heart and, after their breakfast of cereal, fruit and crusty (just out of the oven) bread, get straight into their swimwear and flop on sun lounges by the large rectangular pool overlooking the ocean. The only need to expend energy is walking to the pool bar that's manned from 11am by Spiro, who could also be called Adonis. Spiro is a looker, and he knows it. With sun-kissed olive skin, sparkling blue eyes and short, thick dark hair, he looks a lot like John Stamos when he was on *Full House*, but without the dodgy mullet hairdo. Greek men are a bit like Italian women though; they look great when they're young, but it doesn't last past about forty, when the rigours of smoking, drinking nasty drinks like ouzo and retsina, and too much sun, turn them into looking less like John Stamos and more like Danny DeVito. Still, I'm not planning on marrying the bloke, just admiring him in his current pre-forty state of beauty.

11am-ISH - While the flock relaxes by the pool, listening to the sounds Spiro is cranking out from his mixtapes, I take care of arrangements for the next two days, then retire to my room for a sneaky nap. The clean white sheets, with almost no holes, are cool and soothing to lie on. I strip off to my bra and undies and sigh audibly as I lie down on the bed. I pull an almost hole-free sheet over my body. The ceiling fan makes a gentle clicking noise on each rotation as it bathes me in a gentle breeze. I close my eyes and begin to be 'at one' with the mattress. It doesn't take me long to drift off to the land of nod to catch up on the beauty sleep I need before tonight's toga party.

9pm-ISH - The toga party kicks off with a complimentary shot of ouzo for everyone brave enough to wear a toga and nothing else. And by 'wear nothing else' I mean NOTHING else. Nearly every bed in the hotel has been stripped of its sheets, and they are now wound around bodies in every conceivable way. Most are held together with precarious knots, which will more than likely work their way undone as the night progresses. That's what the boys hope for anyway. I, however, have played this game before. This is not my first rodeo… or toga party, for that matter, and, although I have the obligatory knots for show, I also have a foolproof backup plan. Safety pins secure the sheet so that there is absolutely no chance of it falling to my feet if I attempt an energetic dance move. I may partially be to blame for the hotel's holy bed sheets from previous toga nights.

I arrive at the bar at the same time as flock members Bianca, Candy and Paige, and we throw back a shot of clear liquid together. Hot aniseed burns my throat. The three girls look great: their togas are just long enough to be decent, showing off their tanned, toned legs from all the jumping around that cheerleading requires. They're gathering quite a lot of attention from the males already in the room, including

Justin, who has just arrived with his less-than-happy-looking girlfriend, Clara. Justin and Clara are from Sydney, have been dating for three years and have recently hit a rocky patch. In order to smooth over this difficult period in their relationship, they decided to go on a holiday. Rather than opting for a week in Fiji, where they could relax in a romantic bure, rub suntan lotion on each other and have couples' massages, they have chosen to do a tour of Europe with thirty strangers, including me and Fitzy. Unfortunately for Clara, there are a number of good-looking girls, like the cheerleaders, in the flock, which is not helping Justin concentrate fully on his girlfriend or his relationship problems.

Unlike the cheerleading trios' tanned, toned and shapely legs Clara has that most unfortunate of physical attributes, the 'cankle'. It doesn't matter how thin a girl's legs are, although in Clara's case they aren't very thin, they can be cursed with the 'cankle'. The cankle is where the calf drops to the foot with no change of size where an ankle is supposed to be. Unlike the cheerleaders in their barely decent togas, Clara has attempted to make her toga as long as possible. Her toga makes its way to mid-calf, which, alas, only serves to accentuate her lack of ankle. Clara drags Justin away from the cheerleaders and their shapely ankles decorated with pretty gold chains and plaits of leather, to the other side of the room to join Hennie and Zola from South Africa. Hennie is a Mack truck of an Afrikaans man, with a big box chin. Zola, on the other hand, is just like a real person, only smaller. I fear Hennie could crush her if he rolled over in bed too quickly. Hennie and Zola have been struggling financially thus far on tour; with the South African Rand at ten to the pound, they have found everything very, very expensive. At last, in Greece, things are a bit cheaper, and they feel they can let their hair down.

From my position at the bar looking across the dancefloor, I see Roger. The burning feeling in my throat turns to a tickly butterfly feeling in my stomach. Roger and Skipper arrived in Paxos a couple of days ago and Roger was out sightseeing today when we arrived at the hotel, and as I took my beauty sleep. Skipper, I have been told, is no longer here. He has had to go to Igoumenitsa on the ferry to get their coach repaired, something to do with a rattly thingamabob. This leaves Roger alone here in Paxos with his group... and for me... I mean, with me.

Roger has taken the ancient toga and modernised it. He has dropped altogether the piece of material that traditionally goes over the shoulder and, instead, has his toga knotted neatly around his waist. He has obviously played this game before, too, because his toga isn't the dirty white, just been pulled off the bed variety. It is bright royal purple in colour. In ancient Greece, royal purple meant you were a senator, and Roger looks very much the 'in charge' senatorial man. He has come prepared.

There isn't very much of this purple so-called toga. It sits on his narrow waist and would not have reached mid-thigh if its life had depended on it. He looks up towards where I'm still standing at the bar, now sipping on a blue cocktail that Spiro has placed in front of me. I'm sure Roger must have seen me, so I make my way over to say hi. As I do, he leaves the group he is talking to and disappears into another crowd, and I'm intercepted by Teresa and Deb, who greet me with a rowdy, 'Yamas' (cheers) and clink their blue cocktails against mine. This sets the theme for the evening. Every time I have an opportunity to chat to him and move to find him, he moves on, and I lose him again.

The one time I do get within touching distance, he says, 'I'll catch up with you soon, Shaz, I'm just going to the loo,' as he races away.

His unique toga has obviously made him even more popular with the ladies than usual and every time I catch a glimpse of him, he's surrounded by a group of girls hanging on his every word, or sometimes literally hanging on him. Not that I'm stalking him, of course, I just happen to be very observant about my surroundings, like a highly trained Ninja or Gurkha. I'm having a great time without him anyway, probably more fun than a Gurkha should have. I'm chatting to members of my flock, and knocking back glasses of pretty blue cocktails that are decorated with little Asian-influenced paper umbrellas. Spiro ensures that my glass is never empty, and the little blue drinks give me so much energy that I feel I must burn up the dance floor.

Love Shack by the B-52s comes pounding through the stereo, and the dancefloor is suddenly mobbed. The crowd moves together en masse, as we begin dancing the (God knows who) choreographed dance that even the most uncoordinated person can follow. Right arm up *Saturday Night Fever* style, and then cross over the chest, repeat with the left. Bodies bounce from front to side, to back to side and back to the front again, each keeping in their personally allocated area and all keeping neatly in line. The song comes to an end and the heaving mass on the dance-floor erupts in self-congratulating applause. I look around again for Roger. My now slightly glassy eyes scan the room. Slowly... very slowly. An attempt at a quick scan makes the room spin ever so slightly.

Nutbush City Limits comes on the stereo, and another dance line is formed. I think I see a flash of purple heading up the stairs towards the bedrooms. By the time my beer goggled baby blues focus on the stairs, the only person I see for sure going up is one of the girls off Roger's tour. Surely it can't have been him? It is, after all, only about 11pm; far too early to be leaving the party.

After busting out my best moves to Tina Turner, I wander around aimlessly, hoping to bump into Roger, sipping my blue cocktail, chatting to people, smiling a lot, trying not to sway and feeling quite tipsy. How many of these blue things has Spiro given me so far? I have no idea.

11.30pm-ISH - I take the long route to the bathrooms, swerving by nearly every group of people left in the bar, but still no Roger. In a bathroom cubicle, I sit on the toilet for a minute to relieve myself of a few litres of fluid and catch my breath. The toilet seems to be swaying ever so slightly, as if the hotel has been placed on a lilo in the middle of a big swimming pool.

Deep breaths Shaz… In… Out… In… Out… Inhale… Exhale. The cubicle door next to me closes, and then a voice:

Cubicle: "Hi, how are you?"

Me, trying to pick the voice, American accent, Bianca maybe? "Um… Okay, thanks…"

Cubicle: "So what are you doing?"

Me, thinking this is a bit weird: "I'm just sitting here."

Cubicle: "Can I come over?"

Me (that's crossed the line): "No, I'm kind of busy right now and I'd prefer a bit of privacy!"

Cubicle: "Listen, I'll have to call you back. There's an idiot in the other stall who keeps answering all my questions!"

That is it, I have to get a bloody mobile phone, then I can

be in contact with my friends and organise booty calls even when I'm on the toilet. I won't have any trouble keeping track of Roger then. Mind you, he doesn't have a phone so… Fuck… Why is life so tricky? To avoid further embarrassment, I have no choice but to sit in the carnival ride toilet to wait until the person next door exits the cubicle, spends a ridiculously long time washing her hands and preening herself in the mirror and leaves the bathroom. I think I actually nod off for a bit. Before phone girl exits, the bathroom door swings open again, more people enter, and I hear voices.

American: 'Great night, huh?'

Australian: 'Maaaaaate, I reckon.'

American: 'How hot is our bus driver? Are you, like, totally into him?'

Australian: 'Skipper? I am. I'd love to root him. That curly hair. Those cute little freckles across his nose. I wish he were here tonight.'

Me: Involuntary gagging.

Australian: 'Where's Brandy?'

American: 'She went upstairs… coincidentally just after Roger.'

Australian: 'Such a slapper.'

Both: Giggles.

Me: Gasp! A coincidence, I'm sure. Nothing to worry about. He said he'd catch up with me later.

12.45am-ISH - The dance floor has thinned out enough for me to see that Roger is definitely not here. Spiro calls for last drinks, and I sway towards the bar to get my final little blue friend. Spiro is looking even more Adonis-like than he did at 11am. Nothing to do, I'm sure, with the five or so litres of cocktails swishing around inside me, clouding my judgement.

His teeth glow white under the fluorescent blue bar lighting as he smiles at me while mixing my drink.

'Shaz,' Spiro says as he mixes, 'I finish here in fifteen minutes, then I can walk you back to your room, if you want?'

Suddenly being walked back to my room by Spiro seems like a very good idea indeed. There is, after all, a hazardous flight of stairs to climb and who knows what danger may lurk in the corridors on the way between the bar and my room. I sip my final blue cocktail and concentrate on staying upright on my barstool as I wait for 1am.

1am - The second the hour ticked over, Spiro brought down the metal grate, closing the bar and keeping the alcohol locked securely away. He stepped out from behind the bar and offered me his bent arm. I locked my arm in his and we headed for the stairs.

After Spiro has helped me negotiate the treacherous sixty steps and has made his way inside my room, I'm somewhat at a loss as to what to do. He's certainly very good-looking. There's no denying that his bronzed physique is very well chiselled and worthy of further exploration. The fact that he has bedded a girl from nearly every tour that has stayed at the hotel in the five years he's been the barman here weighs on my mind. That's five times six... months of the year there were tours staying. Multiply that by seven to get how many days there were tours here. Divided by three, the number of nights the tours stayed (Carol Vorderman would have this worked out in a nanosecond), means approximately... Um... A whole bunch of girls who have experienced Spiro's Greek charms. I'm not sure I want to be a notch on his toga belt.

'Spiro, I hate to be a party pooper but I don't think this is a good idea. I have to see you every month or so, and I don't want it to be, you know, awkward. Maybe we should keep this professional.' Where have I heard that before? Is this some kind of romance karma?

Spiro lurches toward me, a dangerous lustful glint in his eye. He has obviously had attempts to fob him off before, and he isn't going to let that distract him from his attempt to get into my toga. He moves towards me quickly with his arms outstretched, ready to grab. I duck.

'Shaz, it no be awkward. I no tell anyone,' he pants, lunging at me again. At the last second, I use my netball skills and dodge. His momentum carries him forward; he trips on the rug on the floor and collapses on my single, sheet-less (because I'm wearing it) bed. 'Just where I want to be,' he says, smiling up at me. He pats the mattress beside him. 'Come join me.'

There's a gentle knock at the door. Who the fuck could that be? I move to the door, stretch up to my tippy toes and peek out the security peephole.

Bugger.

Shit.

Fuck.

Roger.

'Ignore it, Shaz and come here,' Spiro croons from the bed. I raise my finger to my mouth to shush him and assess the situation, my mind racing, albeit not very quickly.

Problem assessed as follows...

Man I want to be in my bed, on the other side of the door.

Man I want to be on the other side of the door, in my bed.

Don't want man I want in my bed, knowing that I have other man I don't want in my bed, in my bed.

Argh!

'Spiro,' I hiss, 'get in the wardrobe.'

'What?' He asks, looking justifiably confused.

'Spiro,' I hiss again, more urgently this time, and I gesticulate towards the wardrobe. He doesn't move. I don't have time for these charades. I take him by the hand and pull him towards the wardrobe. 'Get in and be very quiet. It's my boss at the door.' I'm not sure how my boss suddenly arrived at a hotel on the island of Paxos after midnight, but it's the best I can do at such short notice with an alcohol inhibited brain. 'And he can't know you are here, okay?' I plead. Looking none too happy about it, Spiro folds himself into the wardrobe, and I shove the door closed on him. I hope he'll get enough air through the louvres. All I need is to have to explain why I have a dead Greek toga-wearing barman in my wardrobe.

I open the room door a crack and peer out. Outside my door stands Roger, in all his manly glory. His toga is gloriously dishevelled and I note no longer knotted but now tucked. It's showing a LOT more of his legs than it previously did. It's now, for sure, the shortest toga I've ever seen in my life.

'Shaz, I went to find you downstairs, but you'd gone. Can I come in?' He asks, stepping forward and putting his foot in the doorway.

As he steps forward, his toga splits at the front and I'm suddenly very distracted by what I see, mesmerised even. As if I've been hypnotised by the penile pendulum swaying before me I reply, 'Yes.'

The offer of having Roger and what is under Roger's toga, in my room, is too wonderful to refuse. My brain kicks in just in time, and I remember the Greek in the wardrobe situation and quickly change my response. 'I mean, NO,' I say in what comes out as a high-pitched semi-shout. I breathe deeply to calm my voice. I continue, 'I'm really tired. I'm just about to hit the sack, actually.'

'Don't be mad with me Shaz. I've been trying to find you ALL night to... to... talk to you. I'm leaving tomorrow, come on...' He tilts his head slightly to one side and smiles alluringly at me. It didn't look to me like he was trying to find me all night, more like he was trying to avoid me, but I don't want a fight. Suddenly, I'm bone weary and I don't have the energy to entertain either of these gorgeous men. I think there must be something seriously wrong with me. Maybe I'll ask the dodgy doctor about that when I'm back in London. At my age, my libido should be non-stop. But, right now, all I want is for Roger to leave so I can smuggle Spiro out of my room unnoticed and then collapse on my bed, alone, in an alcohol-induced coma. Maybe a little bit of waiting could be a good thing to pique Roger's interest; treat 'em mean and all that.

'I'm not mad, Roger, honestly. We'll catch up next time we cross paths. Definitely. I'm just really, really, really tired.' I yawn widely to emphasise my tiredness. No sooner have I finished my yawn than a loud crashing noise comes from inside my room. 'You better go, see ya.' I push Roger back from the doorway, slam the door shut and lock it for good measure.

Tentatively, I open the wardrobe door, praying Spiro hasn't fainted or died. Spiro staggers out of the small closet, a large red mark of louvre indentation lines his forehead.

'What the hell happened, Spiro?' Just because I've decided I don't want to sleep with the man doesn't mean I want to be responsible for his brain injury.

'I think I fell asleep, and then BANG.' He demonstrates whacking his palm on his forehead, wincing with pain as he hits the louvre marks. 'And then I wake up. Has your boss gone?' Even with a possible concussion, he is obviously still keen to explore under my toga.

'Yes, he has,' I reply, 'and you have to go too.' At least the bump to the head seems to have lessened his resolve, and he puts up no further protest. Again, I lift myself to my tippy toes and peer through the little hole. The area of the hallway I can see is empty. I unclick the lock and open the door enough to put my head out, looking furtively up and down the dimly lit passage. I'm a secret agent on a stealth-like, covert operation thing. No one lurking in the hallway, no toga-clad party-goers weaving their way home. The coast is clear.

'Right, Spiro,' I say and bundle him out the door, 'see you tomorrow. Bye.' Before he can reply, the door is shut and locked again. I rest my back on it for a moment to catch my breath, and then flop onto my bed, still wearing my safely pinned sheet. I pull the thin blanket up over my shoulders and drift off to sleep, dreaming of what might have been.

Chapter 23

Paxos

Day 15

Groundhog Day in Paxos… It's sunny again. At 8am the day is already threatening to be a scorcher. If I could have placed an order for the weather today, I would have asked for a warm, overcast day. No bright sunlight and certainly no oppressive heat. I don't think my head can cope. Alas, I've no magical weather powers. I dress for the day ahead in my pink and orange 'tartanesque' bikini, slip on a white cotton singlet and very short, white frayed denim shorts and make my way to the breakfast room.

Most members of the flock are already in the breakfast room when I arrive, tucking into scrambled eggs on toast. I see, to my horror, that the server of these beaten eggs is a beaten Spiro. The red mark on his forehead from last night is now a shiny, bright blue bruise. When he turns and sees me, he looks none too happy. Is that look because of said bruise? Or is it because of the early breakfast shift he's doing after a late night on the bar... or perhaps being denied sex and being shoved in the wardrobe has something to do with it?

'*Kaliméra Spiro, ti káneis?*' (Good morning, Spiro, how are you?). I faux cheerily greet him.

'IS it a good morning Shaz?' he shoots back, glaring at me. It obviously *is* going to be awkward, even though we didn't shag. I decide to skip the watery scrambled eggs, which are dripping from the ladle he's holding in a white-knuckled grip and stick to cereal; it might be safer.

10am - ISH Greek timing involves a lot of 'ish'. 'Ish', in Greek time, means give or take an hour or so. Sometimes 'ish' extends to three or four hours. Nothing happens in a hurry here. Once, when I was staying here, my toilet wasn't flushing properly. I asked the hotel manager when it would be fixed. '*Methávrio,*' he replied.

Knowing things could take time, I asked, 'Does *methávrio* mean tomorrow?'

He looked at me and laughed. 'This is Greece,' he snorted. '*Avrio* means tomorrow, *methávrio* means the day *after* tomorrow.'

A *kaiki* (fishing boat), painted in the traditional Greek colours of white and blue, pulls up at the small pier that juts almost apologetically into the sea across the dirt track from the hotel. Drifting up to the hotel, we hear a voice thick with Greek accent calling through a megaphone.

'Hurray up *malákas*! Your boat is leeeeeeeaaaaaaavinnnnggg gg and your breakfast is reeeeeeeeady.'

Chapter 23

'That's our call guys,' I tell the flock waiting in the dining area. They gather up their bags, towels, cameras, sunscreen and hats, and head downstairs towards the pier from which we'll board our vessel. Fitzy joins us just as we're about to board, and he's as excited as a pig who's about to be in muck.

'No driving for me tomorrow Shaz, so I'm ready to p-l-a-y!'

As we each board, Yani, the skipper of the vessel, pours a shot of ouzo into a disposable plastic shot glass cup and offers it up to drink.

'Come on *poústis*. Breakfast,' he says to each passenger.

Yani is the only man I know, aside from Jesus in Barthelona, who can get away with calling some of the large lads in the flock 'poofter', without getting a punch. Each member of the flock, in sheep-like manner, takes the offered ouzo without protest; smiling and thanking Yani as they knock it back. Start the day how you mean to continue is Yani's theory.

Fitzy and me are the last to get on board. As Fitzy reaches Yani, he is greeted with a firm, vigorous handshake and a, 'How are you *poústis*? Still a *poústis*, I can tell by those shorts.'

Yani gives a hearty laugh, which emanates from the depths of his not-so-insignificant belly and hands Fitzy two shots of ouzo. I, however, get the choice of either downing the ouzo or performing a sexual act on Yani. At this early stage of the day, I opt for ouzo. The words 'hell' and 'freezing over' spring to mind when I think about Yani and sex combined. Anyway, I know he's really joking, as he prefers his women much larger than my size 8 frame. Yani's adorable, in a big, hairy Greek way, but is most certainly not in my preferred age bracket, nor is he my type. He crushes me with a bear hug, then reaches behind the bar on the boat to give me a singlet to wear that says, 'SOW YOUR WILD OATS ON YANI'S BOAT' emblazoned across the chest.

'Hey *poústis,*' Yani yells to Fitzy. 'There no enough room on boat for yooooou. You go here.' Yani points to an inflatable rubber ring with handles that is tied to the back of the boat with a dangerously frayed rope. Fitzy eagerly jumps off the boat into the clear blue water and drags himself up into the ring, wedging his bum in the central hole. Yani tosses him a couple of cans of Amstel.

10.30am - ISH We're off! Yani used to use his boat to catch fish for a living, but as Paxos became more of a tourist destination, he took advantage of the opportunity to cash in and swapped his fishing net for a microphone. He built a cabin on the deck with a bar, where he can sell alcoholic beverages for his thirsty tourists and put a toilet on the back, where people can turn their wine back into water. Yani uses the space under the deck as a food storage and preparation area. The whole set-up is rustic, to say the least, but there's plenty of room on the roof of the cabin to sunbathe and it's a great place to jump into the ocean for a swim.

The flock has spread around the boat, finding comfy spots to sit or lie and watch the picture postcard scenery. Yani gives us a commentary about the island of Paxos. I've heard his routine a million times (ish), and it never fails to both shock and amuse his guests. His patter includes a lesson on the Greek language. Why does he do this? Because so many Greek words sound like 'fuck'.

I tune out after Yani says, 'And the Greek word for envelope? *Fákelos,* I'm not joooooking.' The sapphire blue water churns into a white tail behind the boat as we chug along. Fitzy, in his tyre, bobs along on top of it. He waves happily to me and takes a long chug of one of his beers.

When Yani slows the boat and throws down the anchor for our first swim stop, Fitzy tips himself out of his ring and swims up to the side of the deck where I'm reclining.

'Jump in Shaz, it's lovely,' Fitzy enthuses.

I need something to help me shake off the fuzzy feeling in my skull. I pull my new singlet over my head and slide my shorts down to the deck to reveal my tartan-esque bikini. I call it 'tartanesque' as the material is like a traditional Scottish tartan but coloured with playful oranges and lilacs, which would be no use at all for camouflaging one's Scottish self in the Highlands. I step cautiously up onto the edge of the boat, trying to balance in sync with the gentle rocking of the boat on the small sea swell.

I lift my arms to the sky, ready to dive. A dive which, in my head, will be so stylish I will likely be confused with Greg Louganis at the Seoul Olympics (not the bit where he hit his head, obviously). Clean entry, no backsplash. I expect that if judges were watching, I would get a score of at least 9.5. In reality, I misjudge my dive just ever so slightly, as the boat falls away from my feet as I jump. I enter the water at an extremely shallow angle. Actually, there's almost no vertical angle at all. I'm practically horizontal as the water and I meet, and my exposed stomach slaps painfully on the surface of the ocean. My body weight pushes me under the water a bit and when I surface, gasping for breath, I turn to see Fitzy is absolutely killing himself laughing at my display. Colin and Keith from 'Straylia' have entered the water, via equally unstylish but just as effective bombs, before swimming over to Fitzy and I. We tread water together.

'This is fuckin great, innit!' Colin enthuses.

'Reckon,' Keith chips in.

'I have to say, boys… I hate my job on days like today,' I joke, whilst manoeuvring myself from treading water in an upright position to being flat on my back, floating in the turquoise, salty water. I lounge back, exposing my face and my now probably slapped red belly to the sun. The cool water cradles the back of my head and fills my ears, dulling the noise of the world around me. Only my eyes, nose and mouth are in clear air.

'Uh, thasssss,' I hear Fitzy say, at least I think it's Fitzy and I think that's what he said.

'Eh?' I reply, enjoying the sensation of the cool ocean on my head and the warm sun on my face. The fuzzy feeling in my head is starting to recede, at last. The water in my ears makes Fitzy's voice muffled and alien-like.

'Thasssss,' I hear him say again, a little louder but no more clearly than the last time.

Oh, I get it; he must be saying Shaz…

'Yesssssssss, Fitzy.' I languish, slowly moving my arms in a figure eight motion and gently kicking my feet up and down to keep myself afloat. The warm sun deliciously kisses my skin.

Hmmmmmmm. This is so relaxing. I really feel sorry for people with office jobs on days like today. I mean, eight hours stuck inside at a desk, pushing paper around, and here I am getting paid for this.

'Youf hod da hurls out,' I hear Fitzy attempt to communicate again.

'I've hod the hurls out?' I repeat back to him what I've heard without lifting my ears out of the water.

'YOUF HOD THE HURLS OUT.' Fitzy lifts his volume another notch. Why can't he just leave me to enjoy this moment of peace?

'Huh?' Pulling my feet down toward the sea floor, I lift my head out of the ocean and tread water to look around.

A crowd has formed on the side of the boat. I see Colin and Keith staring intently towards me, their eyes directed just below the water line.

What the fuck is everyone looking at? Fear clenches, suddenly and tightly, at my gut.

Fuck! It must be a shark …

I hope it isn't a shark.

I fucking hate sharks.

I'm terrified of the thought of sharks, or other aquatic life with enormous teeth, swimming silently below me, eyeing me up as a source of good protein… a tartan-clad snack to go. Beyond my control, the *Jaws* theme tune, used to build suspense before a shark attack in the movie, starts to play in my head.

Da da…

Da da…

Da da da da da da da da da da da da da DA DA DA DA.

Fearfully, I look down to check for silent aquatic killers. No, thankfully, no shark. But there is a strange white glow where my bikini top should be.

I've been exposing more than my face and my belly to the sun. Shit. My bikini top is a violet and orange plaid blur, sinking slowly to the bottom of the sea. Colin drags his eyes away from my chest and valiantly dives down to retrieve it for me as I try to cover my chest with my hands and tread water at the same time. Kicking my legs like an epileptic octopus, I just about manage to keep my head above the water.

Fitzy, meanwhile, is killing himself laughing, again.

'You'll see much more than that later, boys,' he jokes. 'Just wait for the nude cliff diving.' With the show now over, I'm getting back on the boat for a beer.

Fitzy keeps up a cracking pace, drinking beer all afternoon. He decides to keep lunch liquid as the flock and I tuck into soft, fresh, crusty bread and Greek salad with large chunks of creamy feta cheese and tiny fried fish that Yani has been catching as we swim. The rest of the day is a dreamy haze of warm sun on my body, cool salty water on my skin and cold fizzy Amstel down my throat. The flock is buoyant, relaxed and making the most of their day on the high seas.

5pm - ISH We arrive back at the jetty as the sun sags heavily in the sky. I'm relaxed and mildly numb. Fitzy, on the other hand, is in what can only be described as an alcohol-induced coma and is unable to get off the boat under his own steam. A few of the big lads make a stretcher out of beach towels to lug him off the boat with. They take him back to his room, where they place him in the recovery position and cover him with one of the least sand-encrusted towels. His 'professional driver' armour is slightly dented. Oh well, he's got all day tomorrow to sleep it off.

Chapter 24

⚜

Paxos

Day 16

9am - ISH The bruise on Spiro's head has lost a bit of its brilliant blue colour today, I'm pleased to report. He's obviously still in a grump with me, though, and when I enter the breakfast room, he simply turns his bruised head/ego away from me and leaves. There's no sign of Fitzy. No surprise there. I probably should go and check if he still has a pulse at some point this morning. I think I'll have breakfast first, though. I'll need some energy if I have to perform CPR or some other strenuous life-saving technique to revive him. The only members of the flock present at breakfast are Hennie and Zola, who are sitting over by the windows, staring silently out to sea while they eat their breakfast, and Norman, who is sitting by himself at a small round table in the middle of the room.

Norman is peeling the shell of a boiled egg with a look of complete concentration on his face. His tongue sticks slightly out of the side of his mouth as the egg receives his full focus. His concentration breaks with the last bit of shell removed, and his face lights up when he looks up and sees me. He motions wildly for me to come join him. I look again around the room to see if I can find an excuse not to. I can't. I take my wooden tray, laden with a large glass of UHT orange juice, a cup of strong filter coffee, a bowl of cornflakes and another bowl containing thick creamy Greek yoghurt, or as they call it here in Greece, 'yoghurt', over which I've drizzled an obscenely large amount of runny honey, and make my way over to Norman.

'Hi Thaz,' he begins, machine gun spraying saliva as he speaks. One of the saliva bullets lands right in my bloody cornflakes. I take the bowl off my tray and push it to one side; suddenly I don't feel like cornflakes.

'Hi Norman. How are you?' I take a long sip of my coffee. It's tepid. It joins the cornflakes in the discarded section of my breakfast.

'I'm amazing. I'm having such a good time,' Norman gushes. 'Today I've hired a kayak and I'm going to go exploring.' The 'p' in 'exploring' sends another saliva spray into the atmosphere. I'm suddenly not feeling very hungry at all. Worryingly, I have a flash vision of a Greek search and rescue team having to be deployed to return the exploring Norman to the hotel later on.

'Be careful, won't you Norman. Stay close to the shore, make sure they give you a life jacket... a life jacket that will float, and come back well before dark.' Do I sound like my mother, or what?

'Don't worry Thaz, I will. Now, you eat up.'

Midday - ISH I still haven't seen any sign of Fitzy. As I turn the page of the glossy magazine I'm reading while I lie on the couch in the TV room, it crosses my mind that I still haven't checked if he's breathing. If he's not, I reason, it'll be too late to do anything now anyway, so I may as well not fritter away the rest of this lovely day. I take the magazine and head outside. I pause on the hotel balcony to look over the swimming pool area and across the road to the small pebble beach. I can see quite a few members of the flock are lying on colourful beach towels, soaking up some Greek sun. A few others have hired pedalos from the small beach hut that a local entrepreneur has set up to make some tourist drachmas, and they are happily pedalling around the small bay. A lone kayak is on its way into the middle of the Ionian Sea. Norman will end up on the mainland if he keeps on that heading. Just as I am about to race over the road and perform a Baywatch rescue, Pamela Anderson-style, a bright green pedalo slowly turns towards the kayak. Froth is expelled from the back of it, as Justin and Clara pick up their pedalling speed in order to pull Norman out of the shipping channel and back towards the herd in the safety of the shallows.

Phew, that was a close call… for me… I almost had to *do* something.

The pool area is deserted, so I take up a spot on a lounger and get back to reading my magazine; it's the new edition of *Marie Claire* with Cindy Crawford on the cover. The magazine is actually about three months old but in my book, that IS new. I spend a blissful hour lying in the sun reading about '101 ways to get great hair every day' and how I can 'get liposuction in my lunch hour'. I also find out 'how to manage a career and a relationship' and 'how to have a guaranteed orgasm'. On that note, my mind drifts to Roger. Handsome, divine, aloof, frustrating, mixed message-sending Roger. My eyelids become heavy. I relish the sensation of drifting off, thinking about the man of my dreams.

My hair is looking great today; perfectly coiffed, like it is every day. I run my fingers through it just to check.

Yip, perfect.

Thanks to the liposuction I had in my lunch hour yesterday, my thighs are looking ultra-toned. They're not at all sore either. It's amazing, this new medical technology. I've managed to find this time to myself as I can manage both my amazing career as an international model with my relationship with Roger. He really appreciates, loves and respects me and with him, an orgasm is guaranteed. Here he comes now...

'Hi, babes,' I greet him. No need for words from Roger. He leans over and kisses me deeply. I wriggle beneath him and moan from the pleasure of his kiss. He puts his hand under my perfectly coiffed head and lifts it slightly, pushing us closer together as his tongue and mine dance in perfect harmony.

'Hmmmmmm,' I moan. 'HMMMMMM.'

Suddenly, my face is cold, like a shadow has passed over the sun. The kiss has abruptly stopped, and Roger is no longer here.

'Roger?' I open my eyes to see where Roger has gone, only to see the shadow of Spiro towering over me, blocking the sun. I shake my head a little to get my bearings. I run my hand through my decidedly uncoiffed hair and wipe off the trail of dribble that has escaped from the side of my mouth as I slept.

'Do you always wriggle and moan in your sleep, Shaz?' Spiro enquires.

Fuck.

'Can I help you, Spiro?'

'No, just checking you weren't having some kind of seizure,' he snorts, as he wanders off to open the bar for the afternoon.

3pm - ISH. It's been quite exhausting, lying, first inside on the couch, then outside in the sun. Maybe I'll just have a little lie down in my room where it's cool. There's still no sign of Fitzy. I really should go and check on him... I'll just have another quick nap first.

5.15pm - ISH After a lovely inside nap, I'm all showered and almost ready to take the flock for a 'night out at a traditional Paxos family taverna'. I know Greeks have big families but a taverna that can fit eight or so coach loads of tourists, I would call more a tourist trap than a family taverna, cynic that I am.

I have chosen my wardrobe for this evening carefully. Polyester pants in darkest forest green, which I bought from Sisley (my second favourite shop behind Benetton), last time I was in Venice. The pants cling in, what I hope is, a flattering way to my pert-ish behind. I've paired with them a floral t-shirt with accents of blue and black. The t-shirt has small patches of sheer fabric, giving just a hint of skin underneath. Except where my bra is, then it gives a hint of a black bra. Sensible flat, black loafers complete the ensemble. I check out my reflection in the mirror. Not too bad, but my hair certainly isn't as good as it was in my dream earlier, and I can't remember a single one of the '101 ways' to make it amazing.

5.23pm - Still no sign of Fitzy. I really hope he's not dead. The phone calls I'd have to make would be horrendous, and the paperwork... argh! I don't even want to think about it.

I wander down to the coach. Maybe he'll be there all ready to go. A couple of the flock are starting to appear, in their finery, ready for a scheduled 5.30 departure for their night out. I peer through the glass door on the coach and give the door a prod to see if it will open. It's locked and there's no sign of our trusty driver. I head back into the hotel, up to the first level and knock at his door, gently at first, then harder. I put my ear hard up against the door and listen. Nothing.

Using my fist this time, I pummel at the door and yell, 'FITZY,' at the top of my lungs. I hear a low groan from inside, the sound of which may have come from a wounded animal.

'Fitzy?' I call out. No reply. 'FITZY!' I yell again. I hear the muffled sound of shuffling footsteps on the concrete floor and the door opens, just a crack. What I can see through the crack is one bleary, bloodshot eye and a couple of tufts of what hair Fitzy has left, sticking up at random angles.

'What do you want Shaz?' He asks, rubbing his bloodshot eye.

'I'm just wondering if you're the Fitzy who's driving the big green bus? You know, the one that's parked outside, that's going to the taverna tonight?'

'Funny, Shaz. Very funny. Yes, I'm that Fitzy, but we aren't leaving until half five so fuck off and leave me alone.'

'What IS the time now, Fitzy?'

He opens the door a bit further to let in some more light.

I really wish he hadn't.

There are some things, once seen, you can never unsee or ever erase from your memory. Fitzy, in his boxers, with the fly flap gaping open, is one of them. Ewwww, ginger pubes. He squints his eyes to focus on his watch. When the current time registers through the fog in his hungover brain, he jumps like he's been plugged into a wall socket and 220 volts are shooting through him.

'It's five fucking twenty-five, Shaz,' he barks.

'I know, Fitzy,' I reply calmly.

'We're leaving in five fucking minutes.'

'I know that too. Give me the keys.'

Fitzy dashes back into the gloom of his room, picks up the coach keys and, with a throw that would make a cricketer proud, fires them to me.

'I'll be there in three minutes,' he shrieks, as he slams his bathroom door shut behind him.

7.30pm -ISH It's a fairly quiet night at the taverna. There are only four coach loads of tourists, including our own, sitting at the long wooden bench tables set up under the grapevine-laden trellis. The trellis criss-crosses the open-air seating and the dance floor area at ceiling height, creating shade and ambience.

'How was your breakfast Fitzy?'

'I don't usually have dolmades, lamb, potatoes and Greek salad for breakfast, but do you know what? It was bloody good. How's the retsina?'

'Shit, as usual. It's a shame you can't have any. It's a special mix of chateau de cardboard wine and pine-scented air freshener,' I quip. I try to wave the glass under his nose to see if the smell will make him vomit, but he bats my hand away. A bit spills from my glass into the bowl containing the remains of our now wilted Greek salad.

'It sounds lovely. What a shame I'm driving. It's nearly time for the potato dance. Are you ready for it?' Fitzy asks.

'I think I need more retsina first.' I swig the rest of the glass, wincing with displeasure at the foul-tasting alcohol, and reach for the carafe in the middle of our table for a refill.

The bouzouki player strums, with a flourish, the few final chords of the song the band is playing, before Eleni, the hostess for the evening, takes to the small stage. Eleni's real name is Helen, and she's from Manchester. She's lived in Paxos for decades after meeting, falling in love with and marrying a local boy while she was here on a two-week flop and drop vacation. Eleni looks like she's wearing a disco ball. The lights above the stage glint off her mirrored dress at random angles, temporarily blinding people sitting at the long tables nearest the dance floor. Her bleached blonde hair is piled high in a bird's nest-style on top of her head. She has so much make-up on her face, it's entirely possible that she's just kept putting it on for a few years, without ever bothering to remove the previous day's layer.

'And now,' Eleni announces, pausing for dramatic effect. 'It is time for the…'

Come on, Eleni, spit it out.

'The world famous…'

Yes, come on.

'GREEK POTATO DANCE!'

A shiver of excitement shoots through the crowd, even though they're not exactly sure why they're excited or what a potato dance is. A few people, who can't control their excitement, make a move to the dance floor. Eleni stops them in their tracks with her outstretched arm and outward-facing palm - very Spice Girls.

'Soon, good people… soon it will be your turn. But first… it is the turn of your tour managers and drivers to demonstrate. Please, lovely travel staff, come, come, come… Come choose your potato!' She finishes with a dramatic sweep of her arm to her side and a twirl of her disco ball dress.

'Here we go, Shaz. Make sure you pick us a good spud,' Fitzy directs.

I try to appear casual and look like I'm ambling, while at the same time, moving as quickly as I can without running, towards the bucket of potatoes that have been placed in the middle of the terracotta-tiled dance floor. Fitzy trails behind me. I check out our competition as I go.

Other team, Number One: Must be British, probably from some dodgy package holiday company. She is early twenties and has the tan of someone who has spent their entire summer on the island of Paxos. She has on a pair of white Bermuda shorts and a blue polo shirt with a logo, which must be company-issued and compulsory for her to wear, surely, or why else would she have worn something so hideous for a night out? The polo shirt is pulled tight over her ample bosom and tucked into her shorts, which are held tight on her waist by a tan leather belt. Her boat shoes match the belt exactly, completing the 'I live a life by the ocean and hop on and off yachts a lot' look. He's probably mid-fifties and looks like he could be a local bus driver hired to get the group from their hotel to here. He stubs out his roll-your-own cigarette and places the butt behind his ear before following 'on and off boats' girl to the dance floor. He wipes his hands on his checked shirt, which is stretched to breaking point, over his nine-month pregnant belly, as he waddles.

Other team, Number Two: I would guess they're Spanish... or maybe Italian. She looks like a model and has on a tight black mini-skirt, an orange halter neck top, which leaves no opportunity for any kind of breast support to be worn underneath it, and she has cream-coloured 5cm high heels on her feet. He's mid-thirties and is wearing a designer suit, Armani maybe. His black hair is slicked back in a greasy pile on the top of his head in a do, of which John Travolta of the 1970s would be proud. It looks like he plucks his eyebrows.

Other team, Number Three: Both competitors are men, and my guess is that they are from one of those poncy older people's tour companies that look down their noses at us young folk. Both men look quite old themselves... over thirty-seven, at least... maybe even forty. First guy looks just like a normal man, only smaller; he's about the same height as I am, but probably weighs less. His hips are certainly narrower. The old, small guy gives me a smirk as he heads towards the bucket. The second old guy is well over six feet... 6' 3", maybe. He's just like a normal man, too, but one who's been stretched. His body hasn't filled out at the same rate as it has grown taller. He's what my mother would call 'gangly'. A good gust of wind could probably blow him over.

I side-step in front of the little old guy, so I reach the potato bucket first. I block him by bending over to get first dibs on the potatoes on offer for this dance battle of the titans. Little old guy tries to move around me, to look in the other side of the bucket, but I shuffle around, continuing to block him with my polyester-covered behind. It takes ten seconds, or so, for me to assess the potatoes on offer and spy the perfect spud.

The potato dance requires each couple to hold their potato between their foreheads and perform dance moves instructed by Eleni. The use of hands is not allowed. The couple who manage to hold their potato for the longest, while still performing the required moves, wins. The potato that I remove from the bucket and hold above my head for Fitzy to inspect and approve is about 6cm by 4cm by 4cm. Not too big… not too small. Not too heavy… not too light. Not too hard but… actually, not too hard, full stop. It's perfectly soft and a little bit squishy. Not squishy enough that it'll ooze potato juice down our faces when we push it between our foreheads, but squishy enough that it'll mould to the shape of our heads. Crucially, this potato of perfection is not spherical; it's flat. It should sit nicely between our brows. In the words of Goldilocks, it's just right!

Fitzy's rubbing his palms together in glee as I move across the dance floor towards him.

'Nice work, Shazza.'

'Right, Fitzy, here's the plan: we do what I say… okay?'

'Taking it a bit seriously, aren't you, Shaz?' Fitzy asks.

I put on my serious Winston Churchill addressing the nation voice, 'Fitzy… the honour of the company rides on our shoulders. Our flock is depending on us. We must NOT let the company, or the flock, down. We must crush the opposition. Got it?'

'Um… okay, Shaz. If you say so.'

'Riiiiiiight, competitors,' Eleni begins. 'Do you all have your potatoes?'

There's general nodding from the four pairs on the dance floor.

'Please place your potatoes between your foreheads,' Eleni announces with another dramatic arm waving motion.

'Wipe your forehead, Fitzy.'

'What?'

'Wipe your forehead.'

'Why?'

'So it's not all greasy and the potato doesn't just slide straight off.'

'Are you saying I have a greasy forehead, Shaz?'

'Just... fucking... wipe... it,' I request again, through gritted teeth. Reluctantly, Fitzy drags the cuff of his long-sleeved navy-blue shirt across the back of his forehead. I pull a paper napkin from my pocket that I'd cunningly placed there earlier and gently dab at my brow. When I'm satisfied that it's oil-free, I give the potato the once-over.

'Are we all ready?' Eleni asks, looking directly at Fitzy and I. The other three couples all have their potatoes placed between their foreheads and are waiting for the music to start. I hold our potato between my thumb and forefinger, on its edges that won't touch our skin, so as not to contaminate it with any oil. Slowly, I lift our potato to my forehead and place it gently against my skin.

'Right Fitzy, move on in. Get nice and close. Press up hard against me.'

'I thought you'd never ask.' He laughs. I shoot him a 'this is serious – don't fuck with me' glare and he does as he's told. Soon, we're toe-to-toe, nose tip-to-nose tip. All that's separating us is our chosen tuber. The smell of something acrid reaches my nostrils. I sniff twice in quick succession to try and assess the aroma. Have I stood in something? Is our spud off? I sniff again.

'Have you brushed your teeth today Fitzy?' I hiss.

He doesn't have time to reply, as the band starts playing and Eleni is back behind the microphone, but he does look suitably guilty. The delicate metallic sound of the bouzouki strums a slow beat accompanied by a drummer, a guitar player and an enthusiastic tambourinist, who shakes his instrument to emphasize an eight count. Under Eleni's direction, we are off!

'Righto, dancers… It's time to… DANCE! To begin, step to your left and then to your right, left, then right,' Eleni instructs. Eleni's English has a very Greek feel, and her 'a' sounds like a 'u', so what we hear is, 'Righto duncers… It's time to… DUNCE!'

The command to dunce immediately throws team two into chaos, with model girl going to her right and Armani guy going to his right. Their potato lurches dangerously downwards, and they only just manage to keep it held up, by the bridge of her Roman nose.

'*Il mio moron destra*,' she hisses at him. So they're Italian then.

'On three, Fitzy, we move to YOUR right. 1… 2… 3…' And we are off, carefully stepping from one side to the other. I put my hands on Fitzy's hips. 'Fitzy, hold my hips, then you can feel me moving.'

'This night is just getting better and better.' He smirks, putting his hands further round than my hips and taking the opportunity to have a feel of my behind.

'My hips, Fitzy, NOT my arse! And keep your mouth shut, your breath stinks.'

'Come on,' Eleni encourages. 'Keeeep duncing!'

I turn my eyeballs to the side and see team 1 are in dire straits. Pregnant guy's belly is so big that 'on and off boats' girl has to stand on her tippy toes just to get around his mass and keep her forehead anywhere near his. She's trying to move her feet to the side of his, to avoid his paunch, but she's having trouble getting around the bulk and in a split-second lapse of forehead pressure, the potato slips and lands with a dull thud on the dance floor.

'*Skatá*,' pregnant guy curses, as they head back to their seats, to some lacklustre clapping from their group.

'That's one lot out.'

'Now, duncers… It's time to move around in a circle,' Eleni directs.

I grab one of Fitzy's hands off my hip and hold it tightly.

'I didn't know you cared, Shaz.'

'I'm going to pull you, you idiot.'

'Excellent.' Fitzy laughs.

'Seriously, Fitzy, keep your mouth shut. Did you brush your teeth this morning? The smell of your breath is making me gag.'

'I didn't see this morning, remember? Come on, pull me Shaz. I'm all yours,' he enthuses.

I tug at his left hand with my right, to guide him in the direction we will circle.

'Come on spectators… cheer for your duncing team!' Eleni tries to get the crowd involved in the competition.

From a few tables back comes, 'Come on Shaz and Fitzy. You can DO it.'

And 'Aussie, Aussie, Aussie, oi oi oi!'

'Three teams left.' Eleni states the obvious. She looks at Fitzy and me holding hands and a smile spreads across her face. 'It's time to make it more difficult. Duncers, stretch your arms out wide and keep turning.'

A piece of cake; now we're in our turning groove. While tall old guy is still looking comfortable, with his head bent down resting on their team's potato, short old guy is looking tense. To compensate for his partner's height, and his lack of it, his head is thrown way back, and it looks like he's supporting the weight of his partner's head as well as the potato; his face and neck are red from the strain.

'Duncers...' Eleni sparks up again. 'Now it's time to go down to your knees.'

All teams complete this movement with seemingly no trouble, although team two now have their spud wedged between model girl's cheek and in Armani guy's eye socket.

'Now, sit down on your bottoms,' Eleni instructs.

Again all teams manage to complete the task, albeit slowly and carefully.

'It's time now to stand back up, duncers!' Eleni is piling on the pressure and the band has upped the tempo of the music, creating a feeling that time is of the essence. While Fitzy and I manage to place the soles of our shoes on the tiled surface, get purchase and begin to elevate ourselves back to a standing position, model girl is struggling. She can't quite work out how to stand back up without giving a large section of the audience a view up her itsy-bitsy mini-skirt. Armani guy is getting frustrated. He's yelling instructions while glaring at her with his eye that's not stuffed with spud.

Model girl twists one leg back underneath her bottom and, while squeezing her knees together, slides the sole of her cream high heel onto the tiles and tries to stand. She manages to get her backside about 10cm off the ground and almost gets her second foot underneath her before she loses traction. She slides onto her back on the dance floor, her knees pop apart, and the elderly tourist sitting in direct eye line up her skirt can't believe his luck.

'*Opa*,' he yells and claps his hands together gleefully.

The potato falls out of Armani guy's eye socket, bounces off model girl's Roman nose and rolls onto the dance floor. Armani guy kicks it, as he wanders off, rubbing dirt off the knees of his immaculately pressed pants and leaving model girl to regain her dignity and get herself up off the floor.

'We've got this Fitzy. Only the old guys are left and that bottle of Ouzo is ours! Maybe you could use it as a gargle to freshen your breath?'

'Focus, Shaz. The pride of the company and all that remember?' he reminds me.

'This next move will sort out the real duncers from the pretend duncers,' Eleni announces. 'If you are not a boy/girl couple, you will have to choose one of you to be the girl.' This brings a snigger from the audience. The old guys have a quick chat along the lines of:

'You be the girl.'

'No, you be the girl.'

'No, you be the girl.'

'No, YOU be the girl.'

'Oh, alright then, I'LL DO IT.'

'Girls, put your hands on your partner's shoulders.'

Short old guy reaches up and tentatively places his hands on tall old guy's bony shoulders. He looks none too pleased about it. I firmly place my hands on Fitzy's shoulders, which are only marginally higher than my own.

'We've GOT this Fitzy!'

'Boys, put your hands on the girls' hips.'

'Giddy up,' Fitzy jokes.

There's a moan of disgust from the old boys.

'Righto, duncers. When I say, "*Opa,*" the girls need to jump and put their legs around the boys' hips,' Eleni instructs.

'*Opa, opa, opa,* oi, oi, oi - Fitzy and Shaz!' Colin, or Keith, calls from the crowd.

'Are you ready?' Eleni asks.

'Ready Fitzy?' I ask. Fitzy gives me a look of steely determination as his answer.

Eleni continues, '1… 2… 3… *OPA!*'

While still pressing my forehead firmly onto Fitzy's, I press down hard on his shoulders and jump. Like a scene from *Dirty Dancing,* I leap towards him, wrapping my legs around his waist and locking my ankles behind his back. Nobody puts Baby in the corner! For a split second, I think we've nailed it. I even start to smile smugly. Then I feel Fitzy falling. It's a slow-motion fall, like in the movies. I know it's happening. I know it's not going to end well, but I'm powerless to stop it.

I let out a slow motion, 'Ffffffffffuuuuuuuccccccckkkkkkk,' and manage to untangle my ankles from behind Fitzy so that my feet land, soles first, on the dance floor.

Fitzy lands flat on his back, but thankfully, stops his head from thumping on the unforgiving hard tiles as his body lands. My head whiplashes back, then falls forward, crashing into the potato and pushing Fitzy's head back so that it does indeed crash onto the tiles. The potato - perfectly squishy for keeping it in place for dancing - can't stand these g-forces and is squashed to smithereens. It oozes down the sides of Fitzy's head. My bottom comes crashing down right on Fitzy's groin area and this is how we end up: Fitzy lying flat on his back on the tiles and me straddling him, our foreheads still together like a smashed potato sandwich.

'You okay?' I ask as I lift my head to see two smug old guys holding aloft a bottle of ouzo and bowing to their elderly clients who are applauding them. I pull the tissue out of my pocket again and wipe potato splatter from my forehead. 'I thought we had them.'

I help Fitzy to his feet, and we leave the dancefloor to rowdy

213

applause from the flock and a few comments along the lines of, 'What sort of show is this?'

'Didn't realize we were in Amsterdam already?'

And, 'Get a room.'

10pm - ISH The flock members have tested themselves with the potato dance, consumed litres of retsina and downed dozens of shots of ouzo. They've smashed a few plates, giggled at the Greek dancing men in their white tights, little puff skirts and pointy shoes with pom poms on the toes, and zorba'd 'til they just can't zorba no more! It's now time to pour them out of the door and onto the coach or, as we'll call it tonight, 'the Vomit Comet'.

'I'll park right outside the door, Shaz. You herd them in and get the sick bags ready.'

Opa!

Chapter 25

Ferry

Day 17

6am - ISH There are a few sore heads and a few sick tummies this morning as the flock moves slowly and painfully from the hotel to the coach. The heat, even at this early hour, isn't helping those with hangovers. Everyone's glad of the air-conditioning on the coach for the short drive to the port for our ferry bound for Venice.

'*Kalimera* everyone,' I call out cheerily on the microphone. There are a few groans in response. 'All you have to do today is get on board the ferry, then you'll have ALL day and ALL night to catch up on your rest before we arrive, tomorrow morning, in Venice.' A few subdued, 'Yeahs,' but mainly glassy, vacant stares.

8am - ISH All on board and we're off! Time for a nap.

10am Bingo - excellent. Didn't win, bugger.

11am *Jerry Maguire's* on in the small movie theatre. I love Tom Cruise. Yeah!

1pm I love Tom Cruise. Not as much as Roger, obviously, but still quite a lot.

1.30pm A quick bite of lunch, and then I think a nap is in order.

3pm Bingo - excellent. I didn't win. Bugger.

6pm Fitzy and I meet in the formal dining room for a sit-down, posh dinner, as the company is paying for it. The flock seems to have headed to the cheaper buffet restaurant, so we don't have to make small talk and be nice to anyone. We stare at the menu for a while in companionable silence.

A waiter, resplendent in black pants, a crisp white shirt and a burgundy waistcoat, approaches us.

'*Ti tha thélate na parangeílete?* What would you like to order?' He asks, switching seamlessly between Greek and English.

'To start, I'd like the saganaki with some tzatziki and kalamata olives. Then I'll have the moussaka and, for dessert, the baklava, please… I mean, *parakalo.*'

The waiter acknowledges my order with a brisk, '*Nai,*' (yes) and turns his attention to Fitzy, who requests a Greek salad and a souvlaki.

'Are you sure you want the baklava, Shaz? You could do with losing a few kilos so you don't kill your next potato dance partner,' Fitzy jokes.

'You could do with eating a bit more, Fitzy; build yourself up so you don't drop another one.' And so start the friendly jibes back and forward until our starters arrive and conversation halts, as I'm lost in the creamy saltiness of the saganaki and

Fitzy crunches his way through his Greek rabbit food.

In the break between courses, Fitzy changes the tone to a serious conversation.

'Did you hook up with Spiro?' He enquires.

'NO!' I exclaim. Maybe that NO was a bit too quick and loud. Will he think I'm overcompensating and protesting too much? 'No,' I say again, in a much calmer, more controlled tone. Fuck, maybe answering twice will be more suspicious than one quick loud answer.

'Roger?'

Another emphatic reflex, 'NO!' and then another calmer, 'No.'

'Both of them at the same time?' He pushes on. What is this, the Spanish Inquisition?

'No… What?… NO… why?'

'I just thought I heard both of them in your room around the same time on the night of the toga party.'

He begins eating the souvlaki that has arrived in front of him, playing it cool and pretending that the fact that I may have had a *ménage à trois* with Spyro and Roger is of no consequence to him at all. I plunge my fork into the depths of my moussaka, twirling it around and spreading minced lamb, aubergines, cheese sauce and tomatoes all over my plate. I scoop up about half of the cheesy sauce and slurp it into my mouth in one go. Yum.

'You really like Roger, don't you?' Fitzy asks.

'He's okay.' Play it cool Shaz, be non-committal, you know these boys talk.

'Be careful there.' Fitzy sounds ominous.

He's digging. Don't respond. Play it cool, Shaz… play it cool.

And I do play it cool… for about thirty-seven seconds. Then…

'Why?' I can't help myself.

'He's a player.'

'Do the words pot, kettle and black mean anything to you, Fitzy? He's probably just waiting for the right woman.'

'And that might be you? Don't kid yourself, Shaz. There'll never be anyone that Roger loves as much as himself.'

We don't talk any more about Roger as we finish off our main course. I move onto my dessert, or more accurately, I dissolve my tooth enamel with the sweetness of the honey-soaked pastry of my baklava. I try to keep the conversation light and the feeling upbeat, but I can't help the metaphorical cloud of a downer that Fitzy's words have cast over my metaphorically sunny day.

8.30pm. It must be time for bed. I curl up in the foetal position on the narrow bottom bunk of my womb room and drift off to sleep. It's not a restful sleep though: I toss and turn, thanks to a dream featuring Roger. In my dream, we start off walking hand in hand through a meadow littered with bright yellow buttercups. We're in a happy and playful mood. Roger slips his hand from mine and runs, urging me to chase him. And chase him I do, but I never catch up to him again. All night I run and run, trying to catch Roger.

Chapter 26

Venice

Day 18

My trusty alarm clock goes off at 7am, and I wake up excited, although slightly exhausted from all the running I did in my dream. Venice, here we come! I bounce out of bed and into the tiny bathroom, or is it called a 'head', as we're on a ship? In this 'head', you can sit on the toilet and shower at the same time. It's about the only way you can shower, actually, as there just isn't enough space to stand anywhere, unless you have your back up against the wall and your feet under the toilet, so sit I do. The trickle of water that emanates from the cracked plastic shower head is just enough to get me sufficiently wet to provide the soap with enough lather for me to be able to give my 'pits and bits' a quick wash. The towel is tiny; in keeping with the overall miniature theme. It's more of a flannel than a towel, but it's adequate for me to dry myself enough to be able to get dressed without my clothes sticking to my skin.

I select a pair of black linen shorts from my suitcase and, to go with them, a navy blue and white checked bodysuit that has a Daisy Duke style sweetheart neckline, edged with broderie anglaise; a nod to the lace that we will be seeing in Venice. I pull the bodysuit over my head and fasten the three snaps under my groin, careful not to trap any pubic hair in them. I've made that mistake before. I pull the linen shorts up and button the waist, which comes to just below my rib cage. I slip on a pair of black suede loafers and a zip up fleece jacket to protect me from the morning chill on deck.

After a quick breakfast, I bound up the few flights of stairs that separate me from what I've told the flock will be one of the highlights of their trip around Europe - arriving to Venice by sea. It doesn't disappoint. The early morning sun illuminates the pale pink of the Doge's Palace, turning it a brilliant rose gold. Lines of long black gondolas are bobbing up and down, moored along the front of the entrance to St Mark's Square, waiting for their gondoliers to start work for the day. Stallholders have begun opening their huts, ready to tempt tourists with their imitation gondolier t-shirts and straw hats banded with blood red ribbons.

Fitzy heads off on the coach with our luggage to the hotel on the mainland. The flock and I disembark the ferry on foot. We walk a short distance along the water's edge from our large ferry to board a much smaller boat. This smaller vessel will take us for a cruise around the Venetian lagoon and drop us off on the island of Torcello. There, we'll spend a few hours getting a taste of Venice, before we hit the madness of actual

Chapter 26

Venice tomorrow.

Chapter 27

Venice

Day 19

8.30am I really, really love Venice. Not only is it my favourite city in the whole of Europe, but it's also one of my favourite days on tour. All I have to do is get the flock onto a motoscafi (a large water taxi), which will take us to the islands of Venice. I'll see them safely to a glassblowing demonstration and, at 5pm, meet them again to get them on another motoscafi to get back to the hotel for dinner. In terms of tour managing, this day is a doddle.

The Venetian lagoon is shrouded in clammy mist, which hangs mere inches above the water. It promises to give way to a stunning day when it finally clears. We wait, peering into the pea soup from the small pier near the hotel, for our boat to arrive. The deep sound of a horn to alert other vessels in the area lets us know when it is nearby.

'*Ciao bella,*' Claudio, the motoscafi driver, greets me enthusiastically as I board the boat, once the boat boy has secured it safely to the pier. '*Come stai?*'

'*Ciao* Claudio,' I respond in kind and lean in so we can kiss on each cheek in the traditional Italian way.

I'm all about tradition, especially when the tradition means I get to kiss Claudio. Claudio is just your run-of-the-mill average-looking Italian man, i.e. gorgeous. At around 5'10", he's a good half a foot taller than me. He has the trademark Italian jet black hair, and his piercing blue eyes are made even bluer by the deep tan that seems to cover his whole body (the bits I can see anyway). I take a minute to let my imagination go wild on the rest. What covers the rest, that I can see, is his boat driver's uniform of ink black pants, shiny black leather loafers and a crisp white shirt, accessorised with black Louis Vuitton sunglasses, which probably cost about six months of my meagre salary.

We chat about the weather (when the mist clears, it'll be a stunner), and how well his mother was looking after him (very well, she launders his uniform every day and brings him breakfast in bed every morning), during the half an hour it takes for Claudio to guide the boat to a dock near the Palazzo Ducale. The trip involves a lot of horn honking, listening for a horn in return and watching a reassuring radar screen to make sure we don't crash. I have to stand very close to Claudio to make conversation possible over all the noise. I can feel the green eyes of envy from Fiona drilling into my back for most of the way. Palazzo Ducale, which we saw yesterday in the glow of the rising sun, sits regally on the edge of St Mark's Square and is our drop-off and pick-up point for today.

Arriving in Venice never fails to impress. Those members of the flock who do tear their eyes away from Claudio are madly snapping photos of the bell tower, the massive lions towering over the entry to St Mark's Square and the calming, baby pink tiles of the Palazzo Ducale, which leads on to the Bridge of Sighs, now appearing through lifting fog. The boat bobs on the swell in the lagoon and, as it aligns with the dock, we alight one at a time down a wooden plank. We all stagger a bit as we regain our land legs. Once we straighten up, we take a left turn to walk along the water's edge and, after crossing a couple of bridges, take a right turn into St Mark's Square. Blue sky is now peeking through, and the sun is starting to make an appearance. It's still early enough that the bird seed sellers haven't set up yet, thus the pigeons haven't arrived en masse for the day.

The pigeons are probably still resting in their nests somewhere, building up a supply of poop to launch at unsuspecting tourists later. The air still has a coolness to it, the square is still relatively free of people, and there's a calm, serene feeling. We move towards the middle of the large square that Napoleon once called 'Europe's grandest ballroom'. As we do, THE most gorgeous of Italian men you can ever imagine rushes, actually rushes, to meet me. This God-like creature stands well over 6 feet tall, with raven black hair, milk chocolate eyes and skin that's been kissed by the luckiest of sun rays. He wears a shabby chic ensemble of jeans, torn in all the right places, a baby pink coloured shirt (probably Armani), with a lilac cable knit sweater over his shoulders, knotted loosely around his neck. His Gucci sunglasses are perched casually on top of his head. Not everyone can carry off pink and lilac together, but this man can.

'*Ciao Shaz, come stai?* You look beautiful as always,' he croons, leaning down to kiss me tenderly on each cheek. 'I have missed you; let's get your group over to the glassblowing demonstration so I can be alone with you.' He drapes his arm casually over my shoulders and leads me towards the back corner of the square. The flock follows in our wake. God-like man tilts his beautiful head towards me, leans in close and whispers seductively in my ear, his lips tickling my earlobe as he does.

He looks behind me to the flock as he whispers, making sure they can't hear. 'Your boat back to the hotel might be a bit late, okay?'

I move my lips to his ear, smiling slyly at the flock behind us as I whisper in my best Marilyn Monroe voice, 'No problem,' giggling just a little as though we've just shared a 'known only to us' joke.

By now, most of the girls in the flock would have bought used socks off him just to be able to keep looking at him and listening to his soothing Italian lilt. Little do they know, that as soon as he's got them in the door of the glassblowing demonstration and worked up their shopping juices, he'll be replaced by a much less attractive fat, sweaty Italian glassblower and he'll race out to lure the next tour manager with their flock into his glassblowing lair. He would also be going home that night to his equally gorgeous boyfriend, Paulo.

I do, however, enjoy his undivided attention for the five-minute walk. I also enjoy the envy of the girls who, I guess, think this is my secret Italian lover; a man I rendezvous with each time I'm in Venice, and with whom I'd be spending a romantic day, as they trudge around sightseeing with the masses. If only. You can, though, see why I like Venice so much!

10am Flock safely deposited in the glass shop with the fat, sweaty Italian glassblower and the greasy salesmen. I'm safely ensconced in what is known by Terrific Tours' staff as the 'Italian Office'.

The Italian Office is a small café, just around the corner from the glassblowing place, where tour managers and drivers meet to kill time until their boat back to the mainland at the end of the day, or until they have to ferry their flock to their next activity. The Italian Office is tucked away down a small dark alley just off St Mark's Square, close to the action but out of the way enough to make it unlikely to be stumbled upon by any flock members wandering around the back streets.

The interior is sumptuous, with luxurious red leather booths and dark wood-stained tables. The walls are heavy with gilt-framed pictures of famous Venetians of days gone by. The bar counter, at the entry to the café, is where the locals come for their 'heart starter'. Espresso that can stain your teeth brown in an instant and has enough caffeine to keep any normal person awake for days. The busy locals talking a million miles an hour, with both their mouths and their hands, don't even bother sitting down to drink it, such is their rush for the caffeine 'hit'. Mere mortals like me slide into a booth and sip a tepid café latte in a tall glass, with sugar.

My lazy driver had mumbled something last night about important driver's things he had to do today, as an excuse for not spending the day with me. I know damn well he'll still be in bed, bastard. Still, I'm not going to let that get me down.

After all, Roger is in town and it isn't long before he arrives at the office with, alas, Skipper right behind him. Why can't Skipper be a lazy driver like Fitzy and leave me in peace with Roger? The three of us sit and sip our lukewarm café lattes. I am vigilant for any under-the-table hand-on-leg action, as we discuss how we might fill the nearly seven hours we have until it's time to leave the islands.

'How about the Guggenheim Museum, or the Accademia Gallery?' Skipper suggests.

'Nooooo,' Roger and I groan together.

'No bloody museums,' continues Roger. 'Let's have some fun on this lovely sunny day. How about we all chuck in a bunch of money and go drinking for the day. See some different parts of Venice and have a few laughs along the way.' Roger is in full swing now, running with his idea. 'We shall call this excursion, the Tiny Terrific Tipsy Trek or TTTT for short, AND there shall be rules to keep the day flowing. We will start right here and order a drink of the alcoholic variety… maybe an Aperol Spritz to start? Then we'll take turns to decide whether we go left, right or straight ahead out of the bar, and we'll walk until we find the next bar. Sound good?'

The beauty of Venice is that you can't ever really get lost. If your feet get wet, that generally means you've run out of island and you should turn around. Nearly every building has a sign that points to either St Mark's Square or the Rialto Bridge, both of which are in familiar territory.

'After we hit the next bar, we then order another drink, of course it couldn't be the same as the last one, although…' Roger ponders for a moment, 'in the interest of our health, a cleansing ale is allowed at every 4th stop. We will have our last drink at 4pm. That gives us plenty of time to have a 'sober up' coffee and make our way from wherever we've ended up, back to the dock by 5pm.'

Brilliant plan. What could possibly go wrong?

Roger, event organiser extraordinaire, kicks things off after we knock back an Aperol Spritz (quite refreshing). 'Left', he says in a decisive tone.

Skipper and I trail out of the coffee shop behind him. We begin to negotiate our way through the back streets of Venice, listening for calls of, '*Attenzione!*', which means you're likely to be taken out at the ankles by a man with a trolley if you don't move fast, or you're about the step in a pile of doggy do. The Aperol has given me a spring in my step and a thirst to quench.

10.45am The alleyway we are following spits us out into a small campo, which has a restaurant that's just opening for the day. A brisk waiter, dressed smartly in black and white, lays out trays of freshly made *tramezzini* (crust-free triangle-shaped sandwiches stuffed with delicious tuna mayonnaise, prosciutto, egg and other delights) on top of the counter. A waitress flaps out red tablecloths to cover the chipped wooden tables. The campo is ringed with homes in dusky pink and burnt orange hues. Flower baskets add reds and yellows to the colour palette. Washing lines hang from second floors, window to window, straining not to drop their flapping white cargo onto the campo below.

'It's your call, Shaz,' Roger says, looking at me. 'What do you fancy?'

I try not to blush at the thought of what I fancy. I direct my attention to the waiter and ask for '*Tre prosecco, per favore.*'

After the Aperol started us off, I think some more light

relief, in the form of bubbly, won't go astray. We sit in amiable silence sipping our prosecco, watching Italian nonnas, with their noisy herds of grandchildren heading to school, local men and women impeccably dressed hurrying about their business, and the odd tourist, looking hopelessly at their map; turning it this way and that, trying to figure out where they are and how to get where they want to be. To keep ourselves amused, we spend some time trying to guess where the tourists who stumble upon the campo are from. A middle-aged couple wearing matching clothes and bright white Reeboks are instantly tagged as American. Two men in their twenties with round, frameless glasses and wearing brown Birkenstocks – German. A group of about ten, all with short dark hair and enormous visors covering their faces, scuttle past, cameras hanging around their necks; Japanese for sure.

I lift my elegant long-stemmed glass to my lips and take the final sip of my sweet bubbly wine when Skipper says, 'Straight ahead!' It takes a bit of discussion for us to remember where we had entered the campo and, as there is no alley directly opposite the entry, we have to negotiate some fine print in the rules before we can move on.

Four stops later, after a shot of Grappa (the nastiest stuff on the face of the earth), a glass of red wine (smooth), a shot of limoncello (gave the tonsils a bit of a tingle) and a cleansing ale (ahhhhhh), we emerge from the dim light of an alley to find ourselves at Harry's Bar. This one is a no-brainer: Harry's Bar is where the bellini was created. The marriage made in heaven from prosecco and peach juice. I'm not sure it technically qualifies as a serving of fruit, but it might be the closest I get today. Even though a bellini at Harry's costs an eye-watering 15,000 lire, we decide it's worth it and find a table with a view of the canal. I feel relaxed and happy, the sun is now shining brightly, and it isn't the only thing with a glow on.

'How about some show and tell?' Suggests Roger. 'Tell us something we don't know about you, Skipper?'

Skipper thinks for a moment. 'I volunteered in an orphanage in India for a month in the winter. It was amazing, the children were SO adorable and I really feel like I made a small difference in their lives.'

I smile at Skipper, 'That's a really nice thing to do.'

'Sap,' says Roger, 'what about you Shaz? Tell us something we don't know about you.' He looks at Skipper and gives him a knowing smirk. I cringe, shrinking a little into my wooden chair, feeling hot red creeping up my cheeks.

'Um...' I ponder, 'my dad died when I was six.'

Skipper looks at me in such a caring way it nearly makes me cry, and gently, he puts his hand over mine, patting softly.

'That must've been really hard, Shaz,' he says. I slide my hand out from under his, putting it on my glass and shrug like it was really no big deal, although I fear it actually is a big deal and has a lot to do with the way I go about my love life. I dash the seed of the thought out of my mind before it has a chance to grow. Denial is indeed a happy place. Head in the sand... It's got me this far.

'What about you, Roger?' I ask to divert Skippers attention. 'Spill.'

'I don't really like talking about myself much,' he says then proceeds to do exactly that for a full fifteen minutes all about the languages he speaks (English, French, Italian and German), how he was educated in the finest private schools in Sydney and how much money his family is worth (quite a lot, seemingly). Even though I know I shouldn't be, I'm a bit impressed. All that and looks to die for too.

'OK, Skipper,' Roger says when finally he runs out of breath. 'Back to you... How did you get your nickname?'

'On my training trip,' he begins, starting to blush, looking down at his shoes like they're the most interesting things he's seen today. 'The other trainees all decided I was the one most in charge, like the skipper of a boat, you know.' He trails off, and now his fingers have become very interesting. Roger and I are silent. That's a surprise. I can't imagine Skipper being in charge of anything; he seems so shy and kind of awkward. He demonstrated in bed that he wasn't in charge of EVERYTHING, that was for sure.

Roger turns his attention back to me, 'So, Shaz, is that your natural hair colour?'

Subconsciously, I put my hand up to my short red hair and feel my cheeks start to warm up again.

'You know, Roger, a lady never reveals details like that.'

But Roger will not be put off. 'Well, there's one way to find out, isn't there?'

I'm confused.

'Do the curtains match the carpet, Shaz?'

'What the fuck are you talking about Roger?' I ask.

'Show us your pubes Shaz! That'll tell us if it's your natural hair colour,' he retorts, throwing his head back and laughing at his hilarity.

'Bastard,' I mutter, my face having now gone as red as the hair on my head.

Skipper saves me from further embarrassment and changes the subject to how nice the weather is today. It really is a lovely day now; hardly a cloud in the sky and the sun, nearly at its peak, is heating up the brickwork on the pavements and buildings, radiating warmth at us from all angles. Skipper and I check out some of the boat traffic bobbing and winding its way slowly up the Grand Canal. Roger, meanwhile, checks out the willowy waitress who has come to ask us if we'd like another drink. Roger looks like he'd like to drink her. I decide it is time to move on.

'Right,' I direct.

3pm Another three stops for a fragolino (strawberry liquor, delicious), Campari (made by steeping a secret mix of herbs in alcohol), and another cleansing ale (ahhhhhhhh). We weave our way to the Rialto Bridge. Rialto competes with the Accademia to be Venice's most famous bridge. Where the Accademia has a more temporary-looking wood construction, the Rialto looks strong and stern. Arching across the Grand Canal, its sloping staircases house many shops and market stalls selling 'real Murano glass' trinkets and 'handcrafted' Venetian masks, made in China. We spot a red and white checked cloth-covered table outside a trattoria on the edge of the canal with a view of the bridge and make a slightly wobbly dash to secure it.

Skipper takes a seat while Roger heads to the bar to order our drinks and some desperately needed food. With lightning speed, my brain fires neurons to whizz around (okay, maybe not lightning speed, but faster than a cold knife through butter speed) to weigh the situation and decide that this may be my chance to make a move on Roger.

'I'm just going to the loo,' I say to Skipper and get into Roger's slipstream, tripping ever so slightly over the doorway edge and narrowly avoiding a collision with a waiter delicately balancing four humongous pizzas. Roger, who, as I have recently found out, speaks Italian fluently, is conversing with the barman and ordering us some well-needed food and some more not-so-well-needed alcohol. As he finishes, I'm beside him.

'Roger.' I try leaning into him seductively, but fail and have to instead use him to hold me up. 'What are you doing later?'

'Later when, Shaz?' He smirks.

'You know,' I continue undeterred, 'later, later. After this, later. A bit later. Later tonight. When we get back to the mainland, later.' He's obviously not getting my subtle approach.

'I'm going back to my hotel with my group. What about you?'

I'm not to be put off. 'What's your hotel like?' I ask, swaying alarmingly to my right, so much so that Roger puts out his arm to stop me from falling. I'm about to suggest that if his hotel were nicer than the two-star shoe box I'm staying in, then maybe he'd like to show it to me; his hotel, that is, when Skipper arrives at our side. The man's timing is again off, way off.

'The drinks have arrived,' he says. Roger heads out and, reluctantly, I follow him to the table. The food follows quickly. The quattro stagioni pizza that Roger has ordered is excellent; the saltiness of the artichoke hearts and olives being a nice foil to the slight sweetness of the Moscato wine we are washing it down with. The mozzarella cheese is warm, stringy and drips oil down my chin. I'm too hungry to fully appreciate it, though, and I inhale a number of pieces, barely taking a breath. We sit for a while, and I enjoy listening to the sounds of the hustle and bustle around me: gondoliers touting for business, delivery men pushing trolleys and cursing tourists in their way, the swoosh of the water buses pulling in and out of their stops, spewing people onto the uneven cobblestones.

'It's 4pm,' Roger informs us. 'Time for a caffeine hit, then off to meet the kids.' While I refer to my clients as my flock, Roger calls his 'the kids'. Skipper calls them 'the cargo'. Who knew what my lazy driver would call them, as he was never bloody around to ask.

We negotiate our way, weaving along the alleys in a way that has nothing to do with the tourists this time, but a lot to do with the amount of alcohol we've consumed, back to St Mark's Square and along the water towards the dock. I'm feeling decidedly worse for wear. My leg bones seem to have turned to jelly, and I have to try very hard not to slur my words. Skipper notices this and stops me, putting his hands on my shoulders and turning me to face him.

'Shaz, are you okay?' He asks, seemingly deeply concerned about my well-being.

'Slipper, I… be… fun,' I reply and giggle, 'absloutlbly flun. Now, do we go right or left?' I giggle again as my knees give out just a little, and I would've fallen flat if Skipper hadn't moved swiftly to catch me.

'Roger,' he calls over to him. 'I'm going to help Shaz back. Catcha later.' Gently, he lowers my mirrored sunglasses from the top of my head to cover my eyes and turns me toward my group, putting a protective arm around me for moral support, or to hold me up, whatever.

I smile and nod at my flock and make encouraging noises, as they tell me about their day all the way on the boat and bus rides back to our hotel. Skipper keeps me close and explains that I have a bit of a migraine, so he's helping me out.

Helpfully, he reminds them that their dinner is at 6.30pm, shows them that the dining tables in the reception area are where they will be eating, then guides me to the tiny elevator and up to the door of my shoebox room. It really is lovely of him, but I wish it were Roger.

'Shanks Slipper, I mean Kanks Kipper, I mean… You know wha' I mean. Urrah schtar.'

I sway in to kiss him on the cheek, then sway back into my room, closing the door firmly behind me.

'See ya Shaz,' Skipper says from the other side of the door. I note a little disappointment in his voice. There's a moment of quiet, then I hear his footsteps disappearing down the hall.

One of the first things I learnt at tour manager training school was to set my alarm for the next morning BEFORE going to bed so I would never sleep in. Most important! My Benetton suitcase moves in front of me, tripping me up. I swear at it, as I tip forward and fall, face first, onto my narrow bed. My eyelids are made of lead, and I am sorely tempted to succumb to sleep, but I have a mission.

Must… set… alarm… Fumbling on the bedside table, I knock over the lamp with the hideous gold tassels. There it is - my trusty travel alarm, a gift from my grandmother before I left New Zealand. It has never let me down yet. I strain my grey matter to try and remember where we are going tomorrow and what time we are leaving. After Venice comes? Comes? Comes? Shit.

Starts with an H…

North of here…

Skiing…

Schnapps…

Schnitzel…

Apple strudel...

Rhymes with...

Hopfgarten! Yes, that's it. Hopfgarten doesn't fucking rhyme with anything.

Right, so far, so good. Now, what time are we leaving? I could go down to reception to look at the daily information sheet I put up for the flock, but that would mean expending a lot of energy that, frankly, I just don't have. Come on, Shaz, I pep talk myself: you're an intelligent and not totally unattractive woman... you've done this drive a million times, what time will you leave? 10am, no, wishful thinking. 7am, bit early. 7.30am! Got it. The relief that I've managed to work the details of tomorrow out without having to leave my bed is immense.

Right... to maximise sleeping time, I will leave myself half an hour after my alarm to get up, dressed, packed and get my suitcase to the bus. Breakfast can wait until we stop later in the morning. I have the feeling I won't want to put food in my stomach in the morning anyway. So, 7.30am take away half an hour is... is... is... (Come on Carol Vordeman, help me out!)... 7am! I fumble with the buttons of my alarm clock, squinting to focus my tired, bloodshot baby blues until the numbers flick around to 7 and I flick the switch to turn it on. Triumphant, I reach out and place the clock back beside the toppled-over lamp with the gold tassels, and slump into a drunken coma.

7...The BEEP, BEEP, BEEP, BEEP, BEEP sounds a few decibels louder than is strictly necessary for an alarm clock, or maybe my hearing is extra sensitive today? I try lifting my head to look at it, but the energy required is too much. My bowling ball-weighted head collapses back on the bed. I try, instead, lifting my arm. Yes, that's a bit easier. I reach the clock and snatch it towards me, turning off the ridiculously loud alarm, before throwing it towards my suitcase in one fluid motion. Now that the infernal noise has stopped, it's lovely and quiet. My eyelids are so heavy. It'll be very easy to slip back to a lovely, dreamy sleep after a big day drinking if I don't get up immediately. So get up I do, albeit very gingerly.

After a big day drinking, isn't it funny how you can feel like you've hardly been to sleep? This is definitely one of those mornings. I feel like my eyes have hardly been shut at all. Alarmingly, as well, I still feel quite drunk. That's not unheard of, though. I have experience there too. A can of Red Bull on the coach and I should be fine.

I stumble my way to the bathroom, peeling off yesterday's clothes as I go. My bra comes off just before the door to the bathroom, and I slide my undies to the floor as I step onto the tiles from the worn hotel room rug. Rather than slipping easily out of the undie leg hole, my right foot becomes tangled. I go to step forward, but the undie ankle chain stops me in my tracks and overbalances me. My forward momentum makes me fall into the small bathroom. I twist myself mid-air to prevent myself from taking out my front teeth on the porcelain basin, which pivots me into the shower cubicle. I use the shower curtain as a lifeline to keep me upright. What could have been a disaster now sees me naked and in the shower cubicle, exactly where I want to be.

I turn the shower on full blast. The icy water makes me inhale sharply, and my skin immediately shrivels in goosebumps. My blood starts pumping extra fast, and a little of the fog in my head begins to clear. The water slowly warms. I grab the sliver of soap provided and lather my body to scrub off the lingering smell of alcohol that's emanating from every pore. When I'm done, I turn the water back to cold for a minute to make sure I'm really awake. I dry myself quickly and, peering into the cracked bathroom mirror, I apply an extra-thick layer of makeup.

I look almost presentable.

7.22... Dressing quickly, I shovel the rest of my belongings into my case and sit on it to get it shut and locked. I do a quick check around the room to see if I've left anything behind. The look around is obviously a bit too quick, as the motion makes my head spin, and I have to do a few deep breaths to stop myself from throwing up. I now have only 7.5 minutes to drag my suitcase to the elevator and get out to the coach.

The tiny, one-person, one suitcase, carpet-lined elevator reaches the ground floor and opens up right by the reception desk. My suitcase wheels stick in the entry of the elevator as I stride out of it purposefully, and my arm is nearly detached from its socket. I manage to get my feet back under my body before my face hits the terracotta tiles covering the reception/dining area. Once it's unwedged, I drag my suitcase towards the reception desk and smile at the manager stationed behind it, who, I notice, has a confused look on his face. I also notice that my flock is in the dining room. They're obviously taking their time over their breakfast. They really should hurry up; we are leaving in four minutes.

Wait a minute...

That's a bit odd...

Why are the flock eating spaghetti bolognaise, crusty garlic bread and glasses of red wine for breakfast? I really must talk to the hotel manager about that. Our people really do prefer cereal and toast, with maybe a glass of milk or a cup of tea in the morning.

What is also odd, is that the flock are all wearing the same clothes as they had on yesterday. Alarm bells ring loudly (a bit too loudly) in my tender head. I check my ever-so-reliable Swiss watch: 7.28. I close my eyes slightly, in an attempt to sharpen their focus to look at the letters on the clock that indicate whether it is AM or PM. Slowly, what at first looks like an 'A' for AM sharpens into a 'P' for 'PM'.

Shit.

It's not tomorrow; it's still today.

Shit, shit, shit. I smile at the hotel manager as I hit reverse and start to back towards the lift, hoping like hell that none of the flock has seen me and I might actually get away with this.

One step back.

Two steps back.

The hotel manager is now looking even more confused, but I keep my smile plastered on as I silently will him not to speak.

I'm arm's length away from the elevator door and safety when, from the very back of the dining room, I hear Fitzy's booming voice.

'Hey Shazza, where are you going? Got a date hot enough to take your suitcase?'

SHIT. Fitzy, the bastard, is never around when I need him, and he is when I don't. He's obviously had a lovely, relaxing day, and, by the looks, so has Fiona, who is sitting with him at the dinner table.

I turn my plastered-on smile up a few notches to make it my most dazzling smile ever and call back, 'Hi! I just thought I'd be super orgiamised.' Shit, still having trouble with slurring. 'For tomorrow. Could you help me over here for a minute,

Fitzy?' I don't think anyone noticed that slip. 'Hi, everyone. My migraines lifted a little,' I add, directing my smile at the whole room.

'Please don't blow my cover,' I plead with him as he reaches my side, close enough to smell the alcohol that still determinedly seeps from my every pore. 'Can you just play along and take my suitcase to the coach? I'll head back to my room, no harm done.'

'You'll owe me one Shazza... a BIG one,' he replies, smiling at me in an ever so slightly evil way. Jesus, I wish he'd stop calling my Shazza, probably not the time to raise that though.

'Let's not forget Paxos, eh? Shall we call it even? Fanks Shitzy... Oh, you know what I mean.' He lifts my colourful 'trip up its owner' suitcase with one hand and heads for the door, spinning his coach keys around the index finger on his other hand. He whistles a jaunty tune as he goes.

'Have a great night, everyone,' I say to the flock spread at tables around the room. 'I'd love to join you but I've still got a *bit* of a headache and I've got loads of paperwork, phone calls, and you know... stuff to do.' I gesticulate vaguely to try to emphasize some 'stuff' and I head back to the elevator with as much poise as possible, stopping on the way at reception to set a wakeup call for the following morning for 7.10am; after all, my bag's already packed.

Chapter 28

On the way to Hopfgarten

Day 20

8am - Phil Collins plays a drum solo in my head, my eyes water and my stomach protests for the first part of our drive north from Venice towards Hopfgarten, Austria. Skipping dinner last night and then breakfast this morning hasn't done me any favours. The remnants of yesterday's alcohol and pizza are now well churned with the acid my stomach has released in a desperate attempt to digest it all. This swirling mess of semi-digested alcofood has nothing to soak it up, like it's floating in space without a solid dock to attach to. It rolls, like a boat tossed on a stormy sea from one side of my stomach to the other. Occasionally, a large wave washes a bit up into my oesophagus and I do all I can not to hurl.

To distract myself, I slot a Spice Girls cassette into the tape deck. The chirpy lyrics blast out. This should keep me awake. Actually, the Spice Girls, who are so dear to my heart, make my head hurt even more. I wouldn't have thought that was possible. When the song finishes, I hit the eject button and put in my own mixed tape, which I've labelled in black felt pen 'Mellow Musak'. The Cranberries ease into the airwaves singing *Linger*. This is better.

Soothing.

Virtually no bass at all.

Soothing except that is, for the fact that the lyrics are a bit close to home.

Am I a fool for Roger? Am I wrapped around his finger? The effort of even forming those questions makes my grey matter burn in protest. I turn my focus from The Cranberries singing so accurately about my life, to the road ahead, in the hope this will keep my stomach contents where they belong.

Why did I drink so much yesterday? Why? Why? Why? If I knew it wouldn't be a promise as hollow as a pumpkin carved for Halloween, I'd probably say something like: I am NEVER drinking again. It would be hollow, though, as I know as soon as I see a shot glass of schnapps tonight, I'll be back on the horse that just bucked me off, trampled over me and covered me in manure for good measure.

9.30am After Fitzy parks the coach, I lead the flock past Verona's Roman amphitheatre and down a few pedestrian streets, until we reach an innocuous-looking tunnel entry that leads into a courtyard. The only thing that suggests there may be something of interest inside the courtyard is the myriad of colourful graffiti on the tunnel walls. All the graffiti contains messages of love; red hearts or initials with a '+' in between them. Strangely, there's also an area smothered in chewing gum. Maybe this is some love ritual of sharing spit, then sticking it on a wall for the world to see? My stomach lurches at the thought of spit sharing.

We enter the courtyard, which is ringed by the high, sandy coloured brick walls of the surrounding buildings. Some of the walls are covered in dark green climbing plants. In the far corner of the courtyard, to our right, is a dark coloured brass statue of a young woman. Disturbingly, her right breast has been rubbed shiny. It's cool in the shady courtyard and if it wasn't for the other hundred million tourists jammed into the small area, it could be quite serene. We jostle for a spot, and I move in close to the flock to try to be heard over the rabble. When I have everyone's full attention, I take in a deep breath and release it slowly. I ready myself for my performance. This may take all the energy I have left…

'Romeo, Romeo! Wherefore art thou, Romeo?' I ask loudly to the sky. I bring the back of my right hand to my forehead dramatically. 'Deny thy father and refuse thy name.' I take my hand off my forehead and thrust it out skywards, following it with my gaze in a longing manner. I pause for a moment, both for dramatic effect and to swallow back down the little bit of vomit that has snuck into my mouth. I press the palms of both my hands over my heart and look deep into the eyes of Randy from America, in his perfectly ironed shirt, who just happens to be standing right in front of me…

'Or, if thou wilt not, be but sworn my love, and I'll no longer be a Capulet.' I take a bow and wait for applause.

'What did she say?' I hear Pete ask.

'No flippin' idea,' Belinda responds.

'Where are we anyway?' Asks Margot.

'Philistines,' I mutter under my breath. I stand theatrically straight and try to muster some more energy.

'This, my friends,' I say, as loudly as I'm able, while pointing up to a balcony jutting out of the wall behind me, well above our heads, 'is the very balcony where Juliet Capulet is said to have stood and spoken those words of longing for her true love, Romeo. The statue is of her.'

'I thought Juliet said... "You and me, babe, how 'bout it?"' Muzz bursts into the Dire Straits song named after the Shakespearean play.

The flock springs into life, with laughter and remarks such as, 'Rub her boob!' 'Oh yeah, whatever, Romeo!' 'Take some photos and let's go.'

I give up. I just don't have the energy today. Wearily, I lead the flock back to the coach. As it comes into sight, I see Fitzy knocking back whatever type of coffee is in his hand and leaping up. He rushes to the coach, takes the broom that he's rested against the coach. As he starts furiously brushing the coach stairs, Belinda sidles up to me.

'Maybe that'll be you one day, Shaz?' She says, with a friendly smile.

'Me, what?' My brain isn't up to guessing games.

'You, on a balcony, declaring your undying love. Maybe... to that cute guy we saw you with in Venice!' She nudges me and winks.

'The guy that took us to the glassblowing shop? He's...'

'No, not him.' She interrupts. 'He's as gay as pink ink.'

I really didn't think it was that obvious? Well, there goes my fantasy of making girls green with envy with our little secret whispering on the way to the glass demonstration.

'Who then? Roger? The other tour manager.'

'Nah, not him. He's full of himself. Rumour has it that he's banged half the girls on his bus.'

'What rumour? Who says?' I ask, as the sick feeling in my stomach becomes more pronounced and another sneaky bit of vomit makes it past my tonsils. I gulp it back down, willing it to stay put. Belinda, meanwhile, ignores my questions.

'That loooovely driver who brought you back to the hotel when you had your *headache*.' She gives me another smile and another nudge. This time, she adds a sly wink.

'Skipper? No, he's…'

She cuts me off again. 'Yes, Skipper! You two look so cute together. Our own Romeo and Julia.'

'Juliet,' I correct her.

'Yeah, whatever. So romantic!'

We're back at the coach. Fitzy rests on his broom, watching everyone board.

'Wipe your feet, will ya,' he calls out. 'I've been working like a dog, cleaning while you lot have been swanning around.'

Yeah… whatever.

11am The Dolomite mountains are foreboding shadows ahead of us. We make our way towards them, across the flat, fertile plains of northern Italy. Fitzy takes his eyes off the straight stretch of Autostrada to turn and look at me.

'You okay, Shazza? You look a bit green. Green… Green… Get it?' He snorts at his own joke. 'Cause Green's your last name. Green, like your last name… Ha, ha, ha… Or green like snot. A big glob of snot. Or green like some ham that's been in the fridge too long. You know, when it's gone all slimy and really smelly and, when you put it in your mouth, it tastes a bit like fish-eye milkshake?'

Bile surges up my throat, just stopping this time as it hits my tonsils. I gulp it back down. My body goes hot, then cold. I rip the plastic rubbish bag off the armrest of my seat and put it on my lap, just in case.

'Shut up, Fitzy. Shut up right now. I would give you the evil eye, but I can't look at you. If I do, I'll throw up… I won't throw up from looking at you, you're not THAT ugly… I mean, you're okay to look at.' I cross my fingers behind my back. 'I just can't look away from the road right now.'

'You were fuckin' funny last night, Shaz. You and your big bright suitcase, right through the middle of the dinner…' He can't finish for laughing.

'Shhh, they might hear you.' I flick my head towards the back of the coach without taking my eyes off the road ahead, which is still enough to make my head spin wildly. The flock, though, is sound asleep. Heads are randomly lolling into the aisle, quite comically, like their necks are springs.

'Your secret is safe with me Shaz, don't worry.'

His reassurance does nothing to… well, reassure me. Loose lips sink ships and all that, and I can't afford for my ship to be sunk. Neil has been quite clear: any more fuck ups and I am out of a job. Then what will I do? I don't want to go back to New Zealand and my dull work life; stuck in an office, dealing with morons on a daily basis. Here, I still have to deal with morons on a daily basis, but at least I'm doing it in interesting places and having fun along the way. I want to go home eventually, but I'm hoping it'll be on my terms, with a boyfriend under my arm, or me on his arm at least. I'll have achieved, done something challenging for work, scored a nice man, have a wardrobe full of cool clothes, and be slim and tanned. Tall even. Okay, maybe tall is out of the question at this stage in my life. I'll be a success in the eyes of my family and friends at home.

Hopefully, at least the next time I go home, my mum will recognise me at the airport. My first attempt at a big 'Overseas Experience', when I was twenty, had been a dismal failure. I'd managed to stay away for seven months and put on sixteen kilograms. I had also been the victim of a scandalous Greek barber who, when I asked for a trim of my long, then mousy blonde, shoulder-length hair, had cut it to lengths ranging from 1cm to 5cm in a random pattern around my head. My travelling companions had immediately changed my name from Sharon to Sean. Admittedly, the barber didn't speak English and probably had more experience trimming beards, eyebrows, nose and ear hair, but this Basil Brush he had created with his dastardly scissors had left me follically and mentally scarred. The combination of sixteen extra kilos and bad hair had rendered me unrecognisable to my own mother when she came to collect me from Auckland airport. I arrived home broke, fat, with bad hair and a sense of embarrassment at my lack of travel staying power.

The three years I spent in New Zealand, before venturing to travel again, had been a mixed bag. Professionally, I'd done well; getting a job at an insurance company on my return and making a quick climb of the company ladder, to see me managing a staff of eleven at age 24. Personally, it hadn't been such a success. Even though I looked and looked, there was no boyfriend to speak of the whole time I was home. And trust me, I LOOKED.

This time overseas will be different. I've already been away from home for two and a half years and I've learnt from my mistakes. I avoid all Greek barbers and, thanks to an ongoing stomach upset, stress, and also possibly skipping multiple meals at a time, I've managed to drop to a size 8. I'm determined to go home victorious, conquering the Overseas Experience and returning with my future husband, ready to settle down. Now I just have to convince Roger. He may not be perfect, but I still think he's perfect for me.

12.30pm - Dissecting my life history in my head has taken up most of the drive to the Italian/Austrian border and we're ready to make our second stop of the day. Although, in general, I love Italian food, Italian motorway rest stop food is the worst. Cardboard sandwiches, either cold or toasted, and slices of God only knows how many days old pizza. Urgh. I can't wait to make our first stop in Austria and get stuck into a fall-off-the-plate-it's-so-big, schnitzel and a greasy bowl of fries, washed down with Red Bull for energy. That will keep me going until we get to Hopfgarten.

'Righty-o everybody,' I say into the microphone, jolting all the sleeping beauties back to life. 'We're about to make our first stop in Austria for food.'

A tremor of excitement moves down the coach as everyone wakes and realises they're hungry. 'Have you heard the one about the Austrian sausage?' I ask.

Dramatic pause, for effect...

'No,' Norman yells from the back.

'Thank you, Norman. Austrian sausages... are... the... wurst.' I pause again for laughter.

'Eh?' Norman yells.

Why did I bother? 'You see, Norman, an Austrian sausage is called a wurst.'

A few people together say, 'Oh,' and there's a smattering of laughter, but not enough to make the hassle of telling the joke worthwhile.

'We've got forty-five minutes here. See you back at the bus after that.'

Fitzy and I are quiet, initially, as we sit at the rest stop and hoover up our giant schnitzels. Can anything be better when you're hungover than flattened chicken, smothered in breadcrumbs and deep fried? The flock, too, appears happy to be in the land of meat and potatoes, devouring a variety of Austrian specialities, including wurst. All is calm, serene and peaceful. Then, Fitzy drops the bomb.

'Should be good fun in Hopfgarten. There'll be three tours in, lots of people to play with.'

'Who's there? Us, Liza and Fluro... Who else?'

'Skipper and Roger are there too. I think we're with them nearly the whole way back to London now. That's what Skipper told me anyway. He's got it all worked out. They'll be in Hopfgarten and Amsterdam for sure,' he says, with a smile at my obvious discomfort.

'Great.' My distinct lack of enthusiasm is probably fairly obvious. Roger and Skipper didn't tell me that when we were in Venice. The thought of seeing Skipper so often over the next week doesn't fill me with joy. Even thinking about him gives me flashbacks to the quick romp in London that forced me to see the dodgy doctor, take the pills that made me sleep deprived and nauseous, then mutilate my pubic area with a wayward sanitary towel. However, the upside is, of course, that I'll get to see Roger for the next six days, AND I'll get a chance tonight to grill Liza for whatever information she's harbouring about him.

2pm - We make one more stop on today's drive. The small market town of Wattens is where Daniel Swarovski set up his crystal business. Nowadays, there's a museum, of sorts, where you can see all manner of crystal creations. Fitzy pulls the coach to a halt in front of what looks like a grassy monster lying down. The monster's luminous bluey-green eyes, reminiscent of paua shell, glow ominously. From the monster's mouth gushes a constant flow of saliva in the form of a waterfall. Behind the waterfall is the entry to the museum.

The schnitzel has helped my hungover state, but not cured me completely, and I appreciate the shade and a few cooling splashes from the museum monster's spit as we make our way to the entry. Various designers were apparently given free rein to create art with crystals to be installed here. It looks to me that they possibly also had some chemical help… in the form of hallucinogenic drugs. This place is insane! We are greeted with a two-storey high wall, filled with crystals that are illuminated by coloured lasers pulsing through them. The strobe effect, with glittering crystal, immediately makes my head spin and my stomach begins to grumble and protest. Bile burns the back of my throat again, threatening to add to the technicolour vista the flock is currently absorbed in.

'I'll meet you outside in an hour, guys,' I announce hurriedly. 'Any questions? No, good. Have fun.' And I'm gone. Exit stage left and into the ladies' room.

This does nothing to soothe my sensory overload. My stomach clenches one final and decisive time before I close the cubicle door behind me and eject my schnitzel and fries into the glass toilet bowl, which is lit from below. One of life's great mysteries plays out in front of me. Where the fuck did the carrots come from? The orange is picked up by the floor lights and portrayed in kaleidoscope fashion onto the ceiling of the cubicle. It is both amazing and repulsive in equal measures.

4pm - We arrive in Hopfgarten before the shadow of the Hohe Salve mountain presiding over the town covers it in shade. Ejecting my lunch at the last stop has settled my stomach and, thankfully, I'm feeling marginally better. I raise the microphone to my chin and click it on.

'Here we are folks, Hopfgarten. Woohoo!' I'm trying to inject myself with enthusiasm as much as the flock. 'Hopfgarten is in the Tyrol region of Austria and its claim to fame is being part of Austria's largest connected network of ski runs. However, that doesn't matter a jot to us, as there's no snow in June.'

The mountains surrounding Hopfgarten, including Hohe Salve, are as green as an Irishman's hat on St Patrick's Day. The low-lying parts of the hills are lush meadows where pretty cows graze in the summer, before being shut in barns under homes in winter. The large, lazy-looking brown cows, each wearing a leather collar with a huge bell, wander the meadows, eating their fill.

Mind you, I've never seen a cow anywhere in the world that didn't look lazy; as a species, you could hardly call them 'fit'. Not like leopards, they are the epitome of fit! If Roger were an animal, he would be a leopard. But I digress. Further up the hills, masses of pine trees smother the peaks with deep green. The mass of pine trees has swathes cut through them for ski paths. It's in these very pine trees that, on Christmas Eve, local children rug up against the cold to go looking, by candlelight, for Kris Kringle. This is the spirit child with blond hair and angel wings who delivers gifts to them. Miraculously, the children never see him, but one of their parents will hear a bell when the drop-off has been made. (Parents are so clever like that.) Then the kids rush home to check out their loot. I like the idea of a Christ child angel delivering presents, over a fat old guy in a dodgy red suit who wants them to sit on his knee in order to get gifts. Having said that, Santa is preferable to Zwarte Piet (Black Peter), who hangs out with St Nicholas in the Netherlands and gives lollies and gifts, but only to 'good' children, of course. Zwarte Piet looks shifty and is always crouched down or hiding in shadows - creepy.

Anyway, it's nowhere near Christmas, so I don't have to worry about Kris Kringle or being 'good' enough to qualify for presents. I fear I would fail at this stage of the year. Still, I've got six months to sort that out, and I plan to start being good, the very moment tonight's 'P' party is out of the way.

It does seem ever so slightly weird in this quaint Austrian village, which has homes that would not be out of place on a chocolate box and where wooden shutters cover windows that are adorned with flower boxes sprouting all the colours of the rainbow, to have a bash called a 'P' party. But tradition dictates that we will. I'm not talking about some ancient Austrian tradition, however, I'm talking about a Terrific Tours tradition.

With three tour groups in town staying in adjoining gasthofs (guest houses), the gasthof with the largest bar will host the one hundred or so people for an evening of drinking and dancing. They will come dressed up as everything from priests to prostitutes, wearing plastic and panties. You might see, at the bar, Pippi Longstocking talking to the Pope, a pirate talking to a professor or Pinocchio talking to a platypus. The only thing they have in common is that they'll all be drinking schnapps, at least for some of the evening.

I am, for once, grateful that the gasthofs are short of room space, which means the road crew have to share rooms. As

Liza and I are the only two girls, we're put together. Liza greets me with a bear hug after I deposit my suitcase inside the room. Although the rooms themselves are fairly basic, the Austrian beds are bliss. Big, cloud pillows and duvets that envelope you in comforting, feathery hugs. Although the bedding arrangement is called a 'twin', it consists of two single mattresses stuck on a double bed base. Liza and I can have a good old girly gossip in bed. I chuckle to myself as I think of Skipper and Fluro snuggling up later in their Austrian twin bed.

There's a folded piece of white paper on one of the beds, with 'SHAZ' scrawled on it in black felt-tip pen. I sit down on the bed and pick it up. It's a fax from Terrific Tours' head office in London. Neil's handwriting has been slightly distorted after being facsimiled across Europe. I read it aloud to Liza:

Shaz

How was Venice? Don't forget Europe has ears and a mouth, and it talks to me. Last warning, remember?

Neil

'Wanker,' Liza mutters.

'Fuck, Liza,' Even though saying Europe has ears and a mouth is ridiculous, I get the message. 'I wonder who's been telling tales?'

'Don't worry about it, let's get ready for tonight.'

I have put a lot of thought into my costume for the evening's festivities. I want to look sexy yet demure. Fun yet funky. Sexy yet... well... actually the sexy bit is quite important. We throw a couple of ideas around before finally deciding to go to the party as pussycats.

I pull on a black t-shirt that clings nicely to my torso,

which is performance-enhanced by a lacy, push-up bra. Black leggings and CFM's ('come fuck me' boots - black knee length, with a high heel) take care of the lower half. I have ingeniously turned a pair of black tights into a tail by filling one leg of a pair of tights with scrunched-up toilet paper. Upstairs for thinking, downstairs for dancing! The tail is tucked into the back of my leggings and dangles almost to the floor. When I move, it sways from side to side seductively. Meow.

Liza has the same outfit, but has no need for the push-up bra. Her heaving cleavage is barely contained within her EE cup, and her t-shirt plunges at the neckline to prove the point. She's determined that tonight, Skipper is going to notice her, and I'm keen to help!

'Liza, does my arse look big with this tail stuck on it?' I ask my best buddy. I'm sure, if I live to see forty, I'll look back at photos of my twenty-six year old self and wonder how I could ever have worried about my arse being big in my size 8 leggings. However, in the here and now, I do indeed worry. I don't want Roger being turned off because I have a big behind.

'You look great, stop worrying,' Liza reassures me.

8pm - The 'P' party starts with a talk from Lefty, the barman, about how schnapps is made. You can't say we don't *try* to educate our clientele. Schnapps, although originally invented in Paris in 1810, was brought to Austria by the wife of my favourite short man, Napoleon. She wanted to show off to her friends how nice it tasted when poured on ice cream. The Austrians took to it like Australians took to beer, like Germans took to sausages, like Americans took to hamburgers, like Kiwis took to, er, sheep... You get the idea. Schnapps, in German, means 'liquor' and they take that meaning very seriously; most varieties of schnapps are clear, potent fruit blends with an alcohol content of around 40%. The combined flocks are now sampling their way through the fruit varieties and will finish with a smooth red drop known as 'Rocket Fuel'. A person dressed as a prisoner is sipping pear, Peter Pan knocks back a shot of plum, the Pied Piper gathers as many as he can, and a pilot slugs back some fiery rocket fuel.

'Look, there are the boys in Diesel Corner,' Liza tells me, as we enter the bar just in time to miss Lefty's schnapps lesson. 'Diesel Corner' is the name given to the spot where drivers congregate and, sure enough, in the dingiest, darkest corner of the room, closest to the bar, are Fluro, Fitzy, Skipper and Roger. We make our way over to them.

'I know, Fluro, you've come as pregnant.' Liza takes a jibe at her driver and laughs at her own joke.

'Har-de-bloody-har,' he responds. His beer belly hangs over his Levi's, but the pink face paint, round nose and ears make it obvious that he is aiming for pig.

'You look great, ladies,' Skipper says, all the time keeping his eyes firmly on me.

'Thanks, Skipper,' Liza replies, as she steps slightly in front of me and jiggles a bit to the music to try to divert his attention from me, towards her heaving cleavage. 'So do you. I hope you're not the sort of priest who can't have sex, though. That WOULD be a shame.'

Liza eyes up Skipper like the hungriest of carnivores that hasn't eaten for a week and has just spotted a fine scotch fillet. She's practically drooling. EWWW. I must remember to warn her about his performance, or lack thereof, in bed. It'll be my public service to her, a bit like telling her there's bad weather coming, or not to order the fish at a steak restaurant. I'll warn her that Skipper is like a dull weather day, or that he's worth missing from her sexual menu. It's not like he's not fairly well-endowed. Actually, he's quite well endowed; well hung, shall we say. Maybe his nickname should be horse instead of Skipper. However, I wouldn't want her to waste time and energy to get to the crunch and find it has been a wasted effort, over in seconds. After all, what are friends for?

'Right, let's get this party started. Fitzy, get your lovely bunch of coconuts over to the bar and get us some drinks,' Roger directs. Fitzy has come as a palm tree and, along with the coconut bra he's wearing, he has some kind of half-dead foliage stuck to his head.

'Any chance to get into women's underwear, eh, Roger?' Liza says.

Roger's strangely erotic ensemble (maybe that's just my tainted perspective?) includes a black bra and lacy black women's underpants. Black fishnet stockings cling to his powerful thighs, and the look is topped off with a see-through black negligee. His handsome face is thick with makeup, his lips the brightest shade of red I have ever seen.

'Girls are all keen to experiment with their lesbian side, Liza, you know that,' Roger laughs.

Fitzy, meanwhile, has lined up six shot glasses on the bar, each containing a green layer with a brown layer on top.

'Squashed frogs all round,' he declares.

We each pick up a shot glass in the required manner for one who is partaking in a shooter before midnight: thumb on the rim of the glass and little finger underneath the base. We move back to Diesel Corner and, when all six of us have our glasses in the correct position, Fluro proposes a toast.

'There are long ships, there are tall ships, there are ships that sail the sea. But the best ships are friendships, so here's to you and here's to me.'

Roger makes a slight gagging sound at the syrupy sweet message of the toast. We all touch glasses with each other, careful not to cross over with anyone else and ensuring we make eye contact with the holder of the glass we touch, before we knock the squashed frogs back in a single gulp. Hmmmm, quite tasty. The Midori blazes its way down my throat, leaving the trailing Baileys to tickle my tonsils.

With glasses of wine in hand, Liza and I drift slightly away from the boys, towards the bar, so we can chat more. Two of Liza's flock, from Canada, lean on the dark wooden bar top, deep in a conversation that goes something like this:

Girl 1: "So then, I was like, you know, eh…"

Girl 2: "I know, eh, and then I was like der, and she was like, I know…"

Girl 1: "I know, eh, and then he was like der, and then, you know…"

Girl 2: "I knooooow!"

What the fuck? I'm only about five years older than them, and I've absolutely no idea what these foreign beings are talking about. How they can convey a message using a vocabulary of less than ten words baffles me. We turn our backs on them to avoid any accidental joining of our conversations. I don't think I'd have anything to add to, 'I know, eh, eh, eh.'

Canadians use the word 'eh' (if it can indeed be called a word) in a completely different way from those of us from New Zealand. For Canadians, it's a confirmation of their statement and the 'eh' is uttered with the same tone as the rest of the sentence. Kiwis use it as a question, with the inflexion going up, like 'nice day, eh?' I find it entertaining, the differences in the same language. I once had a Canadian ask if I'd be rooting for him. I slapped him. Confused and with a sore arm, my Canadian friend explained that he was asking if I'd be cheering for him, not... well... rooting as in shagging - very confusing.

I have no such trouble communicating with my Aussie best mate Liza. The only real difference between the Kiwi and Australian versions of English is that the Aussies really mess up their vowel sounds with 'six' sounding like 'sex' and 'fish' sounding like 'feesh.' I don't hold this against Liza, and I barely even notice her accent as I begin to dig for information.

'So, Liza, tell me... what IS it about Skipper?'

'Oh Shaz, he's just soooooo lovely.' I swear her eyes mist over while I look at her. I can actually see the mist roll in from her brain and across her eyeballs, as she turns to catch a glimpse of her priestly perfection. Liza - cool, confident, shag 'em and leave 'em in thirty minutes Liza, is in luuuuurve.

'When did this happen?' I dig further.

'Last tour, I was in Paxos for three days at the same time as Roger and Skipper. The weather was shit and we spent a lot of time over long lunches, chatting about anything and everything. I think he is the kindest, cleverest, most sincere, gentle person I've ever met.'

'Really?' I ask, my voice oddly high-pitched. I clear my throat and try again. 'I mean, really? He doesn't seem your type. You usually go for the tall, dark and handsome bad boy type.'

'And exactly where has that got me? Bloody nowhere, that's where. Shaz, I'm just the same as you. I want the white picket fence... husband... babies,' she says dreamily.

This does actually come as a bit of a shock to me. I've

always imagined Liza would be a road hag; a woman who stays touring forever. She would lead a glamorous lifestyle, always have the most gorgeous clothes, take a serious lover every now and then, and, in the meantime, shag every ski instructor in Austria and possibly Switzerland too. Then, when she felt the need, she'd swan to New Zealand for a holiday. She'd visit only long enough to show off her newest platinum and diamond ring, or Tag watch, or Italian toyboy lover, while I was covered in baby puke. The news that she actually wants the baby puke too, comes as a bit of a surprise.

'And you want all that, with Skipper?'

'Well, I wouldn't mind trying,' she muses. 'After all the long chats we've had, I thought on the toga party night that we might actually get together. I gave it my best shot; shortest toga, flirted up a storm, and plied him with ouzo shots… all the tricks in my book. I thought it was going well for a while, then he said he was going to the loo, and he never came back. At the end of the night, it was just Roger and me at the bar with Spyro.'

This is my in; the break I've been waiting for. 'So, how was Roger when you were with him in Paxos?' I ask, appreciating this chance to turn the conversation to a topic I am really interested in.

'Fine,' she replies. 'I was just at a loss as to what I'd done wrong with Skipper. It had seemed to be going so well.' Damn, she's turned the conversation back to Skipper before I've even had a chance.

'C'mon girls,' Fluro's voice booms out. 'Time for some drinking games.'

Looking around the bar, I see the majority of my flock mingled in with members of Liza's and Roger's flocks. They've made the most of the schnapps tasting, and it has certainly loosened their dancing inhibitions. The dance floor is now a heaving mass of princesses, pop stars and policemen, all bouncing up and down to Chumbawumba's *Tub Thumping*, under the mirrored disco ball. They obviously don't need me to jolly their party along, so drinking games it is.

'What about playing 'I've never'?' Fluro continues. 'Lefty,' he shouts to the barman, 'can you get us a bottle of tequila and six shot glasses?'

Lefty is a fine example of the use of irony in a nickname, for the ginger-tinted Irish barman only has one arm as the result of a nasty motorbike accident a few years ago, and it isn't his left one. His one-armed-ness doesn't stop him from being an excellent bartender, but he does appreciate it when people purchase by the bottle and pour their own. Lefty pushes the bottle of tequila, replete with worm and six glasses, to Fluro. He then marks the purchase on his bar card and gets back to the business of chatting up a prostitute who's leaning over the bar, showing off her hefty bosom.

'The rules of 'I've never' are very simple,' Fluro announces. 'In turn, each person starts a statement with 'I've never'. If you have done whatever this thing is, then you take a shot of tequila.'

The fine print should read, 'The object of the game is to stitch up as many of your friends as possible, while trying to stay sober yourself. This is usually an impossible task'.

'Good luck,' Fluro finishes.

'I'll start,' Fitzy offers. 'I've never... I've never been to Poland.'

A nice, easy, non-controversial start to the game for me. Roger and Fluro have done an Eastern European tour together earlier in the year, so they drink their shot while the rest of us look on.

Liza's turn. 'I've never snogged a girl,' she says. The boys all pick up their shot glasses, I reach to pick up mine, and their eyes turn to me in anticipation, their interest piqued.

'Just kidding,' I say, laughing and putting my glass back down.

'Don't kid around about important things like girl-on-girl action,' Fitzy jibes. 'That would've been a great story for us fellas to remember on long nights alone with our right hands! Maybe you and Liza could snog, now? Or make up a lesbian tale and tell us anyway. Never let the truth get in the way of a good story, I always say.'

'You wish,' I taunt. 'Right, my turn. I've never shagged someone from Austria.'

'Point of order. Clarification needed,' says Fluro. 'Shagged someone *from* Austria or shagged someone *in* Austria?'

'*From* Austria, Fluro. It could have been anywhere,' I clarify. No one likes to have a drink when they don't have to, so these fine points of order are important. Fitzy takes a drink, as does Liza, lucky for her it's only one, as I know for a fact that she has shagged three out of four of the Austrian ski instructors working in the area. She would have done almost anything to get into the fourth's lederhosen, but he played hard to get.

Personally, I've never been that attracted to any Austrians. In general, they seem kinda stiff, if that's the right word? I have, however, tasted a few of the other delights Europe has to offer. My sampling of a Frenchman led me to conclude that the stereotype is correct; they are a bit lacking in the personal hygiene department. This particular Frenchman, let's call him Pierre, had never used underarm deodorant in his twenty-three years. Some may have found this natural smell - his manly pheromones - appealing. Me? Not so much.

My taste of Italy featured the lovely Matteo. He had big, bovine, brown eyes and skin the colour of a double-shot cappuccino. He was (and maybe still is) a water taxi driver in Venice. We met at a midsummer New Year's Eve party - on July 31st. It had followed a midsummer's Christmas - on July 25th. I know this is technically not six months from Christmas, but never let the truth get in the way of a good party, I say. As the crowd at the nearby bar were counting down to midnight, we were having our own countdown on the floor of a water taxi. 10… thrust, 9… groan, 8… oh God, 7… thrust, 6… grind, 5… oh yeah, 4… that's it, 3… thrust, 2… I'm nearly there… And I never quite got to 1. Matteo did, and promptly collapsed on top of me. It was only after, as I was covering up my mosquito bitten behind, that he told me he had to get home to his girlfriend. Typical bloody Italian man. Enough of the trip down memory lane…

Roger's turn. 'I've never had a threesome. Not for lack of trying, though,' he adds. Surprisingly, for me anyway, Skipper takes a drink.

'Long story,' he says.

'We've got time,' Roger encourages him.

'My turn,' Fluro interrupts. 'I've never…' He ponders for a moment, eyes to heaven, then around the room, looking for inspiration. 'I've never slept with Roger.'

'Clarification,' Fitzy asks, 'do you mean shared a room with him or shared bodily fluids?'

'Bodily fluids,' Fluro deadpans, like this is the most normal thing in the world to be talking about.

'I object,' Roger pipes up. He looks anxiously from Liza to

me and back. 'There must be a rule about it not being too personal to those of us involved in the game, or something?' He beseeches.

'No. Overruled,' adjudges Fluro, and, as it is his question, he has the final say. That's somewhere in the fine print of the imaginary rule book.

Reluctantly, I take my shot. I accidentally catch Skipper's eye. He looks deflated. What happens next sure takes the air out of my balloon. Liza reaches over and picks up her shot glass, putting it to her mouth and throwing her head back. What? Liza has slept with Roger?

The world seems to turn more slowly on its axis. The beat of the Duran Duran song blasting through the speakers dulls into a blur, and my head starts to spin. Liza? Roger? Liza and Roger? Together? I can't stay... have... to... get... away.

'Bathroom,' I say to the group, as tears push on the back of my eyeballs and my vision blurs. I bump into a penguin and push between a pilot and the Pink Panther as I struggle to get out. I need some fresh air and space, and I find both outside on a bench with a view of the car park.

How can I marry Roger now? Even if he did know I like him and he wanted to marry me too, I now know that he is a notch on Liza's heavily notched bedpost. Her metaphorical bedpost must be like an old piece of wooden furniture infected with a termite population the size of New York, given the number of notches. It's amazing the metaphorical bedpost is still standing. Sometimes, this industry we work in is just too much. I think back to when I first started in the travel game, I found the immorality of it all quite disturbing. Everyone seemed to shag anything that moved, and occasionally, things that didn't, without a backwards glance. Reality seemed to be suspended, like plankton in the ocean, as we all floated around Europe, showing people a good time and having a good time ourselves. Behaviour that would be considered sordid and deviant in our normal lives was almost celebrated here, as everyone was free to experiment in any way they pleased, with no danger of their mum finding out. I haven't embraced this freedom as much as many of my peers seemed to. I've bent my own moral compass a little, okay, a lot, to find a way to enjoy my time and do a bit of experimenting within my own, slightly modified from home, moral code. This moral code, however, has a section that specifically excludes sharing my future husband with my best friend. While I don't expect my husband to be virginally pure when we marry, I would definitely prefer he didn't know, in the biblical sense, any of my nearest and dearest.

I hear the door behind me open. I turn and see Liza. She plonks her pussycat tail on the seat beside me.

'What's up?' She asks.

'Wh… wh… when did you sleep with Roger?' I ask, developing a stammer from shock and the chilly night mountain air. She offers me her pack of Marlboro Lights. I pull one, pop it in my mouth, and, for a second, the heat of the lighter warms my face. I inhale deeply, the smoke burning my throat and lungs. I only smoke socially and, usually, only when I'm either very drunk or in emergency situations. I think this qualifies.

'Paxos. When I was trying to get with Skipper. Remember, I told you? I was left with only Roger and Spyro at the bar.'

'And you couldn't have bonked Spyro instead?' I demand, remembering my own aborted encounter with him (I wonder if his head is feeling better?). Seriously, we needed a bigger male pond to fish from.

'Why are you so angry with me, Shaz? Liza asks. 'It was just a shag.'

'You think Skipper is your hose reel... well... well, I think Roger is mine. And now you've ruined it. YOU'VE USED MY HOSE REEL! I don't want a secondhand hose reel.'

'Oh hun,' Liza puts her arm around my shoulders. 'I'm sorry. I didn't know. Honestly, how could I? You need to know, though, that Roger is NOT the hose reel type. He's already a well-used hose reel. He unreels his hose all over the show, his hose has been well used... um... You need to be careful, that's all,' she says, giving me a squeeze.

'I can look after myself, Liza,' I say, feeling defensive. 'I'm a big girl.'

We sit quietly for a while, each lost in our own thoughts, inhaling deeply from our cigarettes and blowing the smoke into the crisp night air.

'What are you going to do about Skipper?' I can't really stay mad at Liza, it's not her fault. She didn't know that Roger is my hose reel. What about her revelation? Am I going to confess to her about Skipper? If I am, this would be the moment.

Now.

Right now.

Right now - this minute. Now. Now. Now.

Go on... are you going to confess, Shaz? I ask myself. Oh, why is life so fucking complicated?

And as I procrastinate, the moment has gone.

'Nothing.' She sighs and stares up at the clear, dark sky, smothered in twinkling stars and unobstructed by any city pollution. 'I asked him straight up after you left, if he wanted to come home with me tonight.'

'What did he say?'

Liza knows what she wants, and she isn't afraid to go full steam ahead to get it. I admire that about her.

'Polite to a fault, he says, 'Thanks but no thanks." He thinks I'm attractive… obviously… but he's not attracted to me. He said he thinks he's in love with someone, and he wants to take his time to work that out. He said he didn't think it'd be fair to me to just fool around,' Liza says. 'There's a pretty hot-looking guy in a 'pool' costume in there, maybe I can drown my sorrows in him.'

We laugh together. Our friendship is going to be okay, no man will come between us; hose reel or not.

'Shall we go back inside?' Liza suggests. We clasp hands and navigate our way back to Diesel Corner, past Girl 1 and Girl 2, still leaning on the bar.

Girl 1: 'I know, eh…'

Girl 2: 'And then he was like der, eh…'

'Thought you two might've been having a cat fight,' Roger quips, laughing at his own joke.

'Nope. Just meowing at the moon,' I reply and smile.

He's still looking endearing in his negligee, even though his lipstick is now smeared halfway up his cheeks and his mascara has started to run. I stare at him intently for a moment. Can I move past the knowledge that he has been with Liza? Would it still be okay to be with him, if… if I got the chance? Only time will tell.

12.01am By midnight, the prostitute is now behind the bar with Lefty, and he's calling for last drinks, obviously eager to get away with her. I'm exhausted and ready for a cat nap. Liza feels the night is still young and wants to party on. The last I see of her, she's rounding up Roger, Fluro and a troop of keen party animals in various 'P' outfits and heading down the hill to the only pub that will be open this late in this tiny village. If Liza didn't know how I felt about Roger, I'd be a bit worried about them being out together. But I trust her, and I'm just too tired.

Chapter 29

❧

Hopfgarten

Day 21

9.53am It's more than a bit chilly. The clouds are strangling the top of the Hohe Salve as I meet my flock ahead of the planned 10am mountain bike trip. I'm not feeling too shabby this morning, after having had the foresight and common sense to go to bed reasonably early last night. I'm almost tempted to go for a ride myself, be at one with the great outdoors, and get some fresh mountain air. Conquer some hillocks or whatever mountain bike folk do. Luckily, I remember that I hate bike riding, before I succumb to the urge. I don't get it: all that bouncing around on a tiny, hard piece of plastic laughingly called a seat. My pubic region has mostly recovered from the traumatic hair pulling it was subjected to *en France,* and I've no desire to punish it further.

I've actually tried mountain biking here once. It was winter, and Liza and I were working a ski season in Hopfgarten. I learnt an important life lesson: mountain biking and snow do not go well together. I'd ended up getting up close and personal with a pine tree. That was one of many accidents I'd had that winter. While Liza had a job in a funky bar in the village, the only work I could find was at a restaurant halfway up the mountain, as a kitchen hand, or as I was lovingly referred to, 'The Dish Pig'. The setting was beautiful, and my commute to work was lovely. I'd catch the first chairlift of the day, alongside big metal tubs of milk and crates of vegetables. I enjoyed the crisp mountain air and seeing fresh snow covering the pine trees as I whizzed over their tips on the chair. That's where my enjoyment of the day ended.

My duties at work included preparing side dishes for the chef, cooking ham and cheese toasties, and doing the dishes. The orders from the restaurant came to the kitchen by way of a machine that made a loud noise as the tickets were printed. I came to hate that fucking machine and the god-awful noise it made. As the tickets whizzed out at the speed of light, the chef would take them and yell at me at equal speed.

'ShAZ.' She always raised her voice for the last bit of my name, so she was sure I was paying attention. '*Fünf schinken käse toast, drei schnitzel teller und acht strudel teller bitte.*' My German wasn't great. Who was I kidding? It sucked. So by the time I'd worked out she wanted five ham and cheese toasties, three plates ready for a schnitzel meal and eight plates ready for apple strudel, there were already more orders being shot at me and, behind me, dishes were steadily piling up.

Sometimes I'd get random other jobs to do. One day, the

chef said to me, 'Shaz, can you go and clean the cooler, please. Aunt Helga has killed a pig there.'

When I got there, I found that chef wasn't joking, as I'd thought she might have been. Shrivelled Aunt Helga, who was seventy on a good day, had indeed killed a pig, and there was blood everywhere. It was the Austrian chainsaw massacre. The pièce de résistance was that at the end of the day, long after the chairlift had stopped, if the boss had already left, I had to rodel down the mountain back to the village. A rodel is a toboggan. While tobogganing is great fun on a gentle snow slope on a sunny day, it isn't fun in the dark, down a snow-covered mountain. In fact, it was terrifying. This caused me a few other close encounters with pine trees and, eventually, a neck injury, after which I had to be evacuated back to the relative safety of London to recover for the summer.

As the flock is milling around, waiting for the mountain bike guide dude, I'm approached by flock members Muzza and Pete, good, keen rugby lads from New Zealand. They support the Canterbury rugby team with such fervour that I'm sure, if cut, they'd bleed red AND black. Today, Muzza has on a fine pair of stubbies (very short shorts), that have one red 'leg' and one black 'leg'. Pete has gone for plain black stubbies with a Canterbury rugby jersey. They both have jandals on their feet, oblivious to both the chill and the risk of foot injury.

'Shazza! Me and Muzza were gonna go up that hill this arvo,' Pete says, indicating the general direction of the mountain. 'Do you think this cloud will clear?'

I love meteorological questions. After all, I have a degree in the subject and am intricately familiar with the weather patterns over the whole of continental Europe. I also have plenty of time to watch the weather reports on local TV. Oh, and I have a crystal ball as a backup.

'I dunno Pete, what do you reckon?' I attempt to volley back to him. 'What are you going up there for? Hiking? Nordic walking? Photography?'

'Nah, ya dipstick,' Muzza says, playfully punching my arm. 'To drink glühwein.'

I turn on my most serious, about to impart years of knowledge, voice. 'Well then, boys… it won't fuckin' matter if there are clouds or not, will it?'

'THAT Shazza, is why YOU get the big bucks!' Pete chuckles.

'Thanks, Pete.' I laugh. My chortle evaporates in my throat like a puddle in the sun, as I spot a vision coming over the brow of the hill.

What last night had been a pristine pussy at the top of her game, now looked like a massively mauled moggy. Liza, still in her catsuit, minus the ears and tail, was doing 'the walk of shame' from somewhere down the hill, hoping to make it back to the gasthof just in time to see her flock members off on their slightly later bike trip. A 'walk of shame' involves having to make your own way home from whoever's abode you have spent the night at, in daylight, wearing the same clothes you had on the night before. It's a dead giveaway that you've been 'playing away.'

Catching sight of me, Liza attempts to duck behind a parked car, in the vain hope that my flock won't notice her. Luckily for her, they're distracted by adjusting bike seats and trying to find helmets that fit. I give her a wave and a questioning look as I hold up one finger. She shakes her head. So it wasn't the number one ski instructor she'd hooked up with. I hold up two fingers; more head shaking. No, not number two either. Not to be dissuaded, I hold up three fingers. Again, she shakes her head and looks shame-faced. I go for bust and hold up four fingers. She reluctantly nods that she has indeed finally bagged the fourth of the four ski instructors resident in this tiny village. In horse racing, three out of three is a trifecta, I wonder what shagging four out of four ski instructors is called? In baseball, if a batter is struck out four times in an innings, it's called a Golden Sombrero, but Liza has struck in. She's unbelievable! She keeps low, using the parked cars as a shield to get past my flock unnoticed, before presumably heading for a quick change of clothes, before seeing her own.

1pm - Our room is in darkness as I return after seeing my flock safely back from the bike ride. No major injuries sustained; no toes amputated by bike spokes due to wearing jandals, so that's good. Many of the flock have wandered off happily to make the most of what has turned into a stunning Austrian summer's day, to the 'beer farm', as it's colloquially known. The 'beer farm' is actually a trout farm where, for forty schillings, you hire a rod and try to catch a fish in the trout farm pond. The catch is then cooked for lunch. This really isn't that challenging, as the pond is chokka with trout, hence most of the time is spent lounging on the side of the pond, soaking up sun and drinking beer. I'm going to make the most of this stunning afternoon… by catching a nap.

The air is so much cooler in our darkened room, I realise, as I slowly open the door and sneak in. Liza's gentle snoring is the only noise. I slip off my shoes and shorts, slide under the thick feather duvet and drift off to sleep.

3pm, I start to come out of my deep slumber and roll over, opening my eyes slightly for a second as I do. Liza is staring at me intently.

'You awake?' She asks.

'Hmmmmf,' I respond.

'I'm still really sorry about Roger, you know.'

'I know. It's okay.' I think I mean it. Now would be another really good time to tell her about Skipper. Okay, here I go... I'm going to do it...

'So... fourth ski instructor, eh? Tell me all about it.'

I'm such a wimp.

Chapter 30

꩜

Days 22 & 23

You may be wondering what happened to days 22 and 23. Nothing happened... Nothing at all. They were boring, boring, boring. Day 22 was driving on boring German autobahns, staring at straight, perfectly tarsealed roads and boring countryside.

I think maybe I had 'boringitis', if there was such a thing. I've been finding it very hard to see joy in anything and, as you may have noticed, have been finding things boring, A LOT. I've also been having flashbacks, like some kind of post-traumatic stress, to the moment I saw my best friend lift her glass to drink, affirming that she has shagged my dream future husband. On boring day 22, we'd be driving along a perfectly straight piece of road, and I'd be feeling perfectly fine, if not a little bored, when all of a sudden, an image of Liza straddling

Roger would flash into my head. I'd go from feeling bored to incredibly, heavily, crushingly sad. Liza and I have made our peace, but the memory still digs into my heart like a long dagger. Maybe I should add 'over-dramatic' to 'boring' in my rather short list of how I'm feeling?

To try and erase these feelings, I did the only thing I know how: I drank WAY too much beer out of enormous glass boots at the boring restaurant where we had our boring dinner. Sometime around 11pm, I collapsed into bed and into an alcohol-induced coma sleep.

Day 23, I woke with a really full bladder and a boring hangover in a boring town on the side of the boring Rhine River, which normally I'd find quite picturesque. On this day, the river was just too wide, too murky, too slow, and the castle that clung to a cliff above it, was just too old and boring. We do a boring river cruise to see the Lorelei Rock - can you get more boring? Roger and Skipper are staying in another small village too far away for us to bump into them, so I will have to wait until Amsterdam to see him again. This may be my final chance to make a last-ditch effort to connect with him before our tour schedules may see us ripped apart (very Romeo and Juliet) for the rest of the summer.

Chapter 31

─◦⊱✿⊰◦─

On the way to Amsterdam

Day 24

7am, and the driving day from hell has started already. It would appear that most of the flock members haven't fully opened their eyes yet, given the state of their hair. They've stumbled onto the bus and have already gone back to sleep, with breakfast and check-out now nothing but a hazy dream interrupting their slumber. In an hour, we're out of Switzerland and following the French/German border north, on the first of the excellent German autobahns that will take us whizzing towards the Netherlands.

Neither Fitzy nor I are in the mood for chatting. So I take the time to try and balance my tour accounts. I open my black leather multi-compartmental wallet and remove a thick wad of receipts. Every tour, I vow to keep on top of my finances and not leave it until the last minute. This tour is no different. I've left it to the last minute. And, yet again, I vow next time will be different. I'm now facing accounting hell. I start by unfolding and flattening all the tiny pieces of paper, putting them in date order.

'Fitzy. Do you remember what I would have spent twenty-two francs on, on May 23rd?'

'No.'

'What about six hundred drachmas on May 28th?'

'No.'

'What about twenty-seven thousand lira, on May 31st?'

'Fuck off, Shaz,' he snaps. 'I don't fucking ask you to change gears for me. Do your own job.'

'Well, someone got out of the wrong side of the bed this morning.'

As I'm getting no help from my 'teammate', I ask myself out loud. 'Where were we on May 23rd? France, obviously... maybe Paris? What day did we leave London again? Hmmmm...'

'For fuck's sake, Shaz. Twenty-two francs on May 23rd was for a road toll. Six hundred drachmas on May 28th was probably for gyros for lunch and May 31st we were in Venice, pissed, so it could've been for anything. Put it down for lunch. Neil doesn't speak Italian, he'll be none the wiser.'

Wow, he has a good memory.

'Thanks, Fitzy. How do you remember all that stuff?'

'Training. I'm a lawyer at home, it pays to remember details.'

'WHAT? A lawyer. Why are you driving buses then?' I can't hide my astonishment.

'What's wrong with driving *coaches*?'

'Um, nothing. Just seems a big change from law.'

'That's why I like it,' he responds. 'Until I'm ready for the full-time commitment of a career job and to live with my girlfriend forever, I spend six months of each year in Europe, driving coaches around. I want to have some fun, which I am doing, thank you.'

Chapter 32

Amsterdam

Day 25

11am - As the flock has some free time, I decide some retail therapy for myself is in order and stroll into the nearest department store. I meander in a clockwise direction around the ground floor, taking time to look at every rack and caress nearly every piece of clothing. The feel of cotton, wool and even polyester between my fingers begins to calm my heart rate and slow my breathing. When I've nearly completed a full circle of the ground floor, I come across a shopper's nirvana: the bargain bin.

I take my time as I fossick deeply into the bin, to see what bargains I can unearth. I rule out the bright pink leggings, the gold bikini and the oversized peace sign earrings, before

I come across a pack of three white cotton g-string knickers with pretty lace trim, hanging on a small plastic coat hanger for a mere five guilders. Going with the theory that you can never have too much underwear, I pick up a pack, size small... Okay, medium, and with them safely in hand, wander to the next rack of clothes. As I do, out of the corner of my eye, I see a security guard near the door glance from my face to the underwear in my hand. The slightest change of expression flickers across his not very handsome face, as he pretends to then be looking at something else.

Shit! He thinks I'm a shoplifter and he's on to me. I saunter closer to the guard, holding the coat hanger of undies slightly higher than my waist so he can see I still have them in my hand. For good measure, I hang the coat hanger on my index finger and swing them from side to side, then browse the clothing racks closest to him. He pretends not to notice me and turns to look out of the door. Ah, the double fake. I'll pretend not to look at you while actually tracking your every move. Too much coffee this morning has made me paranoid. I head to the escalator, following sale signs and their promise of more bargains upstairs. As I ride the moving stairs, I glance down at the guard. I catch him looking at me, and he quickly turns away, becoming very interested in an umbrella stand. That's right, security guy, I'm on to you. No one accuses me (in their head) of being a shoplifter.

Deciding to mix it up a little, I walk around the first floor in an anti-clockwise direction. I reach the denim section and am eyeing up a very nice pair of ultra-high waist Levi jeans, when I sense I'm being watched again. I casually walk to the other side of the rack, and I spot another security guard looking my way. He has an officious look with his uniform of blue chambray shirt with epaulettes and his hand hovering over his radio as if it were a gun he's ready to pull at a moment's notice. Obviously he's been alerted by downstairs security dude, and I'm now being actively pursued. I am prey. The adrenaline that had subsided a little after fondling fabric now builds up in me again. Fight or flight? Being a lover, not a fighter, I decide to make a run for it.

I duck behind the fluorescent t-shirt rack and pretend to tie my shoelace. Hmm… no laces on these shoes - doh! I pop up suddenly, to find an officious dude standing on the other side of the fluorescent t-shirts, glaring at me. I smile sweetly. In one swift move, I bend my arm, swinging my hand skywards and hoisting the g-strings over my shoulder, as I walk, head held high, to the swimwear section. My relaxation has now completely evaporated and not only do I feel as tightly wound as a guitar string, but I've decided I actually don't need three pairs of white g-strings. However, I fear that if I don't buy them, I will be strip-searched before I leave the store.

Defeated and still waving my white g-string flag over my shoulder, I head back down the escalator to the cashier, thumping my undies down on the counter. From my enormous black leather wallet, I fish out a five-guilder note and hand it over to the girl behind the counter, who has mastered the 'I'm too cool to be working here and talking to you' look. She hands me a bag full of the undies I don't really want, and I head for the door.

As I pass security guard number one, he turns to me, leers and says, 'Mooi.' Beautiful. Ah, so he didn't think I was a shoplifter. Ewww.

9pm - Not surprisingly, the fact that guests will be taken to a live sex show in Amsterdam is not mentioned in the glossy brochures that Terrific Tours produces to encourage young folk to see Europe with them. Many of the 20-something wannabe holidaymakers, of course, use the Terrific Tours brochures to convey to their mums and dads how safe they'll be when they travel with us. So, advertising this part of the tour wouldn't exactly help seal the deal for the wanderlust-filled youngsters wishing to calm the fears of their anxious parents. I still haven't told my mum that I spent a night in the Netherlands watching a blonde Lois Lane deepthroat a spectacularly well-endowed, dark as midnight Superman. It does, however, provide an ideal spot for me to launch another, and perhaps a final, attempt to sway Roger from his 'let's keep it professional' stance. Where better to get a virile demi-God like Roger in the mood, than a place where pheromones hang heavily with cigarette smoke in the air, where there is limitless alcohol and where naked people are having sex on a stage?

The flock giggles nervously as I lead them into the semi-dark theatre. The manager, with his handlebar moustache and cowboy hat, had once told me that they keep the lights dim on arrival to 'set the mood'. I have a strong suspicion it's a vain attempt to disguise the seediness of the grubby red vinyl chairs (easy to wipe off any mess - yes, don't think about that for too long) and the purple paisley carpet (worn down by the thousands of porn viewers who have preceded us). As soon as the flock is sitting comfortably, I bolt up the narrow, dimly lit staircase to where the road crew and stage performers hang out during the show. In my haste and my concentration on the rickety stairs to avoid tripping, I run headlong into Superman. Superman is rushing, red silk cap flapping behind him, to make his entrance. Lois Lane is on the stage and has started without him. After doing a left, right, left dodge, with a nervous laugh (me), we navigate our way past each other, and I continue my quest to get to the bar.

Doing a quick scan of the dimly lit cupboard they call the bar, I see Fred (the ridiculously well hung stripper), at this stage fully clothed, running his hand through his long blond mane, as he chats to a woman the colour of milk chocolate who very nicely fills out the yellow bikini she has on. A plastic fruit headdress gives her the look of a Caribbean goddess. Fred should be called Horse, seriously. There's a rumour that his appendage isn't real but I have it from a reliable source (a girl on a previous tour that got very close to it) that it was all Fred.

The third member of the group is a gorilla, with a large rubber phallus swinging between its legs. Nothing out of the ordinary here then, and no one of interest to me. As my eyes adjust to the lack of light, I can see two other people towards the very back of the bar, deep in conversation. I move closer to get a better look, and I can see that the larger of the two is Roger. The person with him is of the feminine variety and is one of his clients - Brandy, I think. I've seen her chatting to him before, over the last couple of weeks, since apparently following him upstairs in Paxos. I give her the once-over. Slim but curvy. The high-waist jeans she's wearing show off those curves nicely. Bitch.

Roger spots me and whispers something to her. She turns towards me and gives half a smile, as she heads towards the stairs at the entry to the theatre. As she passes, I notice her classically beautiful face and orthodontist-made straight teeth. I watch her over the mezzanine rail as she takes her seat in the theatre, and many of the men seated in it watch her as she does, perhaps hoping she'll be part of the act. I would have taken some time to be jealous, but Roger is giving me his sexiest smile and has his arms open to give me a welcoming hug.

'Shaz!' He pulls me towards him and holds me longer than would normally be expected for an everyday welcome hug, not that I'm complaining. 'Imagine bumping into you here! Bourbon and Coke?' Before I can either accept or decline, one arrives in my hand, and a backup is placed beside me by the eager-to-please barman.

I decide the time for dithering is over, we'll be back in London the day after tomorrow, and I don't know when the next time will be that we'll see each other. With time running out, I'm just going to ask Roger straight up if he wants to meet later. Carpe diem, as some Roman Emperor once proclaimed a long time ago. I steel myself, take a deep breath, swallow hard and clear my throat... and... I chicken out. Instead, downing half of my drink in one gulp.

I cough and splutter. 'Jesus. A bit light on the coke here, aren't they?'

Roger stares at me intently for a moment, then puts his, oh-so-strong arm around me and draws me in close, really close. Close enough that I can smell the faint aroma of Kouros on his skin and feel the texture of his pink Lacoste polo shirt on my cheek.

'Shaz... how about you come and hang out in my room for a bit later?'

Before I can accept, he places something in my other hand. It's long and it's hard. I look down to see Roger's room key with the number 711 printed on it. The key to my happiness?

'11pm Shaz. I'll be waiting.'

Chapter 32

I am dumbstruck. My mouth moves like a fish gasping for air, but nothing comes out. Before I can formulate a response, the gorilla moves to stand beside us. He removes his head, revealing Skipper's smiling face.

'Skipper, what the fuck are you doing?' I demand.

Skipper puts the gorilla head under one arm.

'They were short-staffed tonight; the usual gorilla has the flu. All I had to do was chase a couple of scared Australian blokes around the stage, waving my plastic willy at them... AND they paid me fifty guilders. Easier than driving for the day, eh? I quite like the costume, actually. I might keep wearing it for a while.' He smiles.

We arrived back at the Dyke View Hotel with a flock buoyant with nervous energy from watching live sex. To burn off this frisson of tension, they head straight to the bar to party. My ever-reliable Swiss watch shows me 10.30. I have half an hour before I'm sure Roger will confess his undying love for me, or at least the desire to see more of me... start a relationship, write love letters, make each other mixtapes, try and coordinate tour sequences and other acts of true love. Half an hour: time enough for some Dutch courage.

Why the fuck was it called that anyway? Have the Dutch been particularly brave in times gone by? I guess you had to be a bit brave to wear clogs in public. It was a fitting saying for me, though, given the setting, and I down yet another bourbon and coke, that's very light on the coke. Seeing that my flock are all well on the way to a big night, I sneak out of the bar. I slink to the tiny, one-person elevator and rattle my way up to head to room 711.

To my destiny.

To where fate will soon tell me... oh, Shaz stop it, for fuck's sake.

Soon, bachelorette-hood will be a thing of the past, a distant memory. Roger and I will be planning our future together and naming our two adorable children, one girl and one boy. The girl will have my blue eyes and the charming mousy blonde hair I'd had before I became bottle orange. We'll call her Bella, and she'll be the apple of her daddy's eye. The boy will have dark hair, like Roger, and his eyes too, green like the ocean. We won't call him Roger Junior, though. I hate that whole name your child after yourself and add a 'Junior' on the end; no imagination. Also, even though Roger IS the most gorgeous man I've ever met, the name Roger conjures up an image of a middle-aged man in a business shirt with a too-fat tie and corduroy shoes, and it SO doesn't suit him. I've never ever seen him wear shoes as offensive as that. Aside from being the name of middle-aged men, it can also be used in too many other ways. 'Roger that, 10-4 over and out,' or, 'Did you give her a good rogering?' You get the idea. But I'm getting ever so slightly ahead of myself.

I slide the key Roger has given me into the lock of room number 711, turn it and push the door into the room. Roger greets me wearing nothing but an itsy-bitsy white hotel towel tied loosely and ever-so seductively around his waist. Beads of water from his obviously just completed shower cling desperately to the dark hairs on his chiselled chest before giving up their grasp and gliding ever so slowly down, disappearing into the teeny towel. The only thing broader than his shoulders is his smile. He takes me by the hand and leads me into the dimly lit room. The door clicks shut behind us.

I put down the key to my own room on the chair by the

door as I pass. Without uttering a word, Roger places his strong hands on either side of my head and lowers his face to mine. His warm lips meet mine and for a moment, I lose myself in the sensation as his tongue explores my mouth. I breathe in the smell of him. He smells fresh from his recent shower, with the faint scent of soap and a hint of aftershave. Jazz or Kouros? Either way he smells GOOD.

Roger moves his hands from encompassing my head to release the spaghetti straps of my dress from my shoulders, gently pushing them down my arms. The smooth fabric caresses me as my dress slides to the ground, leaving me standing in only my (thankfully) matching lacy red lingerie. As my dress hits the floor, my stomach lands with it, and I feel that this is moving all very quickly.

I break the suction between our mouths to speak

'Roger, can we talk for a bit?'

'Come on Shaz, there's plenty of time to talk later,' he replies, moving his mouth back to mine and, at the same time, putting one hand on my breast, rubbing my nipple with his thumb in a hypnotic circular motion over the lace of my bra. I try to resist again, honestly, I do, but my nipple betrays me by standing to attention, and I begin to lose myself in the electric shocks it shoots deep to my core. I rub my hands up and down Roger's back, at first gently, then more urgently, feeling the definition of his muscular body. He releases the towel from his waist and his erect penis makes a plop sound as it hits my stomach just below my breasts. He reaches behind me, releasing my bra while nibbling gently down my neck from my ear, as you perhaps would a particularly juicy corn on the cob.

He takes a break from nibbling to pull me towards the bed.

He sits me down on the edge of it and kneels on the floor in front of me. With one of his manly hands, he pushes me backwards onto the bed. Before I have the chance to sit myself back up, his fingers are under the waistband of my red lacy undies, sliding them down my legs to the floor. Leaning over me, he takes both my breasts in his hands and puts his mouth on one, covering my still erect nipple. He alternates between tugging slowly and nibbling gently, and a moan from deep within me erupts to the surface. He moves his mouth ever so slowly down my stomach… lower… lower.

I give up trying to sit up and surrender, leaving myself exposed and vulnerable to him. His tongue traces a lazy path to my belly button and keeps moving slowly down, circling and caressing every nook of my body. My breathing becomes shallow and raspy, and my mouth tingles, as the excitement in my body builds. My breathing speeds up so much that I momentarily wonder if I might faint from hyperventilating. I can bear it no longer. I hear the sound of a condom wrapper being ripped open and, without moving his mouth from me, Roger quickly rolls the condom onto his impressive manhood.

He moves up my body, supporting himself on his hands and looks at me intently for a moment.

'Oh, Roger,' I sigh. He kisses me deeply, then he enters me in one swift movement, pushing himself until he can go no further. He can't get enough of me, and I can't get enough of him. Our bodies move together; mine, small and fragile under his, strong and masculine. The heat builds between us. A tidal wave builds in my groin. My body tenses. I dig my fingers deep into Roger's back and I let out a long, deep moan as the wave washes over my body, releasing fireworks in my head that would make a 4th of July parade organiser proud. Roger moves more quickly as his own orgasm builds. He arches back, and a primal, guttural sound comes from deep within him.

'YES, YES, YES,' he shouts, collapsing on top of me. We hold each other, gasping, trying desperately to catch our breath.

We stay that way, bodies entwined, as our breathing slows. Roger is spent and his eyes are closed. I stare at him, soaking in every detail of his features, so fine they could've been carved by Michelangelo himself.

Roger opens his eyes and meets my gaze.

'Shaz.'

'Yes,' I reply, nestling closer to his body. This is it. This is when he's going to tell me he wants to be with me... Here it comes... Any moment now... Be cool, Shaz, be cool.

'I think you should probably go. I've got an early start in the morning.'

WHAT? I'm so shocked I can't even protest. Before I formulate a response, he's up off the bed and walking into the bathroom, closing the door behind him. This isn't how I'd played this moment through in my mind on the nine hundred-odd occasions I've envisioned us being naked together. Something must be wrong; maybe he's sick or something. I can hear the tap running in the bathroom, a toothbrush scraping against tooth enamel and, at the same time, a faint tapping at the room door.

Tugging the sheet from the bed and wrapping it around me, I walk to the hotel door, checking my watch on the way. 11.55pm. Quite late for a casual caller. I stretch up to look through the peephole, and I see that Brandy girl who Roger was talking to earlier at the sex show. I turn the handle slowly and open the door in front of me, so all the nocturnal visitor sees is an empty room. Brandy bounces in like a rabbit on speed, without realising it isn't Roger who has let her in.

As she bounces, she says, 'I came a bit early. I hope your safety meeting's finished.' Roger steps out of the bathroom with another small white towel positioned around his waist, as I step out from behind the door. I look from Roger to Brandy to Roger to Brandy, to Roger and back to Brandy, tears welling in my eyes as the realisation of what he's done hits me like a slap in the face from the freakishly large hands of the statue of David.

'BASTARD,' I screech, as I frantically gather my underwear and dress from the floor and race out of the door. Roger doesn't bother to come after me, or even call my name, as I run down the hall to the lift, sheet flapping behind me like Kate Bush in the *Wuthering Heights* video, complete with weird startled eyes, but totally missing her grace.

Tears stream down my face so much that I can barely see the buttons on the stupid, tiny elevator. I get to my room and blindly push against the door.

Locked.

Shit.

Key... where's my key?

It hits me then that I've left my key on the chair in Roger's, or as he shall be known from this moment on, 'That Bastard's', room. Exhaustion and despair crush me as I slump to the floor against my hotel room door.

Tears cascade off my chin. Not to be left out, my nose joins the party and sends out some fluid of its own, as I think of how high my hopes were and how far the realisation of the truth has taken me down. Luckily, I'm wrapped in a massive hanky. My head falls onto my knees, and I weep. The change of angle streams hot, salty tears from my chin to the end of my nose, to combine with snot and drip on the dirty hotel carpet.

I hear footsteps approaching, and a pair of hairy gorilla feet stops in front of me. 'Shaz, are you okay?' Looking up, I see Skipper, kneeling beside me, his face ripped with worry. Well, it's Skipper's head anyway; the body is still encased in the gorilla suit, of which he seemed so fond.

'I...' Gulp. 'Roger.' Sob. I can say no more.

'I'll be back in a minute.' Skipper disappears and returns shortly with the hotel duty manager, who, while avoiding eye contact with the weird, sobbing woman dressed only in a sheet being held by a half-man, half gorilla, opens my room door. Skipper lifts me to my feet as gently as if I'm a porcelain doll and guides me into my room.

I flop, broken, onto my bed. He pulls the duvet cover up over me. I start to shiver, gently at first, then uncontrollably, sobbing with more gusto than before. Skipper lies down beside me and pulls me close, hugging me tightly, as a mother would an upset child. His furry gorilla body is strangely comforting and very handy for soaking up my tears. As I cry, Skipper strokes my hair and talks to me in gentle tones, soothing me with his words and touch.

'You're amazing, Shaz,' he whispers as he holds my head close. 'So beautiful, so clever, so funny. Any man would be crazy not to want you. When I was with you in London, the reason I didn't... You know... pull out in time was because I couldn't believe my luck that I was actually with you. You have the most beautiful blue eyes I've ever seen. Your smile lights up the room.' He talks on and on, his soothing words gently rock my addled brain to sleep.

Chapter 33

~ക്കൈ~

Back to London

Day 26

When I wake, the room is lit by the rising sun, and gorilla Skipper is still beside me. He's holding me tightly and gazing lovingly at me. He kisses my forehead tenderly.

'How are you?' He asks.

'Numb,' I reply, 'but at the same time, everything hurts. Does that make sense?'

As I shower, Skipper runs to his room to change, because he can't very well spend the day dressed as a gorilla. Once he's more appropriately clothed (as a human), he returns to pack my suitcase and proceeds to carry it down to my coach for me. He and Fitzy exchange a 'man look' that communicates I'm not in a good way. Fitzy dutifully takes over my care and gets me ready to face the last day of this tour.

It is, without overstatement or word of a lie, the longest day of my twenty-six years. My soul aches. It is sapping me of my energy, and it takes all the effort I have just to remain upright and keep breathing in and out. I secure sunglasses over my eyes and plaster a smile on my face. Somehow, I manage to get through all the tasks I need to complete on the nondescript drive from Amsterdam to Calais. I chat to my flock: we reminisce about some of the fun we've had on the tour. They fill in tour reports, in which they grade me, Fitzy and the tour itself, which I eventually collect, ready to courier to Neil tonight. Normally, I would worry terribly about what they have said about me, but not today.

Boarding the Calais to Dover ferry, I don't make my usual dash to the driver's room, afraid that 'The Bastard' will be on this ferry too. I visit the duty-free shop to buy a *Marie Claire* magazine, grab a coffee and find a quiet corner to hide in. I lose myself in the glossy pages, filled with useful articles like, 'Will money destroy your marriage?' and, 'Is anal the new oral?'. I also find one hundred ways to wear one little black dress. The catch is, you need forty-seven different pairs of shoes, one hundred pairs of earrings, twenty scarves and twelve hats. It would be hard to fit all that in my Benetton suitcase. Even buying forty-seven pairs of shoes will not heal my leaky heart.

The only way I can even mildly cope is to go into denial. Deep, deep into denial that there is anything wrong in my world. I'm an ostrich and my head is buried firmly in *Marie Claire* sand. I only pull it out of the sand when I sense someone is standing right behind me. Before I turn around, I paste a happy, helpful smile on my face. I needn't have bothered, it's only Skipper.

'Can I sit down?' He asks. I'm tempted to say, 'bugger off, leave me alone', but he's been so kind. Reluctantly, I nod, keeping my eyes firmly affixed to the carpet and concentrating on not crying.

'You okay?'

I really don't have the energy for questions. I nod again.

'Can I do anything?'

Oh, for fuck's sake! A more aggressive shake of the head this time.

'What are you doing tonight?'

'I was going to jump off Tower Bridge or throw myself in front of a Piccadilly line tube train, but I don't have the energy, so I think I'll just have an early night.' I lift my gaze off the floor and give him a weak smile, in the hope that he realises the suicide bit was a weak attempt at humour.

'You'll need to eat. Come to the pub tonight. I'm buying you dinner,' he says in a forceful but caring kind of way.

'But Roger will probably be there and I really, really don't want to see him.'

'You're going to have to see him sooner or later, may as well get it over with. Show him you're not bothered by his disgusting behaviour. Show him that you're better than that. Wouldn't it be better to do it on your terms, rather than run into him when you're not prepared? And I'll be there for moral support,' he adds, giving me an encouraging smile.

I roll the thought over in my head for a moment, weighing up the pros and cons. Although the thought of seeing Roger makes me feel physically sick, Skipper does have a point. It'll be better to see him when I'm psyched for it, rather than running into him randomly, being unprepared and possibly saying something stupid, or bursting into tears on the spot. I mentally prepare scathing things to say to him. There's no way he'll be able to talk me into being his... pause for vomiting noise... 'friend'. Even worse, he might try to convince me I had it all wrong, that I'd made a mistake, then woo me to bed when I fall for his lies. Oh no... that will NOT happen.

'I'll come get you at seven, okay', Skipper asserts, rather than requests. I give a sullen nod and turn my attention back to the happy place of *Marie Claire* land, delving into an article that attempts to answer that age-old question: 'Does Size Matter?'

7pm - A man of his word, Skipper pounds on my door bang on time. Since arriving in my room at 5pm, I've managed to do precisely nothing. Zero, zip, nada. My suitcase lies discarded and unopened just inside the door, and I've neither showered nor changed my clothes. My hair's slightly dishevelled and sticking up at the back after the two hours it's spent in close proximity to my pillow, while I stared at the mouldy ceiling, barely moving. I didn't have the energy to see if *Countdown,* and my hero Carol Vorderman, were on TV. I'm clearly clinically depressed. I'm possibly terminally clinically depressed, if there's such a thing.

'I'm not here', I shout from my prone position.

'Come on, Shaz. This is the best thing to do, honestly', Skipper shouts from the hallway.

I swear my body has doubled in weight since I lay down. It takes all my willpower to stand, unlock the door then flop back down on the edge of my bed, with a groan.

Skipper sits gently down beside me and tentatively drapes his arm over my shoulders.

'You look great! A little tired, but still great.' He's a terrible liar. He gently strokes the back of my head; this could either have been an affectionate gesture or an attempt to try and flatten my hair. Either way, it's quite soothing.

'You need to change your top, put on some lipstick, and you're good to go.' As I don't move, Skipper flicks open my suitcase and tentatively moves some bits around until he finds a bright coloured t-shirt that evidently takes his fancy. He tosses it to me. 'I'll wait outside, you've got two minutes,' he instructs as he moves into the hall, not letting the door lock behind him, so that he can get back in if necessary.

With a clean top on and some fresh lipstick, I do start to feel a little more human. On the short walk to The Blue Pub, Skipper gives me a morale-boosting talk about how great I am and how any man would be lucky to have me on their arm. By the end of the walk, he's convinced me. Damn it, he's right. I AM a catch!

A wall of cigarette smoke hits us as Skipper pushes open the heavy wooden pub door and steps gallantly aside for me to enter ahead of him. Through the haze of nicotine, near the back of the bar, I see a table littered with empty pint glasses and surrounded by Terrific Tours staff. One of them is Roger. The confidence that Skipper has instilled in me drains immediately from my body, and I turn on my heels to leave, only to bump straight into Skipper. He gently turns me around and, with his hand firmly in my lower back, guides me to the bar.

'Two snakebites, please,' Skipper says to the tough-looking barmaid. Drinks in hand, we make our way to the table where our ten or so colleagues look to have been for quite some time.

With a largish group, I manage to get through one whole pint of snakebite and start on my second, without having to speak to Roger at all. Every time he moved in my direction, I ducked off to the toilet or moved a couple of spots around the table to talk to someone else. Every now and then, I catch Skipper's eye, and he gives me an encouraging smile. I'm taking the last sip of my second drink when Roger sneaks up behind me and hands me a fresh drink.

'Thanks,' I acknowledge and attempt to move away.

'Shaz.' Roger grabs my arm to stop my escape. 'I'm really sorry. It was all a misunderstanding.'

I'm not quite sure how lining up multiple women to shag in one night could be deemed a misunderstanding.

'Forget it, Roger, I have.' Wow, I impressed myself there. I think the snakebites may have anaesthetised my emotion valve, or wherever emotions come from.

'But I don't want to forget it, Shaz. I really fucked up. You didn't deserve to be treated like that. You're such a great chick. I'm such an idiot. I've realised now just how special you are to me.'

Chapter 34

~⚬⚭⚬~

London

End of tour + 1

In The Grand Hotel, in a different, grubby room, I wake refreshed, before my alarm. I stretch slowly, like a cat in the sun, roll and put my arm over the manly bulk lying next to me. And I mean RIGHT next to me, in a single bed. He's snoring gently. Normally, snoring would annoy me, but today I find it endearing, charming, and lovely. The manly bulk is toasty warm, and as I roll to spoon his back, I note that he smells great too. Jazz aftershave mixed with lager and his own unique manly smell. I snuggle into him, getting as close as possible, breathing him in and kissing his bare back again for good measure. He stirs and turns his head towards me, a smile spreading across his handsome face.

Chapter 34

'Hi,' he says, 'you look as beautiful as always this morning.'

I kiss the side of his face and continue kissing behind his ear, moving to the back of his neck. He rolls towards me and kisses my mouth; at first gentle and enquiring, then more passionate. He tastes good, not a taste I can easily describe. It's not like I could say 'in the morning, he tastes like strawberry', the taste is sort of musky and maybe a bit salty. I don't need to describe it anyway, I just enjoy it. He turns fully towards me, pulling me closer to him. The hardness of his body is a sharp contrast to the softness of my own. My hands explore his back, the muscles running the length of it dip down to his spine. I trace my finger down until it dips down his firm buttocks. He groans and manoeuvres himself on top of me.

He looks at me for a long time before he says, 'I can't believe how lucky I am.' I guide him to me. This time, he's completely in control, and finally, I understand how he earned his nickname.

'Skipper!' I call out, as he steers me to the peak of the wave of my pleasure.

After we've had our fill of each other, nature calls. I tear myself away from him and get out of bed. I see a note has been pushed under my door. On it, the hotel receptionist has scrawled, 'Neil called. No need to come to the office. Your tour reports were great. Just do on the next tour exactly what you did on this one.'

The End... or is it?

Click HERE to continue Shaz's journey with What Goes on

Tour Too, today!

Get a free prequel, 'A brief tale', by signing up for my mailing list HERE

If you enjoyed What Goes On Tour, please consider leaving a review on Amazon or Goodreads

What Goes On Tour Too

London: Departure Day -2

Monday 10th June 1996

10am - My bladder is about to burst.

Single rooms at The Grand Hotel don't have the luxury of a bathroom. It's desperate times like now when that fact annoys me most.

'Skipper,' I loudly whisper, to try and rouse the warm body lying next to me in the single bed.

He is pushing me up against the wall, stopping my quick exit from both the bed and the room.

'Skipper!' I try again, but a bit louder.

I ruffle his sandy blonde hair at the same time. Nothing.

His rhythmic breathing continues. If I wasn't about to pee the bed, I'd take some time to enjoy the sensation of having this lovely man, so naked, and so close to me. But, instead, I run the risk of ruining our first official sleepover by soaking the mattress with my wee if I can't get out and get to the toilet soon.

I brace my back against the grubby, textured, off-white wall of the hotel room and give him enough of a push that I create a bit of wiggle room and am able to scramble over him. My feet land on the hotel carpet before I remember my cardinal rule of never standing on the hotel carpet in my bare feet. Who knows how many different types of fluids, bodily or otherwise, have been spilled on this floor?

The thought makes me a little ill.

I can't immediately see any shoes that I can slip on. Fuck it. I will have to scrub my feet raw to get them clean later. The floorspace in the single room isn't large and it's currently littered with two enormous suitcases and a variety of clothes that had been ripped off and discarded at random, as Skipper and I made our way to bed last night.

I spot a towel draped on the back of the sole chair in the room. I reach for it and wrap it tightly around my chest. It covers just enough for a quick run to the toilet. As I grab the towel, I notice the envelope that had been handed to me as my coach pulled in yesterday afternoon by a Terrific Tours London team member. I'd dropped it on the table and promptly forgotten about it. I pick it up, leave the room and race down the hall, trying to touch the floor with as little of my bare feet as humanly possible. It's only when I hear the door click behind me that I realise I have forgotten to take a key.

I put the envelope in my mouth to keep it safe, and pull metres of single-ply toilet paper from the toilet roll holder to line the seat of the toilet. I try not to think about how many strangers' pubes I'm going to pick up on my feet. As I relieve myself, I open the envelope that has my name scrawled across the front. The letter inside is written on Terrific Tours' letterhead, in scary operations supervisor Neil's handwriting. It reads:

'Sharon, No need to come to the office. Your tour reports were great. Just do on the next tour exactly what you did on this one. Neil.'

I'm not sure that would be possible. My last tour of Europe had started just over a month ago, with me taking a morning-after pill after accidentally having sex with Skipper, a tour driver I had met 90 minutes earlier. For most of the twenty-six days I was leading my flock of young tourists around Europe, I was trying to woo RHR (Ridiculously Handsome Roger), a fellow tour manager, who was working with Skipper. I finally managed to have a night of passion with RHR in Amsterdam, only to find out he was a two-timing, scum-sucking, untrustworthy lothario. He had lined up a girl to shag on his tour as soon as he'd finished with me.

What I thought would have been my dream night ended with me wrapped only in a sheet from RHR's hotel room and covered in my own tears and snot. While Skipper, who was dressed as a gorilla after an impromptu performance at a live sex show, comforted me.

It's not exactly how I'd like my next tour to go.

While I'm grateful for my supervisor Neil's confidence and not having to make a day-long trek to the office, located many miles away in Kent, I'm determined that on my next tour, I'll be fully focused on the task at hand. The task at hand being providing a quality European tour experience to my group of 18-35 year-olds.

Now that I have discovered Skipper is indeed the man

for me, and we have consummated the arrangement last night... twice... and again this morning... my personal life will be calm, controlled and have no impact on my professional efforts whatsoever.

I am a strong, independent and intelligent woman of the world.

After I have finished in the toilet, I tap gently on the thick wooden door of Room 308, while looking nervously around. The towel I am wrapped in is both short and rather threadbare.

'Skipper,' I call out. 'SKIPPER,' louder but still no reply. I escalate from tapping to rapping to thumping, but there is still no response. Fuck. Think Shaz, what would a strong, independent and intelligent woman of the world do? I bang my fists against the door at the same time as whacking my bare foot into the base and yell Skipper's name.

Damn you, fucking thick fire resistant doors!

10 minutes pass. I decide my only option is to get another key from reception.

Skipper better be dead in there.

There are two ways of getting to the ground floor and the reception desk inside The Grand Hotel - the lift or the stairs. If I take the lift, I can make sure there is no one else in there for the trip down, but... the elevator opens right into the lobby in front of the main hotel door.

The stairs are a little riskier for the journey down; they are the sort of stairs that, if you look up, you can see up the trousers of anyone walking above you. Being clad only in a small hotel towel leaves me vulnerable to other hotel users' prying eyes... but the exit from the stairway is right next to the small hotel reception desk.

I opt for the stairs.

The exit door is another heavy fire door that creaks as I open it a fraction to peer into reception. Thankfully, there is no one visible other than the middle-aged receptionist, who is currently filing her nails while looking undeniably bored.

I use the door for cover and stick my head through the gap.

'Hi,' I call out to the receptionist. She looks up. Her heavy, weary eyes cast around the reception area but seeing no one, she goes back to her nails. 'Hi,' I try again. 'I'm over here... behind the door'. Like one of those robotic clowns whose open mouth you might attempt to fire a ball into at a fairground, she slowly turns towards me.

'Whot the fook are you doin' over thare?' She asks in a thick northern drawl.

'I forgot my key when I went to the loo. Can I get a spare one, please? Room 308.'

She glances down and flicks through the pages of a logbook in front of her, running her finger down one page before stopping and looking up at me.

'You don't look like Andrew Wright.'

Shit. I'd forgotten that Skipper had registered for the single room. I'd actually forgotten his real name was Andrew Wright as well.

While, technically, there was a maximum occupancy of one person, by Skipper and I sharing the tiny, shabby room with one single bed, we each saved £11 a night. That's a lot of beer money when you're on a budget.

Think fast, Shaz. Strong, independent and intelligent woman of the world, remember.

That's my code name?

He's my brother?

I've been abducted?

All good options, but what comes out of my mouth is, 'I'm in the witness protection programme. They told me never to use my real name,' I say, as confidently as I can.

'What *is* your real name?' The receptionist asks.

'Sharon Green.'

'Why the fook are you telling me it? If they've told you not to tell anyone your real name, and you are actually in the witness protection programme?' Northern reception woman asks.

Shit.

Excellent point.

'I've only just gone in. I'm still getting the hang of it,' I babble. 'Please don't blow my cover.' For good measure, I tremble my bottom lip and look a bit teary.

She reaches into a drawer beside her, pulls out a key attached to a long metal stick, about a foot long, and hands it to me.

10.45am - I slot the key in the door of Room 308. I'm itching for a fight.

Bloody Skipper, what a knob.

I swing the door open as hard as I can. I'm hoping for a dent in the wall or a satisfying bang at least. Sadly, the hydraulic door thing stops either. I raise myself up to my full 5'4", tighten the towel around my chest and stride in.

'SKIPPER!' I shout at the top of my lungs. He sits bolt upright. The sheet that was caressing his neck slides slowly down to his waist, revealing a strong chest with just a smattering of hair. A darker line of hair leads the way from his navel further south. He's too cute for me to be angry with

306

him. Instead, I regale him with my recent escapades. After he's stopped laughing, he pulls me to him, and the next hour is a blur of sweaty intertwined bodies.

2pm - We roll out of The Moon Underwater pub, after a huge lunch of bangers and mash drowned in onion gravy, washed down with lager, and into Leicester Square. We find ourselves blinking our eyes to adjust from the dingy pub light to the unusually bright London summer's afternoon.

'Shall we get the Tube and go back to the hotel?' I ask, through a yawn. The large lunch and pint of lager has made me lethargic.

'Why don't we walk? It's a lovely day for it, and it's still hours before I have to be at my tour pre-departure meeting.'

Walk? WALK? Is he fucking mad? Clearly he still has a lot to get to know about me. Like, I hate walking. I want to impress Skipper, though, so I gaze up at him, make my tired blue eyes sparkle just a little and say, 'Sure, I'd love to.'

He takes my hand and leads me past Chiquito - my favourite Mexican restaurant, which serves the best frozen margaritas in huge frosty jugs - and down Cranbourn Street. We pass souvenir shops flogging the latest royal memorabilia featuring Charles and Diana, now on separate china cups, and booths with discount tickets for the latest London shows. Skipper stops suddenly outside a shop I've never seen before. He looks down at me with a silly grin on his clean-cut, handsome face.

'Shaz,' he enthuses, 'let's get mobile phones! Then we can contact each other all the time. Even when we are at different ends of Europe, we'll still be able to keep in touch!'

The thought of being able to keep tabs on my new boyfriend does sound appealing. Not that I don't trust him, of course. I just don't trust all those girls who will be sitting on the coach behind him, drooling over his driving skills and asking him how he 'gets that big thing through those tight bends'. Coach driver keys have magical powers. Perhaps if he were getting regular calls from his hot new girlfriend, it would counteract some of his appeal to them? I step nearer towards the shop window to have a closer look.

'Twenty quid, Skipper! That's a lot of money. Then there's the £100 monthly charge, and I've heard you have to pay for each call and message as well.'

'They're the latest technology and you can make them ring with different tunes,' he beams at me. 'We can call each other to say goodnight... every night. It will be like we're in the same city.' Before I can resist further, he drags me into the shop. When we come out, we are each carrying a bag. Inside each bag is a box, and inside each box is a Nokia 1610 Plus mobile phone.

We walk back towards the hotel, holding hands and swinging the bags containing our new mobile phones in our free hands. To pass the time during our walk, and because I'm nosey, I quiz Skipper.

'Tell me about your last girlfriend,' I ask.

'Why, Shaz? It's in the past. Now it's just you.' He squeezes my hand.

'I'm interested, go on, tell me about her,' I beg, 'pleeeeaaase.'

'Okay then,' he submits to my pressure. 'I met her when I was working on a farm just out of Glencoe... in Scotland,' he adds, obviously assuming I don't know where Glencoe is. He's right, I have no clue. 'It was over the off-season. I didn't want to go back to Australia, so I got a job up north and spent a freezing Scottish Highland winter on a farm,' he laughs at the memory. 'I used to drink at a pub in Glencoe, and she worked behind the bar. She was a local Highland lassie with flaming red Celtic hair and sparkly green eyes. Pretty girl, she was.'

I feel jealousy prickle my skin. 'So, what happened?'

'We both got drunk on New Year's Eve and ended up… you know… together,' he says, sparing me the intimate details. 'We saw each other for about a month after that.'

'Why did it end?' I ask, hoping to learn from her mistake.

'She had an on-again, off-again boyfriend. He was from Zimbabwe originally, the only black man in Glencoe! He'd gone back to Zimbabwe for Christmas, for a month or so. They'd broken up before he left. Then he came back and it was on again and she gave me the flick!'

'Aw, poor you.' I squeeze his hand in sympathy.

'It all worked out for the best,' Skipper replies. He gives me one of his most beaming, wholesome smiles, then lowers his head and plants his lips on mine.

4pm - To enter the hotel I march past the Northern reception gargoyle. Greeting her with a loud 'HELLO', as I head to the stairs, to distract her, while Skipper slips from the main door across to the elevator.

'You're blimmin' loud for someone who is in the witness protection programme,' she says.

'It's a double bluff,' I quip. 'The louder I am, the less likely people are to think that I'm in hiding.'

She scoffs and goes back to her work.

I flop onto the single, unmade bed after turning on the small TV, which is perched on a chipped wooden veneer chest of drawers in the corner of the room, opposite the avocado green basin. *Countdown* is on, my favourite TV show. I immerse myself in it while Skipper opens up our phone boxes, one at a time. He discards the VHS cassettes that have 'quick start instructions' printed on them. We have no VCR in the room to watch them on. He also casts aside the instruction manuals, opting instead to snap the battery on the back of each phone and plug them into the wall. He focuses on his phone first and turns it on by holding down the on/off button. A soothing *dong dong dong dooonnnnggg* tune comes out of it and the screen lights up. I turn my attention back to the TV as Skipper presses various buttons to see what he can make happen.

Countdown presenter Richard looks his usual nerdy self with a grey plaid suit and clashing tan paisley tie. Carol Vorderman, my hero and girl crush, has on a fetching canary yellow pantsuit with a risqué V-neck and short sleeves showing off her slender, tanned arms. She lifts a slender, tanned arm to hit the magic button that creates a random number answer. The two contestants immediately start scribbling on pieces of paper in front of them, to try and make the smaller numbers Carol has already placed on the board, equate to the magic answer number, using maths.

4.50pm - What the fuck is that noise?
Da da dum dum, da da dum dum, da da dum dum duuuu-ummmm. Da da dum dum, da da dum dum, da da dum dum duuuuummmm. Da da dum dum, da da dum dum, da da dum dum duuuuummmm.
I must've nodded off.
I crack one eye open and cast it around the room.
Da da dum dum, da da dum dum, da da dum dum duuuuum-

mmm.

The TV is still on, but it's not that that is making the noise.

Da da dum dum, da da dum dum, da da dum dum duuuuum- mmm. I notice Skipper has gone.

Da da dum dum, da da dum dum, da da dum dum duuuuum- mmm. I get up and follow the noise. Behind an open suitcase on the floor, a brand new mobile phone is ringing. I pick it up, press the green phone button and put it tentatively to my ear.

'Hello?'

'Shaz, it's me!' Skipper's voice is full of the joys of spring. 'Isn't it cool that I can just phone you whenever I want? You were snoring really cutely, so I left you to it. I've just come down to The Pit for my pre-departure meeting. Come down and we can have a beer before it starts.'

'Okay, I'll be there in 5 minutes,' I respond. 'I forgot to ask you, who is your tour manager anyway?'

'It's really weird, I don't know yet. My driver manager, Scotty, just told me to be at the meeting at 5.30pm. He said my tour manager will be coming into London this afternoon and will arrive just in time. Bit of a mystery,' Skipper says.

He's such a kind driver.

Most coach drivers skip the pre-departure meeting, with the excuse that they have to get up super early the next morning to pick up their coach on the outskirts of London and get back into the hotel by about 6.30am on the morning the tour departs.

As I sit on the edge of the bed, I reach for my tan leather boat shoes and slide them onto my bare feet. They go nicely with my high-waisted stonewashed jeans and dark denim shirt, I think, as I quickly check my reflection in the mirror and wipe off a bit of smeared mascara from under my eyes that's smudged during my nap. I run my fingers through my short reddish-brown hair and apply a swish of shiny lip gloss, tinged every-so-slightly pink.

That'll do.

I slide my new phone into my Florentine leather handbag-cum-backpack and head out the door.

5.15pm - I happily trot down the industrial metal stairs that lead to The Pit, excited to see my boyfriend. I still get excited just saying 'boyfriend'.

A waft of heat and cigarette smoke hits me as I slide past the heavy door and into The Pit, making a beeline for the lime green staff shirts I can see near the u-shaped bar. Skipper looks up when he hears the door open and beams at me. He looks cute in his lime green Terrific Tour polo shirt and dark Levi's 501s.

'I got you a drink.' He slides a frothy-topped pint of lager towards me.

'Hi Scooter! Hi Julie!' I greet the other staff standing with Skipper, 'Quiet day, eh? Only two tours leaving tomorrow?'

'Yip, so there's a 50% chance that babe in the corner is with me,' Scooter says, leering at a girl with a Rachel Hunter-esque figure and long ringlet curls who is chatting to two other girls in the corner of the room.

'You can have her, Scooter,' Skipper says as he puts his arm around my waist and gives me a squeeze. Julie clocks this show of affection out of the corner of her eye and flashes me a questioning look.

'How long is your tour, Julie?' I ask to divert her attention rather than actually caring about the answer.

'Nice quick one,' Julie replies in her Australian drawl. 'Seven days and we'll be back in London. Hardly time to scratch ourselves, but also not enough time to get sick of the group either.'

The only other staff member in the room is Boring Barry from the office. Boring Barry tried to be a tour manager once. He made it onto the six-week European training trip but got kicked off in Rome after not being able to remember the difference between Doric and Corinthian columns or Gothic and Baroque architecture, or the names of any Roman Emperors or French Kings. He seemed to be both date and directionally dyslexic. When he was doing practice spiels during city tours, he'd constantly be telling people to look out of the coach windows completely the opposite way to where they should be looking to see what he was talking about. Once he found his way back to London from Rome, he managed to land himself an office job with the company instead. Part of this job was to come to the pre-departure meetings and kick things off before blending back into the carpet and reappearing the next night.

5.29pm - Boring Barry drags the corded microphone from its resting place on the bar to the step in front of The Pit's door to the outside world. It makes a 'click' as he switches it on.

'Hi,' he drones into the microphone. While me and the crew in green shirts stop talking and look at him, the rest of the eighty or so people in the bar and dancefloor area ignore him. 'Hi... Hello... HI!' He finally shouts. The din in the room lowers, and people start to gravitate towards where he is standing.

'Where the fuck is your tour manager?' I whisper to

Skipper.

He shrugs his shoulders in response. If I were about to be swamped by forty people and had no paperwork to know who they were, I'd be a nervous wreck. But Skipper looks totally calm and in control… and very sexy.

'My name is Barry.' Boring Barry states in his low, monotone voice. As he is about to launch into his spiel and introduce the road crew, there is a loud noise behind him and a black-wheeled suitcase tumbles down the steps and into view through the glass in the doors, followed by a loud noise from the top of the stairs…

'FUCK!'

A few seconds later, the door swings open, nearly knocking Barry off his step. The green-shirted female blur screeches to a halt next to Boring Barry, flicks the long dark hair back off her face and smiles.

When I see who it is, I realise I am in shit…

Deep…

Deep shit.

Continue reading What Goes On Tour Too now by clicking HERE

About the Author

Gillian Scott lives at the bottom of the world in beautiful New Zealand, but her heart has always been on the move. Bitten by the travel bug at eighteen, she has spent decades exploring the globe, first as a tour rep and manager in Europe during the 1990s, then leading groups through New Zealand, Australia, Canada, the U.S., India, and, recently, back through Europe, Australia and South America.

In 2011, Gillian, her husband, and their two young children swapped routine for adventure, packing up their lives to backpack around the world for nine unforgettable months.

Drawing on her years behind the microphone of a coach and in front of hundreds of travellers, Gillian turned her experiences into fiction. Her debut series, *What Goes On Tour,* and the follow-up Terrific Tour series capture the humour, heart, and chaos of life on the road, where the stories are as unpredictable as the passengers.

You can connect with me on:

○ https://gillianscottcreative.com

◪ https://www.facebook.com/GillianScottCreative

⌗ https://www.instagram.com/gillianscottcreative

Subscribe to my newsletter:

✉ http://eepurl.com/hHgCfX

Also by Gillian Scott

If you enjoyed What Goes On Tour, then you'll love reading about the continuing exploits of Shaz.

What Goes On Tour Too

I, Sharon 'Shaz' Green, am officially happy. My mantra of, 'you are a 26-year-old, strong, independent, intelligent, woman of the world', is paying off. I have just successfully finished leading a tour around Europe and am on my way to do another. For the most part, 1996 is looking to be a great year.

Only a month ago I was a mess. Then, I was lusting after Ridiculously Handsome Roger, who was bad for me, and not wanting the man who was right for me. Skipper. Now Skipper is by my side and Roger is a distant memory. The only slight problem is my best friend Liza also thinks Skipper is the right man for her and doesn't know that he and I are now together.

What can possibly go wrong? Liza, finding out, an unseasonable snowstorm and a late period. That's what. Can I keep my boyfriend AND my best friend, at the same time as leading my flock of tourists? Join me on another jaunt around Europe and find out.

What Goes On Tour - Camping
The third book in the What Goes On Tour series

I, Shaz Green (26 and a half), have an actual boyfriend. The lovely, kind and caring, coach driving, Skipper.

Things were going great until his ex-girlfriend showed up with some disturbing news.

While I struggle with the fall-out I get some more bad news from the Terrific Tours office. After years of leading tours through Europe enjoying the comfort of hotels, I'm being sent on a camping tour! No indoor showers, no crisp white linen, no waiter service at dinner. CAMPING!

Can I survive a broken heart and camping? Can I resist the charms of the inexperienced but handsome driver, Guy? And what's up with Michelle, the mobile cook? Why is she so bad at cooking?

Come on another jaunt around Europe with me and find out.

A Fish Out of Sparkling Water

A laugh-out-loud, heart-tugging romantic comedy about finding purpose, falling in love, and learning that the best things in life can't be bought.

Esther Smith's life in South Africa is all champagne and silk sheets — until her father sends her to rural France for the summer to "learn responsibility." Arriving at Château Vin Rouge in designer heels, Esther is horrified to find she's expected to *work*. Scrubbing floors, cooking for guests, and sharing a stable room with strangers were not on her packing list.

Then there's Benji — the maddeningly calm, quietly magnetic Head Cleaner who sees right through her privileged façade. Between disastrous chores, late-night kitchen raids, and a growing connection she never expected, Esther starts to discover who she really is — and what she truly wants.

But when her family calls her home with news that changes everything, Esther must decide whether to return to the life she knew or fight for the one she's fallen in love with.

Warm, funny, and full of heart, A Fish Out of Sparkling Water is a sparkling escape for fans of *Emily Henry, Sophie Kinsella,* and *The Summer I Turned Pretty.*

Love, Lies & Lemon Trees

An irresistible romantic comedy set on the sun-drenched Amalfi Coast — where love tastes sweet, secrets run deep, and danger hides in paradise.

When Clare takes a summer job in Italy, she expects sunshine, gelato, and adventure — not a man like Luca. Brooding, beautiful, and bound by family ties, Luca draws her in from the start. But behind his charm lies a web of secrets that threaten to pull them both under.

As their connection deepens, Clare finds herself caught between love and loyalty, truth and survival. With Luca's family watching her every move, she must decide how much she's willing to risk for the man she's falling for.

Love, Lies & Lemon Trees is a heart-stopping romance about passion, courage, and the fight for happiness when love comes with consequences. Perfect for fans of *Emily Henry*, *Sophie Kinsella*, and sweeping European escapes.

Paint Me A Lie

A glamorous French Riviera rock star romance about secrets, second chances, and the lies we tell to protect our hearts.

Bella's summer job at a bustling campground in Antibes is hardly five-star, but her nightly escapes to Monaco let her pretend she belongs in that glittering world. Then she meets Jock — a charming Scotsman who claims he's just a house painter helping family nearby.

He's easy-going, funny, and far too good to be true. And as their paths keep crossing under the Riviera lights, Bella starts to suspect Jock's story has more layers than a freshly painted wall. When the truth comes out, it could destroy the fragile trust — and unexpected love — they've built between them.

Paint Me a Lie is a witty, heartfelt romantic comedy about love, deception, and discovering what's real in a world obsessed with appearances. Perfect for fans of *Josie Silver* and *Sophie Kinsella*.